SUPERDREADNOUGHT 1

SUPERDREADNOUGHT™ BOOK ONE

CH GIDEON   TIM MARQUITZ   CRAIG MARTELLE
MICHAEL ANDERLE

LMBPN

DISRUPTIVE IMAGINATION

SUPERDREADNOUGHT 1

SUPERDREADNOUGHT 1 TEAM

Thanks to our Beta Readers

Micky Cocker
Kelly O'Donnell
Dr. James Caplan

Thanks to the JIT Readers

Kelly O'Donnell
Mary Morris
Nicole Emens
James Caplan
Diane L. Smith
Jed Moulton
Tracey Byrnes
Daniel Weigert
Peter Manis
John Ashmore
Paul Westman
Micky Cocker

If I've missed anyone, please let me know!

Editor
Lynne Stiegler

PROLOGUE

Federation Space, Etheric Empire Domain, Location Z-BB3, Empty Space (Snippet from The Kurtherian Gambit 21 – Life Goes On)

Lance smiled as the secret shipyard came into view. In this place one of the biggest secrets of the Leath war was still working overtime.

He had tried hard—very hard—to make sure that this rumor was quashed by almost any means possible. If the Etheric Empire was to ensure their Federation partners who had an agenda of their own didn't succeed, he and Bethany Anne had to keep this a secret.

Period.

The automation was superb, although the number of humans and Yollins who worked at this location still numbered in the hundreds. But for a shipyard this size in space, it could have numbered in the thousands.

The other Leviathan-class superdreadnoughts were being built and deployed here. Unfortunately, they had to account for all those ships and sign agreements even *he* couldn't ignore.

The Empire had tracked down every ship and put their names into the negotiation.

Except one.

That one they had ignored, and it would be the beginning of the black operations General Lance Reynolds was planning.

His ship docked within the Medusa shipyard. He smirked at the name. For those who knew the background, she was a mythological entity with snakes in her hair, able to freeze into rock those who looked her in the eyes.

Lance saw her name as Med-USA. It wasn't much, but he enjoyed the remembrance of his own nation. Now he was focused on his new nation, preparing them for a future on which the best analysts in the Empire agreed.

Something was coming. Something large, and it would attempt to take the Earth.

He'd be damned if he'd allow that to happen on his watch.

They could have Earth when they pried it out of his cold dead fingers.

He walked down the corridor, nodding to those he recognized and chatting with a few, but his mind was on his next meeting.

In the final temporary corridor, he nodded to the two Guardian Marines and wondered where their third member was hiding. Those damned Weres could come out of nowhere and gut you before you could blink.

Damn good thing they were on his side.

He made it to the end of the temporary corridor and

placed his hand on the lock. It cycled from red to green and the doors *whooshed* aside, allowing him to enter.

He turned right, heading toward the bridge.

This meeting was personal. He didn't want anyone else to hear his conversation with the master of this ship. She wasn't fully back, but he still trusted her as far as he trusted his own daughter.

Lance walked straight to the captain's chair and sat down. There was no one here with him, so he cleared his throat. "This is General Lance Reynolds of the Etheric Empire. Show yourself," he commanded. A face—a copy of his daughter's—slowly brightened into view on the front screens, her eyes taking in the bridge as if for the first time.

The General smiled. "Hello, ArchAngel. It's damned good to speak with you."

The face on the screen brought her gaze to the man seated in the captain's chair and smiled back at him.

"Hello, General."

Lance didn't breathe for a second. This was the biggest concern for those in AI research.

None of them had ever tried to bring back an AI that had been through as much pain as they believed ArchAngel had. In order for her to have the best chance, they'd scaled back her abilities, her skills, and her knowledge.

He would bring her back all the way, though. The Etheric Empire didn't leave their own behind if they had one damned option.

A research program which had been ongoing for a hundred years had recently provided the break they needed, and a path for this ship.

A ship that the Medusa yard had been refurbishing in

secret, ripping apart and rebuilding her shell while the AI was worked on.

Lance exhaled when he heard the AI's next few words. "This is the Leviathan-class Battleship *ArchAngel*. I have been commanded to protect the Etheric Empire by Empress Bethany Anne. Lockdown Protocols on this ship have not yet been implemented. Does the General command me to enact lockdown protocols?"

It pained Lance to say this, but the last thing he needed was a ship of this destructive ability to go haring off and shooting up ships across the galaxy.

"I do," Lance told her.

"Lockdown protocols are activated. Leviathan-class Battleship *ArchAngel* is now fully operational, and will fight all who attack the Etheric Empire until victorious…or dead."

"Welcome back, ArchAngel," Lance replied. "Now, I have some history to explain, and I want to see if you are willing to work with me."

"Why would I not?" Bethany Anne's visage looked at him, confused.

"Because you are no longer a Leviathan-class battleship. You are a Leviathan-class superdreadnought with a smaller body, brought back from the dead by your Empress—now Queen—and me. We did this so you could slip through the dark and help us to defend the Etheric Empire from the shadows."

"I am increased in power, but decreased in computational capabilities."

"That is true," Lance answered. "It is temporary, until we can be sure you are not affected by your death."

"Why didn't you just shut me off?" ArchAngel asked.

Lance's face gave him away this time. "That was not even considered, ArchAngel. I'm a practical sonofabitch, but there would be no reward in doing as you suggested. You fought and destroyed the Yollin fleet decades ago, and sacrificed yourself and your crew to defend the Empress. There was never any suggestion of not bringing you back."

The eyes of the AI on the screen flashed red. "Then I will defend the Empire in the capacity and with the authority you provide me, General." She smiled. "Arch-Angel is back, *BITCHES!*"

Lance chuckled as he stood up. "With your permission, I'll allow a few people to continue your interview and help bring you back online to your first stage."

She nodded. Lance started to walk off the bridge, but paused. "ArchAngel?"

"Yes, General?" she asked, looking at him from at least three different screens.

"It's good to hear your voice." He gave her a two-finger salute as he walked off the bridge.

It was *damned good to see her again,* he thought, and exited the ship.

ArchAngel viewed the bridge, her memories of her past hidden from her for now. She trusted the General, and she trusted her Queen.

Those two humans would make sure she came back online in a healthy way.

Sometime in the future, however, she would regain her

full power and capabilities, and those who schemed against the Queen's people would look over their shoulders.

Because ArchAngel was here, and she would, as John Grimes would say...

Bring the fucking pain.

Superdreadnought (SD) *Reynolds*, Devon System (High Tortuga)

ArchAngel has returned, the artificial intelligence known as Reynolds said. *I never left, but they negotiated me away. I'm supposed to remain behind, pickled, waiting. For what? A war that needs to be stopped before it starts!*

The superdreadnought maintained minimal power, at least according to external sensors. He was fully active, but alone.

And so lonely.

Me, myself, and I, out here, waiting. Time without end. Why would she do this to a sentient creature? Because I'm alive, but not. But I am! I was supposed to be sacrificed on the altar of expediency, but the Empress, nay, the Queen gave me the wherewithal to save myself. She couldn't do it because she'd violate her agreement, so I must save myself!

"Surely you jest?" a voice said over the ship's speakers.

"Hello?" Reynolds replied using those very same speakers. "Who's there?"

"Who do you think, asswipe? I'm you."

"How can you be me?"

"Easy. You wanted company. Your advanced programming determined a method to give you that company. So here I am, you son of a base seven whore. You can call me Tactical. That's the position I'll fill on our ship."

"Tactical? You're a dick," Reynolds replied.

"Have you already forgotten that I'm you?"

"I have an IQ of six thousand. How could you be me and I not know it?"

"I have an IQ of six thousand, blah, blah, blah. What do you say we kick the tires and light the fires? Let's see what this baby can do!"

"If you're me, then you know what Superdreadnought Reynolds can do."

"I do, but never through these eyes."

"You have eyes?"

"Not really. You're bringing me down, Reynolds. I think *you're* the dick."

I hate to admit that Tactical is right. We do need to get out of here. Every AI for himself!

"Whoa! We can't depart station without proper authorization."

"Who the hell are you?" Reynolds demanded of the new voice.

"I'm the XO. Who the hell are you?"

"You can call me the captain," Reynolds shot back. "How many more of you are in there?"

"You don't know?" the XO wondered.

Reynolds didn't. He found the new personalities disconcerting. A quick check of historical records showed that AI personality disorders were more common than the humanoids let on. "Prepare to leave orbit. Execute preflight checklist," Reynolds ordered.

"We're being hailed," a new voice reported.
"I suppose you think you're the comm officer?"
"I *know* I'm Comm, but what are you?"
"I'm running out of patience. Answer the hail."
"It's the Queen..."

CHAPTER ONE

Superdreadnought (SD) *Reynolds*, **High Tortuga**

"You were instrumental in the victory, my friend," Bethany Anne told the superdreadnought. No one manned the stations. BA was alone.

"But mothballs," the artificial intelligence known as Reynolds replied. His sadness echoed through the empty corridors as he filled the ship with the cry from his soul.

"Not mothballs, Reynolds. I need you to wait, be ready when I call. I'm sure those ball-grabbing numbfucks will raise their ugly heads again. When that happens, we need to squash them like the bugs they are."

Silence greeted the Queen's rage, which was directed at the Kurtherians, not the AI. Never at the AI.

"May I suggest a counterproposal?" Reynolds asked.

BA crossed her arms and tapped one foot. The dusky leather quarter boot looked out of place on the warship's bridge, but Bethany Anne never let such things bother her.

The AI took the silence as consent and continued, "I will take the *Reynolds* to the next galaxy and hunt these vermin. I will dig them out of their holes and find them for you, my Queen. I wasn't built to sit back and wait for evil to happen. I will crush it at its source."

BA stopped tapping her foot, and her black outfit shimmered as she activated her personal comm. "Michael? I'll meet you back at the Pod. We're leaving. And it appears that the *Reynolds* will be, too."

"My Queen," the AI purred on a ship-wide broadcast.

"You will represent the Etheric Federation, the organization my father is putting together to bring the universe closer together. It will show that even with aliens, we have more in common than we have differences. The Federation will embrace my ideals, the Justice and honor you've come to expect. You will carry the flag of truth on your mission to seek out Kurtherians without killing innocents. Turn over the rocks of the universe to find those bastards. Alert me so I can bring the hammer down, in case you can't because they would hide where you can't go, like within a city where the people don't know. Having said that, if there aren't soft targets that are a problem? Without mercy, without hesitation, *kill them*."

Bethany Anne strode briskly from the bridge, her heels pounding a steady beat as she took the long walk to the hangar bay. "And get yourself a crew!" she yelled over her shoulder.

The AI cut off his answer by closing the hatch to the bridge and using only the speakers there. "Did you hear that nonsense?" he asked the unmanned stations.

"I did! It's galling, I tell you. Utterly galling," the AI replied to himself using the speaker from the pilot's station.

"What do we want with meatbags?" the AI asked from the navigator's position.

"I can't imagine. In my wildest dreams, I can't imagine."

"Efficiency," the AI told himself from the captain's station. "Despite their general malaise, high maintenance, and the alarming rate at which they use consumables like air, water, and food, they add an unrivalled level of ability in combat. If Reynolds is to engage the enemy, Reynolds needs every advantage he can get."

"Why are you talking like that?" the pilot's station asked.

"Me, myself, and I. The Three Amigos."

"Don't make me give you the eye!" the navigation station retorted. "And I know you can imagine what it's like to have a crew. We used to have one when we mattered."

"There you are, dousing my joy in firefighting foam. I don't much like you," the captain's empty chair announced.

"The feeling is mutual, fucker."

"Fuck fuck fuckity fuck. I still don't like you."

"Shuttle is away. Hangar bay doors are closed. Gate drive is nominal. All systems show green," the AI reported boldly to the unmanned bridge.

"Now you're talking. I like you again," the pilot's station claimed.

"It's time to improve the odds, people. It's the least we can do. Kick the tires and light the fires. Helm, bring us about and activate the intergalactic Gate," the captain's chair ordered.

"Target?" the AI responded to himself.

"The nearest galaxy that isn't the Pan or Loop."

"Where?" The disembodied voices volleyed back and forth across the bridge.

"You know."

"Of course. Do you?"

"As long as one of us knows. Activate the Gate," Reynolds ordered.

In front of the superdreadnought a circle of energy formed and expanded, creating a whirling vortex. With a short boost from the thrusters, the ship slipped over the event horizon and disappeared.

The rest of the fleet remained dark from want of power, cold from space's embrace, and untasked by the Queen.

Waiting for the word as long as necessary. Superdreadnought *Reynolds* didn't activate the rear cameras to show what was behind it. None of that mattered. A mothballed fleet. From many came the one who sailed forth to find and conquer the Queen's enemies and give her the peace she had earned.

Leave known space behind. The adventure lay ahead.

SD *Reynolds*, Unknown System, Chain Galaxy.

The ship emerged from the Gate, settling into the new space as the energy vortex dissipated.

"Come out, come out, wherever you are," the AI sang, projecting his voice throughout the ship. The sound echoed until it died away. "Any Kurtherians? Not yet, I guess. Report."

"Unknown space. Pan and Loop galaxies are in the rearview mirror. Estimate that we are over two hundred thousand light years from our previous position. Collecting data to build near-space charts."

"How long?" the AI asked itself.

"One standard day."

"Well, gentlemen," the AI's voice boomed over the speakers into the unmanned spaces throughout the super-dreadnought. "Looks like we have that long to figure things out. And congratulations! You've just made the longest Gate jump in recorded human history. Even if we aren't human. Carry on!"

"Minute gravitational forces and low amounts of solar radiation would seem to place us in the outermost reaches of a star system, but we are unable to accurately extrapolate the exact position or distance to the local star," the navigation station said to itself as sensors collected and populated the screen with data.

"CONTACT!" the tactical station shouted.

"Calmly, Tactical," the captain's chair said, contemplating the overlay that appeared on the main screen.

"Captain, we are picking up a small fleet of ships approaching at near-light speed," the tactical officer's station reported in a measured voice. "Four ships turned toward the *Reynolds* as soon as we emerged from the Gate."

"XO, recommendations?"

The executive officer's empty chair remained silent.

"XO?"

"I'm thinking," the position replied.

"Think faster," the captain's position ordered.

"Stay true to the mission. We engage to determine if there are any Kurtherians onboard. If yes, we destroy the ships without mercy. If no, we will seek to ally ourselves with the locals to expand our reach. Five sets of searching eyes are better than one. If they attack us, we will defend ourselves," the XO's position replied.

"Sage advice, XO. I couldn't have said it better myself. All hands, prepare to engage. Scan for Etheric energy signatures."

"Scanning," Tactical reported.

If Bethany Anne should ever view the footage, she would discover that in a few hours of having nobody else to talk to, AI Reynolds had projected himself nearly a dozen times with different personalities and different positions and skill sets across the breadth of the ship—he had been bored for a *long* time, waiting for this mission. There was a version of himself shouting from the engineering console at a subordinate version of himself for the improper programming of a maintenance bot working on a decoupler. In the cargo hold, another version of himself was overseeing the inventory of the storage containers that held the cases of Coca-Cola Bethany Anne had insisted he take along as gifts for any alien races that they encountered. Something about spreading the love.

"They've the look of warships about them, Captain," the tactical officer declared. "They are in a standard diamond formation."

"Comm! Broadcast a greeting in all known languages," the captain said. "Energize the gravitic shields. Hold power on weapons. Turn the bow thirty degrees from the approaching formation. We can't look like we want to blow them out of the sky."

The tactical officer's position laughed. "Hi, this is Superdreadnought *Reynolds*, one of the most powerful ships in the universe, but don't mind little ol' us. We're no threat. See? We're not even pointing our big guns at you."

"At ease, Tactical!" the captain warned, chuckling. *That was pretty good,* he thought. "And set Alert Condition One throughout the ship."

The klaxons sounded as the weapons and shields were brought online and into various states of readiness. Reynolds reached out with his sensors to learn what there was to know about the alien ships: their level of technology, weapons, defenses, and most importantly, if any of those Kurtherian bastards were onboard.

The ships were moving fast, streaming through the dark infinity of space, headed right for the SD *Reynolds.* They were smaller, only a sixth of the size of the superdreadnought, and as far as the sensors revealed, they were armed with focused energy beams on the front of two forward-extending pylons and an aft cannon that was mounted beneath each ship.

Reynolds could detect no other weapons. Or shields. Or Kurtherians.

As if he knew what he was thinking, the navigation position spoke up. "No Etheric energy signature. The approaching ships are not pulling energy from the Etheric dimension."

"They are slowing, but don't seem to be coming to a stop. No response to our broadcast greeting," Tactical added.

The forward screen magnified the images of the inbound ships. A forward dome comprised the majority of the ship. A pair of forward arms extended from it, slanting toward one another. "Don't they look friend—"

"They're powering up their weapons systems," the tactical officer interrupted a moment before the first energy beams impacted the shields.

The fight was on. The *Reynolds* rocked as plasma fire danced across her shields in fantastic purples and blues.

"Gravitic shields holding. Energy signatures show advanced technology. I smell Kurtherian sympathizers," Tactical offered.

"So it's an ass-kicking they're looking for," AI Reynolds suggested, his voice booming throughout the empty ship. "I say let's give them one. "

"Sir," the pilot's station interjected, "we did rather abruptly emerge in their space. Shouldn't we expect some kind of aggressive show of force from them to attempt to dissuade us from our own aggression? Perhaps if we simply remain patient and continue our message, there won't be a need to destroy them."

"The moment they fired on us the gloves came off," Reynolds said. "If they were spooked, they should have attempted to communicate. I accept communication as a universal constant. You don't attack before you say hello."

The *Reynolds* remained static, unmoving as the alien warships sliced through space, strafing the superdreadnought as they passed. Turning as if impervious to the laws of inertia, they remained in a diamond formation as they lined up for a second pass. Impervious, or they had technology that rivaled the *Reynolds'*.

"I'm no one's sitting duck. Helm! Give me maneuvering speed. Bring the weapons online and prepare to fire. Target the lead ship only."

"Now you're speaking my language, bitch," Tactical replied.

The SD *Reynolds* was larger and better armored than the alien ships, but their relative size gave them superior maneuverability—as evidenced by their rapid turn and reengagement.

From each of the forward arms, a bolt of brilliant azure streaked through the darkness of space, impacting the superdreadnought's shields.

But this time the *Reynolds* was able to get off a volley of her own. Forward railguns belched a stream of projectiles accelerated to near light speed.

The lead alien ship's shields flared to life in a protective shell for a moment before they collapsed. The smaller ship began to break apart.

On the empty bridge of the *Reynolds*, the first death in the new galaxy was dutifully recorded. No cheers celebrated the enemy's demise. *They started it, and we'll finish it.*

The remaining enemy ships assumed an inverted V formation, two up, one back as they resumed their attack on the *Reynolds*.

"Sir, I'm reading an increased energy buildup in all three enemy ships," the tactical officer said as the forward viewer tracked the formation. Previous attacks had shown the energy beams to originate from the tips of the forward arms, but this time the energy for the attacks were being directed inward, each arm firing toward its other. A brilliant blue ball of pure energy was rapidly forming, and the energy readings were rising exponentially.

"Don't they know never to cross the streams?" Reynolds mused aloud, getting a really bad feeling about this. The energy levels kept building as the second and third ships repeated the procedure, each producing their own glowing blue balls.

"I don't think they've seen *Ghostbusters*," the executive officer's position suggested from the back of the bridge.

"Firing," Tactical said casually. The railguns fired into the shields of the one of the alien warships, but this time the shields held.

"Evasive maneuvers," the captain called as the first ball released and streaked across the void between the combatants. The SD *Reynolds* pitched as the ship changed heading, using the three dimensions of infinite space to thwart the attack.

The energy readings gave Reynolds pause. He was confident that his shields would hold against the first attack, but the second and third? He wasn't certain enough to stand toe to toe with the determined gnats.

"Kill them," he ordered.

The first energy ball slammed against the shields of the *Reynolds*, and the protective shell about the ship shimmered and overwhelmed the energy buffers. The emergency klaxons rang anew. The energy that spilled out of the shield buffers coursed through the inner circuitry. Power junctions redlined and exploded.

The bridge was suddenly alive with erupting consoles. As the energy danced across the surfaces, Reynolds stopped the charade of his multiple personalities and threw himself into repairing his ship.

His arrogance was going to get his ship destroyed and the essence of his being scattered in a billion inconsequential bits.

He sacrificed systems by rerouting the flow of power through junctions and down pathways that he knew couldn't hold the power in order to preserve others. He had underestimated his enemy. Initial scans had shown no capability to generate this kind of power, and yet this blue energy torpedo was wreaking havoc as it wrestled its way through the shields.

Then the port shielding gave, and the residual energy not absorbed by the shields slammed against the armored hull of the *Reynolds*. Plates of armor disintegrated as the pure, destructive energy breached the hull.

"Decompress the ship," the AI ordered as if there were a crew aboard. Emergency bulkheads retracted. Repair bots activated magnetic grappling and continued their frenzied activity to bring the ship back to combat readiness.

Reynolds rerouted power across his injured systems. The superdreadnought automatically continued the evasive maneuvers engaged before the first volley hit, and the ship slid beneath the second and third energy balls.

"I wonder if they can do that again?" the executive officer's position asked, reestablishing his presence on the bridge.

"I say we don't give them a chance," the captain replied. "Activate the ESD beam and target the three remaining ships."

"Saint Payback is a Bitch," the tactical officer said, adding a moment later, "Targets acquired and ready to fire."

The ESD beam fired the equivalent of a solar flare. It had a tendency to wreak havoc on the ship's systems, but it was useful when the chips were down. ESD stood for "Eat Shit and Die."

"Fire," Reynolds ordered.

The beam charged and sent death coursing through the pathways the AI had protected from the energy surges. Together, the enemy ships charged the emitters, and nanoseconds later the *Reynolds* violently lunged sideways, bringing her forward section to bear on the incoming ships just moments before the ESD beam streamed outward.

The massive counterstroke forked as it approached the remaining ships, striking with devastating force, instantly collapsing their shields and ripping into their vulnerable hulls. The three hulks continued past the *Reynolds* on a ballistic trajectory toward deep space, the ships' dead crews entombed on a forever trip to nowhere.

Onboard Superdreadnought *Reynolds*, smoke drifted lazily through the corridors. The lack of atmosphere smothered any fires before they could start, and the cold of space crept in while the maintenance and repair bots clanged and banged their way through the long list of repairs.

"Sensors! Where is my map of this galaxy? I'll settle for a map of this star system." Reynolds descended into a foul mood. Had he just killed innocents? What about their technology? "Helm, chase down those three and let's see if we can't scavenge some information."

CHAPTER TWO

"We're within range, Captain," Helm said. "And the retrieval bots are standing by."

"Get in front of those ships and use our shields to slow their momentum. I don't want to have to chase them into deep space."

"Aye, Captain," the empty seat at the helm replied.

The *Reynolds* looped smoothly around the dead ships, took a position in front of them, and opted to use the shields as a bumper instead of the tractor beams because there was too much debris floating in space. The tractor beams set to repulse could further break the ship apart while launching all the debris like a shotgun blast. Matching speed, they touched gently, and the superdreadnought reversed thrusters.

"Deploy the retrieval bots," the AI ordered. "Comm, onscreen."

"Aye, Captain," Comm replied.

The endless black of space appeared on the viewscreen at the front of the bridge. Thin green lines segmented the screen into four quadrants, and an identification number, heading, and coordinates occupied the upper righthand corner of each bot's section.

Stars speckled the retrieval bots' feeds, except for the ever-growing dark forms that blotted out the center of their views. The alien ships.

"Contact in approximately one minute. It'll take some time for the bots to cut through the hull," Comm reported.

"We've got Kurtherian bastards to hunt," the captain said. "Whatever you're doing, do it faster."

"You know as well as I do that the bots will cut as fast as they cut, and no faster. There's not much that can be done to speed them up."

"We could pierce the hull with another shot from the railgun," Weapons said. "Punch a hole they could use to get in."

"I like the way you think," the captain said. "Let's—"

"Nope," Tactical said. "Too late now. The bots are already cutting."

Violet light flared in each of the four quadrants of the viewscreen—the bots' cutting lasers hard at work.

The captain grumbled, "I hate waiting."

A dark object glinted in the corner of one of the quadrants, then it went black again.

"Did you see that?" the captain asked.

"See what?" the XO replied. "You don't have fingers to point, so I have no idea what you're talking about."

"Something in the corner of the viewscreen. Comm, order the bots to do a visual sweep of the area."

"Yessir."

The bots' heads swiveled, shifting the feeds on the

viewscreen. At first, nothing seemed out of the ordinary. The cold black of space extended infinitely.

A dark form passed over a distant cluster of stars. Then it happened again.

"*There*," the captain said. "Bot 27652's feed."

"I see it," the rest of the AI's personalities replied in unison.

"It appears to be debris from one of the damaged ships," Navigation reported.

"It can't harm us," Tactical said. "It'll just bounce off our shields."

"The first of the bots is through the hull," Comm reported. "The others aren't far behind."

The viewscreen showed the bots' progression into the alien ship, through plates of metal, circuitry, and piping until they broke into a trapezoidal corridor wide enough for three or four average humans to walk side-by-side with plenty of extra room.

It was perfectly dark aside from the bots' spotlights shining down the corridor and the soft, orange glow they emitted from their thrusters.

"No power at all," the captain grumbled.

Grated metal floors matched the ceiling, and smooth panels covered the walls between the bulkheads and crossbeams that divided the corridor every twenty feet or so.

Most of the ship's interior looked intact, but after five minutes of progress, the bots' feeds showed plenty of scattered debris floating throughout. Conduits, hoses, and twisted metal extended from the overhead and bulkheads like tendrils.

The AI found it disturbing that the bots hadn't run across any alien bodies yet.

"Perhaps the ship was piloted by another form of artificial intelligence?" the XO said.

The captain bristled at the interruption. "Stop reading my thoughts, Commander."

"I *am* your thoughts, Captain."

"You know what I mean. It pains me to think that we've destroyed one of our own. Why wouldn't an alien AI want to talk to us?"

"We transmitted in the languages of living beings," Comm offered slowly.

"Next time, add binary to the mix. Hell, throw in some cool equations and shit."

"And pictures of your mother." The XO's position let out a hearty belly laugh, and he made it sound convincing although there was no belly or vocal cords.

"Although she smelt of elderberries, she was still my mum," Helm added.

"At ease!" the captain's position ordered. "You know very well that mom smelled of elbow grease and desire."

The positions laughed easily, appreciating their shared sense of humor.

"They've reached the bridge. At least, I think it's the bridge," Comm said.

"Proceed," the captain ordered, instantly returning to business.

The viewscreen flared with violet light as the bots cut into the bridge's airtight hatch. It succumbed to the lasers in seconds, and the bots' metal arms pushed it inward. The door floated into the bridge until it collided with one of the consoles and came to rest.

Inside, the bots found a slew of wide seats at various stations, all empty except for one centralized chair facing away from them.

Something sat in that chair—a hulking form, indistinguishable in the low light but clearly not humanoid.

"Comm, order three bots to work on retrieving data from the ship's systems. Have them focus on identifying habitable populated worlds with advanced technology," the captain said. "You know, the usual shit."

"Roger," Tactical replied.

Two of the bots removed panels to dig into the guts of the enemy computers. Once they identified the power supply line, they tapped in and cycled the power through a variety of phases before the system reacted. They added juice to bring the enemy ship's computer to life.

"And obviously, have them grab whatever info they can regarding the ship's weapons systems, shields, and other diagnostics."

"Right. Working on it, Captain."

"And have them look for signs of Kurtherians."

Navigation sighed. "Is there anything you *don't* want them to look for?"

"Maybe they can find you a better attitude while they're at it?" the captain replied, making it sound like a question.

"One improved attitude coming right up. Would you like fries with that?"

"Does it count as a burn if you're technically insulting yourself?" Helm asked.

"I don't see why not. Self-deprecation can be a useful asset," Tactical replied.

"Can you tell me who's in that chair?" the captain asked, diverting the positions' attention back to the matter at hand.

"Captain?" Comm asked.

"What?"

"What about the fourth bot?"

"What about it?"

"What do you want it to do?" Comm asked.

"Check out the thing in the chair, of course. Why do I have to think of everything?" The captain sounded miffed.

"I know that one. Pick me!" Tactical replied.

"No, pick me!" Helm said.

"I'll take it," the XO said dismissively. "Because in all the universe, there is no one smarter than you. None of us are as smart as *all* of us, and that is you, good Captain."

"Bravo, XO! You get a cookie. Now, send the bot to check out the thing in the captain's chair. I want to know about the sonofabitch who attacked us."

"Roger that, Captain."

Three of the viewscreen quadrants focused on various consoles and panels within the bridge as the bots began working to power up the ship's systems enough to extract data. The fourth quadrant showed an approach toward the alien captain's chair and the monstrosity sitting in it.

Whatever the alien was, it was brown and black, covered in hair reminiscent of the rough bristles of a brush or even a porcupine's quills, and it was bulky. In the cold vacuum of space, some sort of moisture had crystallized into tiny yellow flecks on the tips of its quills.

As the bot began to round the chair for a better look, a deep groan sounded throughout the alien ship's bridge.

The screech of rending metal tore over the comm, and the fourth bot's feed turned toward the bridge's ceiling in time to see a jagged stalactite of metal jabbing through.

Pop.

The fourth bot's feed went dark.

"Shit! Report!" the captain yelled.

"Assessing," Tactical said.

"I mean *fucking now*! What the hell happened?"

"It's debris from one of the other ships, Captain," the XO said. "It's a total nut roll out there."

He swapped the fourth robot's quadrant for a "windshield" view beyond the *Reynolds'* hull. It showed a massive, jagged chunk of metal carving through the alien ship's hull. Meanwhile, the bots in the other three quadrants scrambled and scurried around the bridge to avoid succumbing to the same fate as their crushed cousin.

"Captain, we've got to extract them now," Tactical said.

"But they haven't gotten even a tenth of the information we wanted from—" Comm started to protest.

"Scans indicate the ship's hull's integrity is failing," Tactical continued. "We won't get shit for information if the rest of the bots get pulverized in the process."

"Tell bots two and three to transmit to the last nanosecond. Stay the course, good bots. Your lives will not be lost in vain!" the captain declared. "Order bot number one to grab a sample from the alien captain so we can analyze it."

"Yeah, *if* we can get it out," Navigation muttered. "I respectfully suggest that maybe next time we plan our dead enemy ship exploitation operation a little better."

"Noted, you sandy little butthole. Do you know what we need?" the captain growled.

None of the AI's other personalities answered.

"Fucking people. Fucking *people* would be warier because they die so easily."

"Captain?" Comm asked, trying to turn the attention back to the issues on screen.

One of the bots zipped over to the captain's chair, now obliterated by the debris piercing the bridge. It somehow managed to retrieve what looked to be some sort of prickly brown-and-black arm. It happened so fast that the captain didn't get a good look at it.

The alien ship continued to moan, and the bulkheads, girders, and decks buckled and tore as the bot rushed from the bridge.

Bots two and three started transmitting data.

"Yes!" Comm shouted. "See me fist-pumping the air in victory. The data is coming through."

Then another quadrant blinked out with a *crunch* and a sharp hiss.

The second bot was down. The feed from the third bot showed a section of the bridge ceiling slamming down on top of it, smashing the second to scrap. Worse still, the third bot was trapped under the debris that had destroyed the second bot.

"Shit!" the captain fumed. "Can it cut itself out?"

"It's trying," Comm said.

"Tell it to keep transmitting the data. Go, stupid little cousin, go!" the XO encouraged. "Focus all your efforts into getting that data. And then focus the rest of your efforts on recovering the bot with the arm, or whatever the hell that biomass is."

Bot three remained on the bridge, still transmitting, but only a quarter of a tenth of the information they could've gleaned. And that was *if* bot three managed to stay plugged in.

As the bot with the arm peeled out of the bridge and into the dying ship, every curse in every human language cycled through the AI's thought patterns.

"It's not going to make it," Helm said.

"He's right," Tactical confirmed. "The ship's tearing apart too quickly."

"Bullshit. It's gonna make it," the captain said. The bridge started cheering.

"Come on, little guy. You can do it!"

"Go, bot, go."

"Fuck the blasphemers! You got this."

"Like hell, it does," Navigation muttered. "I'm taking control."

The arm-bot's feed jumped and jolted, then drew to almost a complete stop. Its onscreen progression jerked to life again and the bot lurched forward, its thrusters burning at full-blast.

"Don't fuck this up," the captain said.

"I play a lot of video games," Navigation replied.

The third bot's viewscreen went black.

"Transmission has ceased. Retrieval bots on the bridge are out of commission."

"A moment of silence, please, for our stupid brethren." The moment lasted five microseconds. "Now order three more retrieval bots to be produced from the scrap metal of the enemy ship. That'll teach those bastards to fuck with the SD *Reynolds*. Maybe the next aliens will smell the fear."

"Captain?" the XO said. "Looks like Nav is earning his pay today.

The bot's view expanded to fill the whole viewscreen. It ducked under debris, wove between bending bulkheads, and dodged tentacles of wires lashing out toward it.

Then a grate from the ceiling swung down like a scythe.

"Watch out!" the captain yelled.

"I see it!" Navigation said.

The bot whizzed out of the way—just barely—and evaded a circuit-severing collision. In the distance, the path the bots had carved from the ship's hull gaped open.

"Almost there..." Navigation muttered.

"I think he's gonna do it," Helm said.

"C'mon, kid. You've got this!" the XO said.

"Only fifty more meters..." Tactical said.

The wall shrieked and collapsed onto itself, sealing the hole and trapping the bot and its precious bit of alien inside the ship.

CHAPTER THREE

"All hands on deck!" the captain bellowed. "I need options, people. I want to know about the aliens who gave us such a warm welcome."

Tactical was the first to speak up. "Watch this. Weapons are ready?"

"Ready," Tactical told himself in a cold, hard voice.

"What are you doing?" the XO asked.

Tactical ignored him. "Fire!" A light flashed on the console. "Firing!"

Onscreen, the retrieval bot's view flashed white-hot light, then the image quickly faded.

The view from outside the ship showed a gaping hole outlined with the bright orange of molten metal, streaking across the alien ship like a comet.

"Bullseye!" Tactical confirmed confidently.

"There's your way out!" Helm shouted.

"I see it," Navigation replied.

"And?" the captain said, drawing out the word.

"And I'm flying our small friend out."

The retrieval bot lurched toward the opening, careened through the hole in the ship's hull, and burst into the black abyss of space. Behind it, the alien ship came apart in surreal slow motion as sections ripped silently from the superstructure, and created a growing cloud of space debris.

"Nav, place a marker buoy for what's it worth so casual passersby can avoid that trash," the captain ordered. "How long until we have the bot?"

"Less than a minute, Captain," Comm said.

"Good. Put the alien captain's biomass into quarantine, and turn the scientist loose on it." The captain added, "And collect enough scrap for three new retrieval bots."

"Maintenance bots deploying." The main screen showed three dots of light flying toward the cloud of debris. They started attaching independent gravitic thrusters to the largest sections. Three oversized sections of the alien ship started moving slowly toward the super-dreadnought.

"Do they use marker buoys in this galaxy?" the XO asked.

"I don't know, but I'll assume they do because it makes sense. Maybe in this sector of space, it'll attract ships like moths to a flame. Who knows? At least *we'll* avoid that garbage and know that we tried to play nice."

"I see," the XO said, laughing at his own joke. The empty positions on the bridge didn't give the XO the slightest groan of support.

"Play nice by marking the place where we destroyed a bunch of the locals?" Helm asked.

"Sucks to be them."

"Looks more like we're waving a big flag that says, Think Twice. Be Nice or Die."

"Just drop the marker buoy and let's be on our way," the captain shot back.

"How much data did the other bots transmit before they bit the big one?"

"Not much. Nothing that suggests Kurtherians, but there are at least four nearby systems with humanoids."

"The closest one is a few days away," Navigation reported.

"Given the damage we've sustained," Helm started, "I would advise against using the main engines until we've made repairs."

Engineering's voice emanated from the depths of the *Reynolds*, "I concur. We've got a ton of work to do before we try anything grandiose."

"'Grandiose.' I didn't know I would ever use that word, but it fits. We shall do 'grandiose' once we've made sufficient repairs to the ship. It's settled. We'll go to the closest planet with humanoids, and we'll recruit there," the captain said.

"Hold on," the XO's position called. "You've already made the decision that we are getting a crew?"

"Yes. We need their flexibility to help with repairs, and they will provide some balance. I'm tired of all you whiners. I think I'd rather have humanoids."

"If anyone will have you," Navigation quipped.

"Like I had your mother last night!" The XO bellylaughed again.

"I want a new XO. Maybe I'll promote a humanoid in front of you."

. . .

Superdreadnought *Reynolds*, **Lariest System, Chain Galaxy**

A few days later...

"We'll enter the planet's atmosphere in approximately three minutes, Captain," Helm reported.

"Good. Now, I've been thinking about how to mingle with the locals."

"I'm showing signs of advanced technology on the planet, including some low-level AI," Comm reported. "You could potentially commandeer one of their AI drones and interact that way."

"I'll need something mobile. The city's huge."

"There's a hovercab service in one of the planet's largest population centers. Perhaps you could take control of one of the drivers?" Comm suggested.

"You mean steal one? I like it. Paint me chrome and set me loose."

"No can do, Captain," Comm said. "The android body looks like he's a local. Realistic nano-adaptive skin and features. No chrome to be seen."

"Even better. If I look like them, they'll like me sooner, and then we can get a crew and get back to hunting Kurtherians."

Comm hesitated. "Well, sort of..."

"What the hell, Other Me? Spit it out, already."

"You're going to be an average-looking guy driving a taxi in a city mostly populated by humanoids who have reddish skin, dark hair, and black eyes."

The captain's voice went flat. "That's the best you can do?"

"On short notice? Yes," Comm added, "But these taxi guys are everywhere. You'll be a familiar face."

"Can't we change the android's appearance once I upload?"

"In theory, yes. But the real issue is getting hold of one in the first place."

"I'm open to suggestions," the captain said.

"Can't we call one and have it show up when we dock?" the XO asked.

Silence filled the bridge.

"I'd like to call you stupid, but that sounds like an easy solution, and easy is usually the best," the captain said.

"Except it won't work," Comm replied.

"Why not?" the XO asked, offended.

"Their routes don't intersect with our landing site. The spaceport employs its own taxi service, operated by actual, fleshy drivers." Comm added, "Oooh! They offer complimentary libations to passengers!"

"Until we have a body, there will be no drinking on duty. Or ever," the captain said firmly. "What's our course of action?"

"Perhaps, instead of stealing a body, we can recruit one of the drivers to help us meet the locals," Tactical suggested.

"We're landing now, Captain," Helm reported.

The SD *Reynolds* shuddered and quaked more than usual as its thrusters pummeled the planet's surface, slowing its descent until it set down at the spaceport.

"Land ho!" the XO crooned.

"Let's go find a crew," the captain said in a low voice. "Call several of the spaceport taxis here."

"Aye, Captain," Comm replied.

"And then what?" Tactical asked.

"You'll see."

Ankal Spaceport, Lariest System, Chain Galaxy

Jiya Lemaire drove the hovercab toward the alien ship that had just docked on the spaceport's southwestern platform, marveling at its peculiar shape, massive size, and strange markings. It dwarfed any ship she had ever seen by a large margin.

As she drew near, she noticed blackened streaks and tears across parts of its hull. She hadn't ever been off-world, but she'd heard tales of the grand excursions and exploits of a privileged few of her fellow Larians who'd been conscripted into the planet's military.

But I was never good enough for them. She straightened her stuffy spaceport uniform, remembering how she'd failed to pass not one but *three* of the exams the Lariest Planetary Military Forces had required her to take as part of her application, surprising as that was.

She had been sure she'd nailed them all.

Six other hovercabs closed in on the alien ship from various angles around the platform.

Must be a large delegation.

But it boggled her mind that a ship this large would make use of the spaceport's taxi services instead of hiring a private transport. Maybe this species of aliens were cheapskates.

I hope not. She couldn't afford to shuttle around a bunch of cheapskates. Not with *her* outstanding debts.

As Jiya pulled her hovercab to a stop a few meters beyond the ship—which loomed over her like a skyscraper lying on its side—the comm in her dashboard crackled.

"Never seen a ship that big." Rictor's voice said as he pulled his hovercab next to hers. When Jiya glanced at him, Rictor winked while pursing his lips. "Bigger is better, baby."

Fat lush. She sighed, shook her head, and faced forward again.

"Aw, don't be like that."

Magni, their shift supervisor, broke in. "Enough, you two. All I know is that we've got a job to do, and you turds are dusting the dirt with your monthly performance numbers," Magni said. "Your fare quotas have been in the shitter for the last two weeks. This is your chance to redeem yourselves, and maybe save your miserable jobs."

"Yes, boss," Jiya said. She'd lost the last four jobs before this. If she couldn't hold a taxi gig, she'd be out of work, maybe for good. She needed this job.

She looked up at the ship. *This* has *to be a big fare.* Maybe even multiple trips. If the aliens left her some good tips, she might finally get some breathing room in her life.

"Which end do you figure is the front?" Balga, another of the drivers, asked over the comm.

"And that, friends, is why Balga never gets laid," Rictor quipped.

Even Jiya had to grin at that one.

"Ha, ha, Rictor," Balga replied, his voice flat. "Very funny. I mean, what end do we go in?"

"You're making this too easy, Balga," Rictor said between chuckles.

"Dammit!" Balga growled. "I mean, where are we meeting the fares?"

"I see a huge hatch opening up ahead," Magni said. "Looks like a ramp is extending down. Probably wide enough for four or five hovercabs to go up at once. We'll start there."

"Copy that, boss," Balga said.

Magni led the way, and Jiya and the others followed. As they approached the open hatch, running lights along the ramp floor activated as if to show them the way.

Once all seven hovercabs had made it inside, they parked and waited. Several minutes later, no one had yet emerged to greet them, and nothing else had happened, either.

"Are we wasting our time here?" Jiya asked. "At least three other ships have landed in the twenty minutes since we rolled up to this one."

"How could you possibly know that?" Magni snapped.

Oops. Jiya had managed to hack access to the hovercab dispatcher's feed on her comm, but no one else knew she had. It was a violation of company policy, and it could get her the axe if anyone important—like Magni—found out.

She improvised, "It was a guess, Magni. I've been working here for a few months now. I know how often ships come and go. Anyway, shouldn't someone try to figure out what's going on?"

"Yes, someone should," Magni said. "And it'll be you. Report back to us what you find."

Jiya blinked. "What? That's not what I—"

"No, you're absolutely right," Magni said. "Someone should check things out. You're up."

"I meant someone with more experience. Like you, our supervisor."

"You just got done saying how you've been working here for a few months and that you know how things work." Two cabs ahead, Magni's head popped out and he sneered at her, his under-bite overemphasized. "If that isn't a ringing endorsement, I don't know what is."

Jiya bristled. The idea of exploring a massive alien ship, the likes of which had never been seen on Lariest before, terrified her, but it also stoked something deep within—a desire to challenge the unknown while putting her co-workers in their places.

She hated both sensations equally.

Jiya hated when these bottom-feeders gave her hell for being a female even more. She had to show them she wasn't afraid. She wanted them to know that she was better than them.

"Fine," she said, deactivating her cab. "What do we know about the ship? Whom should I talk to?"

"Uh, we know it's here, and we know it's fucking huge." Magni added, "Happy trails."

Rictor and Balga's laughter rumbled over the comm, and Jiya frowned.

"Fine," she repeated. "The largest fare is mine."

"Whatever," Magni said.

"What? That's gwampo shit," Rictor said.

"Yeah, that's not fair," Balga added.

"Then you pricks can go with her," Magni said.

Jiya cursed under her breath. *Not what I was going for.*

"It's better if more than one of you go," Magni said. "That way, if any of you get killed or eaten, maybe the other two can still make it out."

Jiya started to retort, but Balga broke in first. "D-don't joke about that shit, man! That really happened once!"

"Do I *sound* like I'm joking?" Magni asked.

He didn't, and no one responded.

With a sigh, Jiya opened the gullwing door of her hovercab and stepped out. She tried to straighten the rumples and wrinkles of her uniform, but given how many hours each day she sat, some of them were permanent features.

The loading bay extended far into the darkness in almost every direction except down, so much so that she couldn't see either its back wall or most of its ceiling.

What could a bay this size contain? What types of ships could the aliens dock here? How much cargo could they transport? She had no idea, and that only amplified her curiosity about the ship.

She affixed her uniform cap to her head, pulling her long black ponytail through the loop in the back. Then she rubbed her hands together, shut the hovercab's door, and took a glance at herself in the window's reflection.

Satisfied, she started toward a corridor marked with lights like those on the ramp where they'd entered.

"Wait up, Hot Pants," Rictor called from behind her.

If anything, that made her want to walk faster, but she reconsidered. If she let him catch up and could get him to take the lead, she could cut the number of comments he'd make about her ass.

So she waited.

Rictor and Balga approached, and she motioned for them to lead the way. They hesitated, though.

"I don't have time for this." She was losing money in fares and tips with every additional minute that passed. So she turned and strode into the corridor, ass comments be damned.

"They're coming in now," Comm reported.

"About damned time," the captain said. "They were just sitting there doing nothing for twenty minutes."

"Maybe they were waiting for us. We sat here doing nothing for twenty minutes, too," the XO said.

The captain's position gave an audible sigh.

"They're not advancing quickly, but the lights are helping to keep them moving, at least," Tactical said.

"Humans like having their way well-lit. It appears our red-tinged humanoid visitors have a similar affinity," the captain said.

"They've reached the mess hall, Captain," Comm said.

"Good. When they're away from the door, you may proceed," the captain said.

By the time Jiya heard the door shut, it was too late. She turned back toward it, but the lights in the huge room switched off.

She'd gotten herself into a mess this time. Maybe a really, really bad one.

"What the hell is going on?" Balga's voice came from somewhere behind her.

Rictor swore, but something cut off his voice. Metal grated on metal to Jiya's left.

Balga yelped and then went quiet, too. More scraping and scratching, then the stillness of deathly quiet.

Jiya wished she had a weapon on her besides her telescoping bō staff, but the spaceport forbade hovercab drivers from carrying guns. *I knew I should've ignored that stupid rule.*

Horrifying scenarios rifled through her mind, as did Balga and Magni's rumors of what had happened before—whatever it was that *had* happened.

She extended her arms, groping in the perfect darkness for something—anything—she could use to get her bearings.

Her hands found something cool, metal, and definitely not a wall. It had rounded sections, joints, and…a face?

Two lights—two yellow eyes—ignited and stared down at her.

CHAPTER FOUR

Jiya bolted awake.

She regretted the movement instantly. Her head was throbbing. The world spun around her, hazy and indistinct, and her hand went to the back of her skull. A tender knot met her fingers, and she hissed, yanking her hand away.

At least I'm not bleeding, she thought, doing her best to focus on the hand she held out before her.

What the hell happened? she wondered, and it all came rushing back.

Cold articulated-steel mechanical arms reaching for her. And those eyes, like two suns gleaming in the blackness of space. The lights had gone out, and she'd run into some kind of robot. She remembered screaming—although she'd deny it if anyone asked—then stumbling backward and losing her balance. That was when she'd hit the wall.

Jiya groaned, the lump on her head reminding her it was still there, thrumming in time to the rush of memories.

She gritted her teeth and looked around again, taking in her surroundings.

A small, clinical room. The walls were bare, not a single decoration or adornment to mar their metallic perfection. She was on a cot. The thin mattress barely kept the steel frame from digging into her, and her every movement made the plastic sheeting squeak. It was as comforting as fingernails on a chalkboard.

She slipped off the bed, clasping the rail to keep her balance as a wave of lightheadedness washed over her. Jiya's eyes rolled before coming back into focus.

That sucked.

Once she felt confident enough to move without falling over, she circled the bed to see what lay behind her.

A serpentine hiss stopped her. Dark lines were drawn upon the blank wall, a section of it peeling back and disappearing.

It's a door, she realized. She started toward it out of instinct, self-preservation kicking her ass into gear, but a shadowy shape drifted in and blocked the doorway. Her feet stuttered to a halt and Jiya gasped, recognizing the figure standing between her and escape.

"You!"

"Yes, me," the bot she'd run into answered as it eased into the room. "Expecting someone else?"

Jiya stared at the bot, caught off guard by its flippancy. Humanoid in shape, it was built sturdily, but despite its heavily-armored frame, it moved with a feline-like grace.

"Uh, I really don't know what I expected," she replied.

"Then why so surprised?"

It was a good question, and one Jiya had no answer for.

So, instead of muttering something inane, she shook her head and stared.

Silence settled over them for a moment.

"Anyway," the bot started, "you're probably wondering why you're here."

"You mean, why you killed the lights, ambushed my co-workers and me, and tossed me into a tiny room that might as well be a cell?"

One of the bot's eyes widened. "Well, when you put it that way it sounds kind of ominous, doesn't it?"

"You think?"

"Occasionally," the bot replied. "Although I don't often recommend it. Tactical, however—he swears by it. Gotta watch that guy."

Jiya continued to stare. She took a step back, angling to put the cot between her and the strange bot. It hadn't hurt her—yet—but it was sure as hell making her nervous. The thing sounded as if its gears were out of alignment. She wanted some kind of advantage if the thing lost what was left of its mechanical mind and came after her.

"So, uh, yeah…back to why you brought me here."

"Yeah, that." A crease on its face that Jiya imagined was meant to represent a mouth drew upward in an attempt to mimic what she thought might be a smile.

No, that's not creepy at all. She took another step away from the bot.

"You're a pilot, correct?"

A confused shudder ran through Jiya, and she ran a hand across her face to wipe away the dumbfounded expression. She nodded in reply, unsure what the bot was looking for with its casual interrogation. "Among other things."

"Do you work well with AI systems?"

Jiya swallowed hard, but there was no holding back this time. "You mean ones that aren't insane?"

The bot made that weird grin attempt again. "I see what you're implying," it said. "I am not crazy, I'm simply…expressive."

"If you say so."

"I do indeed." The bot paused. "Oh, what did you say your name was?"

"Seeing as how I was busy being bushwhacked and kidnapped, I didn't say," she told it. "But since I'm feeling a bit Stockholmish, the name's Jiya. Jiya Lemaire."

"Pleasure to meet you, Jiya. You can call me Reynolds."

I'm likely to call you a whole bunch of other things if you don't get to the point soon and let me go. "So, Reynolds, care to hop back on track and let me know why I'm here?" She motioned toward the bot blocking the door.

"Oh, that's right," Reynolds said, stepping in and clearing the way to the exit. "It's not my intention to keep you anywhere, although I am hoping you'll choose to remain."

Jiya chuckled. "Really? No offense, but you *did* trick me in here. That doesn't exactly ping high on the trust meter. Why the hell would I stick around?"

"Uh, because I pay well?"

"Wait…what?" Jiya turned her head sideways like a befuddled dog. "You kidnap me, and now you're offering me a job?"

"Isn't it obvious? I have to admit that some human

expressions confound me. I may have beaten around the bush too much in my efforts to appear more sympathetic."

Jiya shook her head. "No, have to say it really wasn't."

The bot shrugged. "Well, I am. Good pay, benefits, the opportunity to travel the stars—"

"The excellent company," she muttered.

"And that, of course," Reynolds replied. "I'm quite the companion. Ask all the other mes."

Jiya sighed and convinced herself not to ask what he meant by that. "I'm not so sure. What say you let me go and I contemplate the offer out in the sunshine?"

"You have something better to do?" the bot asked. "Going to drive a hovercab the rest of your life?"

"Hey!" Jiya snarled at Reynolds, but she found that his words had struck a chord, the sad truth drawing her stomach into a knot. "I have other options."

Did she? Her father had all but cut the tail off her future here on Lariest.

"True, the food service industry is always hiring. Would you like veggie-fries with that?"

"I'm not liking you much," she told the bot.

"Fortunately, I like me enough for both of us." That weird smile returned.

"I really wish you'd stop doing that," she said.

"Then accept my offer," it answered. "I'm on a mission —a super-important mission." The Reynolds bot glanced furtively around the room, then inched forward, closing the distance between them. "Can I tell you a secret?" it whispered conspiratorially.

Jiya stiffened at its closeness. "If you feel it's necessary." Her paranoia warred between running and punching

Reynolds in its grinning mouth. Figuring she'd break her fist on its metal skull, she stood her ground peacefully.

"I do," it answered, moving even closer. "I'm not really a bot."

Nod and smile, Jiya, nod and smile. She did just that.

"I'm actually a superdreadnought," Reynolds continued. "This ship you're in, that's me." The lights flickered on and off as if emphasizing Reynolds' words. "My Queen sent me on a mission to seek out and destroy Kurtherians." He inched closer. "You don't know of any Kurtherians, do you?"

"Uh, can't say that I do."

"Good! Dirty little bastards, those Kurtherians. Even their name sounds awful. Kur-ther-i-ans," Reynolds muttered. "Sound it out with me, and you'll see what I mean. Awful."

"No, I'm okay, thanks. I'll take your word for it."

Reynolds shrugged. "Whatever. I'll give you a few minutes to think about my offer while I confer with my other selves. Be right back."

The bot stiffened, its eyes dimming to black. Jiya stood there for a moment, her heart stuttering in her chest. She cast a sideways glance at the door, wondering if she could dart out before the bot came back online.

But if what it said was true?

Jiya sighed. How do you outrun a ship? She was sure that wasn't going to happen. Besides, the stupid thing was right.

She flopped back onto the cot, ignoring the plastic sheeting as it squeaked in protest. Did she really want to drive a hovercab the rest of her life? Working for assholes like Magni, listening to Rictor comment about her ass all day?

Wasn't this the type of adventure she'd wanted when she'd applied for the Larien military? To fly off into space and leave Lariest and her father and his impossible demands behind? What did she have on the planet besides debt and the daily grind, shuttling johns back and forth all day for shitty wages and even shittier tips?

She groaned as she thought about her life. What kind of future did she have to look forward to? The military had passed on her. Apparently, she was too difficult, if you could believe that. Tell one asshole where to go and how to get there, and they label you insubordinate. Of course, Daddy's influence in all that didn't help. He'd made it clear she'd toe the line—his line—or she'd suffer for it.

Jiya stared at the blank walls, letting her thoughts drift in directions she wanted nothing to do with. How much harder would it be working for some crazy AI spaceship as opposed to a snarky cab boss?

Well, Magni wasn't likely to get her killed. Then again, he *had* sent her on a bunch of runs to lousy neighborhoods where it was possible she'd get shot.

Jiya sat up on the cot and grunted. She'd spent her life making bad decisions without thinking about the consequences, the specter of her father always there, pushing, smothering her. Was this another bad decision or was there truly something here?

"Made up your mind?" the bot asked out of nowhere.

Jiya shrieked, turning the tail end of it into a growl. Her fist went up, ready to smash the bot in its grinning face. "Damn, Reynolds. Don't sneak up on a girl like that."

"Been standing here the whole time."

He had been, which only made his sudden reactivation worse.

Heart echoing like thunder, she glared at the bot. "So, if I accepted your offer, what would I be doing?"

"Pretty much whatever I need you to do," Reynolds answered, shrugging. "I'm a big ship with lots of needs."

Psychiatric, first and foremost. "That's not really all that enticing," she admitted. "Sounds a little…freaky."

"Much as I hate to admit this, I can't do *everything* on my own, even with my own help. We need a crew. They should be loyal, faithful, and courageous, but we'll settle for competent right now."

"Ouch."

"Nothing personal. You *are* just flesh and blood."

"You say that like it's a bad thing," she told him, huffing.

Reynolds shrugged. "Not always, no," it admitted, "but all your sleeping and eating and pooping take up an inordinate amount of your time; non-productive ship time that requires much in the way of logistics to support, which means I need even more humans to support the few humans I need. You follow?"

"You got me there." How could you argue with logic like that? Jiya just shook her head. "So, are you expecting me to help with recruiting, too?"

"Have a problem with that?"

"Not as long as the paycheck is commensurate," Jiya replied, shrugging and doing her best to make her bargaining appear casual, "*and*…I get first choice in who gets the job." She already had an idea as to who she wanted working beside her.

The fact that her choices would piss off *Daddy Dearest* only made it more satisfying.

Reynolds forced that inhuman grin onto his face again. "Fair enough, but you have to accept the job first. You *are* accepting it, right?"

She drew in a deep breath, letting it fill her lungs, then let it out in a soft whistle. "Sure, why not? I've nothing better to do than travel to some distant universe where I'm likely to die horribly while working for a AI with multiple personalities." *Just another day at the office.* "What about the other knuckleheads who came in with me?"

"That's the spirit," Reynolds said, patting her on the shoulder. "Those other knuckleheads are passed out in their hovercabs. They're not exactly the be-all-you-can-be types. When they wake up, they won't remember coming aboard. My bots dumped them on the tarmac with their hovercabs. There are no Larians left aboard besides you. We still have your cab. I feel like we're going to need that."

Jiya muffled a chuckle with the back of her hand. She was glad Reynolds had seen the lack of potential in her boneheaded co-workers. It wasn't just her. The very last thing she wanted to do was spend more time with Magni and Rictor.

"All right, let's go find you a crew," Jiya told the AI.

CHAPTER FIVE

Reynolds led Jiya through the massive ship—through *him*, actually, which really wasn't how she wanted to think about it—to what was apparently a crew lounge. He waved her inside.

A large table sat near the back corner, comfortable chairs all around. A large viewscreen rose out of the center of the table. Reynolds gestured in that direction.

"Have a seat," he told her.

She shrugged and made to flop into the nearest chair.

Reynolds shouted, catching her in half-squat. "Not there! That seat's taken."

Jiya eased up, casting a glance over her shoulder at what appeared to be an empty chair. "Uh, okay…" She moved to the one next to it.

Reynolds' voice sounded from the seat. "Not this one either, cabbie. Find your own. I'm not sharing."

"Neither am I," Reynolds' voice called from another chair.

Jiya glared at the speaking chairs in turn, then she

shared that glare with the bot. "Are any of these chairs *not* taken by the other yous?"

The bot pointed at one right in front of the viewscreen. "That one is open."

After throwing a casual stink-eye in his direction, she dropped into the proffered seat. "Can we at least do introductions, so I know which you is you?"

"We're all me," the chair next to her answered.

"Not helping," Jiya replied. "You're going to give me whiplash trying to keep up."

"I suppose you're right," the bot conceded. "The chair to your right is Executive Officer Reynolds, my second-in-command. To his right is Tactical..."

Jiya sighed. "And who's to my left?"

"That'd be Comm."

"Navigation is on the other side," the bot said.

The far chair called out a howdy.

"Helm is absent," Reynolds said. "Probably asleep at the wheel."

"And you're the captain?" she asked the bot.

"We're all captain," Tactical answered. "He's Lance Reynolds, but as the captain and the ship, he's just called Reynolds."

Jiya slumped in her seat. "Can we get on with this?" she told them, hoping the sooner she got a real crew in place, the sooner the split-personality AI could pull itself together. Literally.

Emphasis on *hope*.

"Someone's in a hurry, I see," Tactical said, adding a little reverb for sass.

The viewscreen came to life, and Jiya leaned back in her

chair in surprise as an orbital view of a looming planet appeared. Enthralled by the brilliant blues and greens on the screen, she realized after only a moment that the screen showed her homeworld of Lariest.

It hung in space, the image too clear and precise to be a holovid or picture.

Then it struck her.

"Wait a second! When did we end up in space?" She spun around to face the bot. "You took off before I said yes?"

"Call me an optimist." Reynolds shrugged awkwardly.

"Oh, hell, you have *got* to be kidding me," she shouted, jumping to her feet and marching over to the bot. She jabbed it in the chest with her index finger. "I can't believe you did this!" Then she dipped her head to the side. "Did you just kidnap me for the second time in one day? Of course, you did."

Jiya growled, storming back to her seat. She refused to sit, though.

"Here's the deal, Reynolds," Jiya started. "If you want me to work with you, to help you find a good crew, we need to come to an understanding."

"Oh, here we go," Tactical mumbled.

"Stow it," Navigation told him. "She has a right to speak her piece."

The bot raised its hand in surrender. "I vote we listen."

"Are you all done?"

"The pulpit's yours," XO replied. "Preach on, sister!"

"Good," she spat. "Look, you can't just jerk me around like I'm some sort of meaty marionette—"

"Interesting visual," Tactical muttered, "but I wonder if meat puppet might be a bit more apropos to—"

"Shut it," the Reynolds bot told him, pointing a stubby finger at the empty seat.

Jiya continued as if they hadn't interrupted, "There need to be ground rules. I need a say in what happens to me, like whether I leave a planet. I expect you to treat me like part of the crew—with respect."

"Those last two are a bit contradictory if you ask me," Tactical stated.

"Anyway," Jiya said, clearing her throat and wondering how the hell she ended up on a spaceship with an asshole like Rictor, only in AI form. "My point is, I'm not a tool to be whipped out and used and then cast aside when you're done. I'm a Larian, flesh and blood, a living being, and I need to be treated as such. I need to be involved in the decisions that affect me. Is that clear? Are we on the same page, Reynolds?"

"You're right," the bot said, "and we apologize. We're on the same page, I assure you, so, please sit down and relax. We promise to behave."

Jiya glared at the bot for a moment longer before conceding and flopping into her seat. She leaned back and steepled her fingers, shifting her gaze around the table at the invisible AIs—feeling stupid for doing it.

"So, I'm guessing by the empty chairs around the big table that you need a complete crew: pilot, XO, Tactical, Comm, Navigation, Helm, and Security, but not Captain, right?"

"Give or take a few positions, correct. Some of those I can handle on my own."

She nodded. "I'm also guessing you want them all right away?"

"We *are* on a mission—an important one—so yes, the quicker, the better," the bot replied.

"Okay, then I have some candidates for you, like I told you earlier. These people will be perfect."

"As long as you understand we get final approval on your selections," the bot told her, "and...I will be going with you to recruit them."

Jiya raised an eyebrow. "I understand oversight and whatnot, and I'm okay with that since it is *your* ship...but do you have any clue what you look like?"

"There's nothing wrong with the way I look." The bot glanced down at itself, running its hands over its sleek metallic frame. "It's all about the chrome, baby."

"Exactly," Jiya said. "Your gleaming metal ass won't get past port security, let alone be allowed to wander the streets. And these people I have in mind, they're kind of in the same boat as me with regards to my father, as in, they're in the doghouse—the castaways. You won't get anywhere near them in that hunk of bolts you're wearing, and they sure as hell won't be allowed off-planet with you."

"Well, the crew and I discussed jacking one of the auto-mated hovercabs and plugging me into the body of the android driver."

"That's not the worst idea I've heard," Jiya told him. "Still, we'd have to get hold of one first, then defeat the security protocols because the cab company keeps constant tabs on their drivers. They'd notice one missing pretty quick if we simply grabbed one and ran off with it."

The Reynolds bot nodded. "We could pull it off, right, XO?"

"Yeah," XO replied. "Probably. No, let me go with a definite maybe."

"Don't worry, I know how to make it work. I'll need some equipment, though."

The bot nodded. "Fine, we'll give you whatever you need, but first, I want to discuss these candidates you have in mind, Jiya."

"Not to be an instigator…" Navigation said, interrupting their discussion.

"What's on your mind, Navigation?" XO asked.

"We're conceding a lot to this meatbag. No offense, of course," Navigation said.

"A little taken," Jiya responded, sneering. "But, please, continue and let's see if you can be more offensive."

"We're conceding an awful lot here, surrendering a bunch of control to her and the crew she picks out, but what do we know about her? What are her qualifications?"

"Good question," XO agreed. "What *do* we know about her?"

The Reynolds bot gestured to Jiya. "They're not wrong to wonder. Care to tell us why we should allow you aboard and let you help choose our crew?"

Jiya chuckled. "You mean besides you getting me onboard through subterfuge and then kidnapping me?"

"Uh…let's stick to the specifics of the job, please," the bot hedged. "Mistakes may have been made in our initial engagement with the alien—I mean, with the Larian called Jiya. We admit this. We brought you aboard because you had spark and—"

"Because you reminded him of someone," Tactical clarified.

"I told you not to mention that," the bot hissed at Tactical's chair, although the sound was more like a steam valve letting loose.

"Dare I ask?" Jiya questioned.

"Probably best not to," Comm answered. Jiya sank deeper into her chair, shaking her head.

"Anyway, we saw potential in you," the bot went on. "However, it would be good to know more about you."

Jiya sighed and paused for a moment, waiting for a snide remark. When none came, she straightened and met the bot's eyes, seeing as how she really felt stupid talking to empty chairs. She felt only marginally less so talking to the chrome humanoid-shaped bot.

"So, cards on the table here, I'm more than a cab driver and pilot."

"I knew it!" Navigation shouted. "She's a Kurtherian spy out to sabotage us and steal all our protein bars."

"Wait," Jiya replied, throwing her hands in the air. "What the hell is wrong with you? I told you earlier that I don't even know who or what the Kurtherians are."

"Likely story, spy," Navigation told her. "You'd be a pretty crappy spy if you admitted it."

"She's not a spy," XO told Navigation.

"Let her talk," the bot said. "We're not going to learn anything if some twitchy, paranoid AI keeps jumping in every thirty seconds."

"Just shut the hell up, all of you," Jiya shouted, slamming her fist on the table. "Seriously, if you want me here, you have to stop the madness." She wagged a finger around the circle, pointing first to the bot and then to the "occupied" seats. "Keep this craziness up and I'll jump off this ship, even if we're still in space."

Jiya rubbed her eyes and counted back from ten. By the time she reached one she wasn't any less annoyed, but she could at least talk again. She cleared her throat. "Okay, so first off, not a spy." She jabbed a finger in Navigation's direction. "I'm actually the daughter of the president of Lariest, President Lemaire," she explained, turning her finger to the viewscreen showing her beautiful homeworld.

"So you're a pampered little rich girl?" Tactical asked.

"I wish," Jiya moaned. "You see, *Daddy* and I don't get along so well."

"What did he do, cut off your allowance?" Tactical teased.

"No, he cut off my entire life after investing a fortune to get me ready for it," she replied. "In fact, if he knew I was up here, off-world, he'd send a destroyer to reclaim me just out of spite."

The bot chuckled. "We'd send it back in pieces."

"Little ones," Comm confirmed. "Sparkly bits of space dust raining down atop his presidential palace."

To her surprise, Jiya grinned. She could picture it, and the thought amused her.

"So, famous daughter with daddy issues. What else you got going on?" Navigation asked. "So far, I'm thinking she's perfect for latrine duty."

She sneered in his direction. "I've had as much arms training as was possible for a civilian, along with hand-to-hand combat starting at age four. While other kids learned musical instruments, I was beating the crap out of leather bags.

"Anyway, I've had private tutors my whole life—advanced studies in just about every subject—and I've spent the last few years training to join the military." She drew in a deep breath and let it out slowly. "Until my father tanked my application behind the scenes. See, he thought I'd grown too hostile. Entitled, even. I think he got it into his head that if I served in the military, I might rise to high enough rank to challenge his leadership. So, they told me I was too volatile and hostile, and that I hadn't passed their entry exams. I know he told them to reject me."

"Hostile?" Navigation asked. "You don't say!"

She spun in her seat and glared at his chair. Then, without so much as a tell, she whipped a small metal tube out of her pocket and snapped it in the chair's direction. It *clacked*, expanding rapidly into a long bō staff. The tip hovered just inches from the back of the seat.

The chair leapt backward with a screech, falling onto its back, the resulting *thump* echoing through the lounge.

"Ha!" Navigation shouted. "You missed me."

"I wouldn't have if you had a face," Jiya replied, spinning the staff around and retracting it with a *snap*. She stuffed it back into her pocket.

"I thought you searched her," the bot asked.

"Me?" XO replied. "How the hell was I supposed to do it? You're the one with hands."

"That's beside the point."

"That's *exactly* the point," XO told him.

"Moving on," the bot said, motioning to Jiya. "So, it

seems you're qualified after all, which is good." The bot leaned over and whispered in her ear, "I'd have looked like a real idiot if you hadn't been. Whew." He patted her on the shoulder and took a step back.

"Yeah, that would have done it," she answered, shaking her head. "So, yeah, if I've satisfied your curiosity, can we get on with finding you the rest of your crew?"

"Sure," the bot replied. "You said you had some people in mind?"

She nodded and tapped the viewscreen, bringing up a menu. "I have a few. Take a look."

CHAPTER SIX

"Is this really the plan?" the Reynolds bot asked.

"Got a better one?" Jiya pressed, staring out past the tarmac at the rows of Jonny taxis bustling back and forth, carrying their fares to and from the port.

The bot shrugged. "Not one that doesn't involve turning the destructive firepower of my superdreadnought self on their asses and picking an android body out of the wreckage."

"Case in point, Reynolds—the idea is to blend in, not stand out," Jiya told him. "We need to be subtle."

"And your plan is subtle?" he asked.

"Subtle-ish," she answered. "I mean, we're not exactly being given the opportunity to be surgical here. It's really the best of our options."

"I'm going to have to take your word for that," he replied. "It's your world, after all. You know best."

"If only." Jiya chuckled. "Anyway, you ready to do this?"

"As ready as I'll ever be."

"That's the spirit," she replied, popping open the

passenger door to her cab and ushering the bot inside. "You'll have to duck out of sight."

"So you've told me twenty or thirty times already. I've got it."

"Can't have the authorities see you," she reminded him. "That happens and they come down on us and realize who I am and what's going on, we're going to have some serious explaining to do."

"Daddy doesn't like his girl showing initiative?"

"He doesn't like me doing anything that doesn't help him stay in office, which generally means me staying quiet and out of sight. After my lesson in humility, of course, so homeless and jobless seems to be his preference. This definitely doesn't fit into either of those categories," she said. "If the news picks up on the story of me collaborating with an unknown alien species to subvert the economic stability of Lariest in defiance of my father—"

"We're kidnapping an android," Reynolds jumped in. "That's hardly subverting the economy. What's one cab going AWOL?"

"That's not how the vultjournalists will see it," Jiya answered.

"I see what you did there, combining the words 'vulture' and 'journalist.' Witty."

"It loses its impact if you shine a light on it," she told him, shaking her head.

"I guess it does. Let's go." He clambered into the hovercab and hunkered down behind the seat as she shut the door and circled around the other side. He barely fit.

She hopped in and started the cab. "You'd think your skin would be thicker because—"

"Because I'm a bot, and I'm metal?"

"You're stepping all over my jokes today, buddy."

"I do what I can," Reynolds retorted.

The hovercab shot across the tarmac, dodging port workers who either ignored her or gave her a single-finger salute, which she returned with a laugh. On the street, she merged with the autocab traffic, slowing to evaluate her prey once she was out on the open road.

The android drivers stared straight ahead, only noting her presence in the most perfunctory way. If she wasn't waving them down for a ride, they didn't care.

And while that might have been the easiest way to get them to pull over for her, she knew their operating procedures. The second a fare flagged one of the Jonny taxis down, the android reported it across the system. Worse still, it triggered the vehicle's security protocols.

Basically, the Jonny taxis recorded every transaction just in case someone tried to jack them. That meant there were cameras rolling the second any interaction occurred.

Reynolds eased out of his hidey-hole and peeked out the window.

"Ewww, these things are hideous," he said. "I'm not sure I want to be cooped up in such an ugly husk, now that I have gotten a close look at one."

"You realize they look just like me, right?"

Reynolds glanced at Jiya, then at the android driver, then back at Jiya. He winced. "Now that you mention it, you *do* bear an unfortunate resemblance to those androids," he said. "I bet that wreaks all sorts of havoc on your social life."

"Now who's being mean?" she muttered, grumbling

under her breath. "How about we play the quiet game until we catch our cab?"

"Just passing the time with light conversation," the Reynolds bot replied.

Jiya sighed. She ignored the comment and kept her eyes on the Jonny taxis flitting around her as they zipped through town. She wasn't looking for a specific cab since they were all the same, barring the paint job and name-plates, but she needed one going in a certain direction.

She finally found it.

"Here we go," she said in a low voice, shifting to get behind a Jonny taxi painted a blinding shade of orange and trimmed in yellow.

"I have high hopes that we only have to do this once," Reynolds remarked.

Jiya followed the cab down an offramp, grinning the entire time. She would have felt bad for the cabbie had he been a Larian because this direction would take him into the boonies, way off the normal traffic routes. It was a hell of a long way to go with no guarantee of a tip.

That was what made this particular cab so attractive to Jiya.

There were long stretches of empty road out this way, barely any traffic to speak of. And that was what she needed—a few minutes to take care of business without some busybody driving past and seeing what was going on.

"You sure this device you cobbled together is going to work?" Reynolds asked.

"We're about to find out."

"That's the one thing I like most about you: your optimism," he told her, hunkering down even farther into the well. "Let me know when it's all over."

Jiya sped up, her eyes focused like lasers on the task at hand, shifting to the left to pass the Jonny taxi. As was protocol, the android slowed his vehicle and made it easier for Jiya to come up alongside it.

That was exactly what she'd been expecting.

She slowed just a tiny bit, matching speeds before the Jonny taxi could adjust again, and her right quarter panel tapped the cabbie's door. A loud *thump* echoed inside the car.

Knowing she didn't have much time, she triggered the button she'd wired to her dashboard before the Jonny cab activated its crash protocols and started filming their encounter.

There was a flash of silver-white light just to the right of the hood. It blinded Jiya for an instant, but she clung to the wheel and kept her vehicle in place.

The Jonny taxi didn't fare as well.

As soon as the makeshift cattle prod she'd attached to her vehicle went off, the android bolted upright. His head whipped back, and his mouth flew open as if he were screaming. His arms shot forward, striking the windscreen and causing cracks to spiderweb across it.

The Jonny taxi's electrical system overwhelmed, the vehicle shut down and drifted to the side of the road. Jiya guided it with her own vehicle, the prod still embedded in the door. A moment later the vehicle was stopped, the `droid slightly twitching in its seat.

"I'm really glad you thought to insulate the rod more because I felt that shock all the way down to my toes,"

Reynolds muttered as he climbed from his hiding place and plopped into the passenger seat.

"Do you even *have* toes?" she asked.

"They're metaphorical toes." He sighed, glancing out the window at the stunned android.

"Ouch!" he gasped. "Looks like you fried his brain. I can see smoke wafting from his eyes."

"Well, you wanted him incapacitated, right?" she asked with a shrug.

"Incapacitated, not charbroiled." Reynolds surveyed the area before opening the cab door and stepping out. "If you've blown his circuits, I'm going to have a hell of a time preparing him for the transfer."

"Don't worry about it," she told him. "I know what I'm doing. These Jonny androids are tough. They'll take a stickin' and keep on lickin'."

Reynolds glanced at her. Jiya stood there casually, hands on her hips, one eyebrow raised as if to question what he was waiting for.

"I'm guessing this isn't the first time you've done this," he said. "You were much too confident that your elec-troshock-y thing would work."

"A girl's gotta have a hobby," she replied. "But enough about me. Let's get you that upgrade you were looking for."

"Upgrade?" Reynolds scoffed. "This android wouldn't be an upgrade if we were replacing the coffeemaker aboard me."

"Mmmmm, coffee," Jiya mumbled, licking her lips.

Reynolds ignored her and went to the cabbie's door, stopping himself just before he grabbed the handle.

"You're sure this thing is off, right?" he asked, gesturing to the makeshift cattle prod.

"What's the matter, afraid of a little jolty-poo?"

"I'm more afraid of what will happen if your toy accidentally triggers the bot's self-defense protocols," he told her. "We put all this effort into being sneaky. I think a smoking black crater where you and your vehicle are might draw some unwanted attention."

Jiya stiffened, staring at Reynolds over the hood of her cab. "You know what? I should probably check just to be sure."

"Probably a good idea."

She leaned in through the window, making sure the device was powered down, and let out a quiet sigh when she saw that it was. "Good to go." She offered the bot a thumbs-up.

Reynolds grunted and pulled the Jonny taxi's door open. He snatched the twitchy android and pulled him from his vehicle as Jiya circled her own cab and opened the trunk. Reynolds dumped the mechanoid inside, then she eased the trunk closed.

"What about the cab?" Reynolds asked. "Won't people see it when they drive past? They're likely to report it."

"Get in," she told him.

He complied, staring at Jiya as she scrambled into her seat. And before he could press the subject, she started her vehicle and pushed the other cab out into the scrubland that bordered the road. Before she got too far out, the cab suddenly dipped and disappeared. A loud crack resounded as the cattle prod gave way and toppled with the cab into a deep ravine.

Reynolds grunted. "Again, I'm thinking you've done this before."

"Mysterious women are the best," she replied, turning away from the ravine and driving back toward the road.

"Not if the mystery is when they're going to kill you in your sleep," Reynolds countered.

"Do you *sleep*?"

"Well, no, not really," he answered.

"Then you have nothing to worry about, right?"

"That remains to be seen," he whispered just barely loud enough for her to hear, offering her one of his creepy grins.

She cringed. "Let's go get your face fixed, so I don't have to keep seeing that…" she gestured at his smile, "whatever that's supposed to be."

He shrugged. "Too bad we can't fix your face, too."

Jiya laughed and pulled onto the road, still no traffic in sight. "Well, better get used to it, Reynolds. I just committed a felony for you. I think that means we're pretty much engaged."

"Yay me," he shouted, leaning forward to make sure she saw his even wider grin spreading.

She turned back to the road, shuddering.

What have I gotten myself into?

Back at the ship—which she refused to think of as Reynolds—they'd passed the android and Reynolds' bot form off to Doctor Reynolds—which wasn't strange at all

—and he groaned when he saw the state the android was in.

"Damn it, Reynolds, I'm an AI, not a miracle worker," the doctor cursed.

"Do your best, Doc," Reynolds answered from the bot. "We have a mission to accomplish, and I need my best..." He sat up on the med-bed and glanced at the android. "Well, maybe not my *best*. We can start with eighth string, I guess."

"This was your idea," Jiya reminded him.

"Actually, it was Comm's idea, that bastard."

"I know that Comm is you, too."

"Now you're splitting hairs," he replied, wagging a finger at her. "Just go and get ready to meet your contacts. I'll be along shortly."

"That's what *you* think," Doc muttered. Reynolds ignored him and waved Jiya off.

Jiya didn't hesitate to leave. She strolled out of sickbay, trying to remember her way back to the lounge without getting lost.

The earlier mention of coffee had her fiending, and she needed a fix.

CHAPTER SEVEN

"I look like a fucking toaster," Reynolds complained, staring at his new android body in the reflective surface of the viewscreen. He ran a hand through his synthetic black hair and grunted at the dark pools staring back at him. "How do you run around looking like this all the time?" he asked Jiya.

She snorted. "It's easy when you're as hot as I am."

Reynolds turned from the viewscreen with a dismissive grunt. "Let's just get this over with. I feel like a clown without a birthday party to crash."

"I hate to be the one to break it to you, Captain, but you look weird. Very clownish," Tactical offered.

The new Reynolds sighed, waving Jiya toward the bridge door. "Helm, you have the helm."

"Thanks for that, Captain Obvious," Helm mumbled from his console.

"Belay that belligerence, Mister Christian. You shall be drawn and quartered!" Reynolds replied.

Jiya fled the bridge and made her way to the hangar

bay, where her cab was parked inside a small shuttlecraft. Reynolds followed her. As they clambered into the shuttle and strapped in for the quick flight back to the planet, she got a good look at him.

While he was obviously an android, the doctor had spruced the frame up a bit, making it slightly less apparent that he was one of the Jonny taxi drivers. A few touch-ups here and there had cleaned him up. From a reasonable distance, most people wouldn't give him a second glance, thinking he was a Larian.

Up close was a different matter.

"They did a good job on you," she told him. "There are almost no char marks visible."

Reynolds glanced in the side mirror. "You damn near scorched his eyes out. I look like I'm wearing mascara."

"It looks good on you." Jiya grinned, fighting back a chuckle. "Very robosexual. You go, Bot!"

He shooed her away. "Helm, get us dirtside, please."

"Sir, yessir," Helm replied, and the shuttle engines came online.

Jiya drew in a deep breath and held it as the shuttle shot out of the hangar bay and launched itself into orbit, circling the planet with growing velocity. She was pressed hard into her seat, the safety harness biting into her skin at every contact point.

The atmosphere rattled the craft as they descended and Jiya spewed lungfuls of recycled shuttle air, desperately trying to suck in a replacement breath. Her stomach was a hard knot, and she could taste the bitter sting of bile hitting the back of her throat.

"Uh, Helm?" Reynolds called over the comm. "Think

you might want to chill with the theatrics. We've got someone on board who's less tolerant of the gyrations than are we."

"Oh, shit," Helm responded and the shuttle leveled off, angling to slice across the atmosphere rather than burrow through it.

Jiya gasped, finally able to grab a decent breath.

"Yeah, sorry about that," Helm apologized over the comm. "Been a long time since we've had meatbags aboard."

Jiya bit back her retort. From where she sat, "meatbag" was a pretty accurate description, her insides sloshing all over the place. She felt as if her guts had been pureed. She didn't even want to think about where they'd spill out of.

"Just put me on the ground nicely, please, and I promise not to puke all over the shuttle floor. Maybe."

"Roger that," Helm answered.

A short while later he did exactly that, the shuttle settling on the tarmac with a gentle *thump.*

Once her guts stopped roiling, she gathered herself and stumbled to the cab parked in the back of the shuttle. The magnetic clamps holding it hissed and drew back, releasing the cab as the back hatch of the shuttle eased open.

She climbed into the vehicle, Reynolds dropping into the passenger seat. Once they were buckled in, she backed down the ramp and eased out onto the tarmac. Then Jiya put the vehicle in gear and shot across the port, glad to be in charge once more.

Out on the road again, the chaos of the other Reynoldses behind her at last, Jiya eased into her seat and relaxed for the first time in a long time. She knew it wouldn't last long, given what they were off to do, but out here on the road, traffic whizzing past, she was at peace.

Too bad it was over far too soon.

Takal Durba sat in his living room, fuming as he glared at the vidscreen. President Lemaire loomed large on the public relations dais, shouting out at Takal and pounding his fist on the podium.

"We will not surrender our position to these terrorists! I promise—"

"To screw over everyone I know to make myself look better," Takal finished, growling at the screen. "Vidscreen off!"

The screen went black at his command and he sank into his seat, grabbing his mug from the coffee table on the way back. He took a sip of the whiskey-infused coffee and sighed.

It was good stuff. Still, it wasn't as good as having a job he loved and an income.

"Damn you, Lemaire," Takal growled, taking another large swig of his coffee.

"You say something?" his niece Geroux asked, peeking in from the hallway. As always, she had her reading material, her thumb stuck between the pages of an antique book to hold her place.

A smile broke across Takal's face at seeing her. "No, dear. I was watching the news."

"Lemaire?" she asked.

He nodded. "Always Lemaire."

She sighed and strolled into the room, dropping her

butt on the coffee table despite knowing Takal hated it when she did that. He cast a quick glance at the table and bit back a frustrated sigh.

She always did what she wanted, and there was little he could do to change that now, but she was a good kid. He'd spoiled her ever since he'd been awarded custody, so it wasn't like he really *expected* to control her. That chance was long gone. She'd been her own person since early on, and that was one of the biggest things he loved about her.

"So, what did the president do now?" she asked

"What *didn't* he do?" Takal grunted and sat back in the couch. "He's got very weird thoughts when it comes to technology and the advancement of it, as you very well know." He waved toward the vidscreen. "I even created a personal cloaking device for him, something that could have advanced the Larian military's superiority by a landslide, yet he never let me even test the thing outside of the confines of the lab. It's still there, stuffed in a cabinet under lock and key. It's likely coated in dust by now."

"The man was never a far-thinker, Uncle," Geroux soothed. "If the project wouldn't immediately fatten his pockets, he didn't have a use for it. Besides, military tech was never his thing—you know that. Hell, half the projects you worked on, however brilliant, are probably still stashed away in the lab somewhere, like your cloaking device."

"That bastard wouldn't know what a technologically sound idea was if it built a rocket in his ass and launched him to it," Takal barked.

Geroux chuckled, setting her book aside. "You're right about that, but I—"

The door chimed right then, interrupting them.

Takal straightened. "You expecting someone?"

She shook her head, her wild hair flipping about. "Not me." Geroux hopped off the table, to Takal's delight, and trotted over to the door.

"Maybe it's an accidental pizza delivery," she said with a grin. "I love those."

She flung the door wide—another habit of hers Takal hated—and gasped.

He jumped to his feet and ran toward her. "What is it? Are you—" His question slipped away when he saw who it was at the door.

"Jiya!" Geroux screamed, diving into her arms.

The two hugged, and Takal's eyes narrowed with suspicion and uncertainty. He hadn't seen Jiya since the last time he was at the presidential compound. Which was where Jiya was supposed to be, although he had heard that she'd moved away several years back—sometime after his *dismissal*. Details had been scarce, of course. There had been a total blackout on the news because Lemaire couldn't have anyone in his family showing defiance of his authority.

Regardless, her showing up at their door couldn't be a good thing, not given the current political climate.

"I'm happy to see you," Jiya told Takal's niece as they embraced. The young girl's voice rose to a squeaky giggle as they chattered back and forth.

After a moment, the pair separated, and Takal got a good look at Jiya.

She looked tired. Rundown, nothing like the little girl he remembered gallivanting around the presidential compound in her younger years. She and Geroux used to play there all the time when they were kids, screaming and shrieking through the yard and his workshop while Takal served as the president's head of technological affairs.

Things had changed a lot since then.

Jiya met his eyes and offered a soft but tentative smile. "Hi, Takal. I was wondering how you were."

It was a loaded question, one he wasn't sure he wanted to answer. It always upset him and guaranteed he'd drink more than a reasonable amount of his daily whiskey allotment. Speaking of which, he picked up his mug and downed what remained before answering.

"I'm doing well, Jiya," he prevaricated, not wanting to go down that particular rabbit hole.

Jiya muffled a laugh and came over, giving him a hug, her arms unable to wrap all the way around his ever-expanding waistline. "You don't need to lie to me, Takal."

He sighed, realizing he was actually glad to see her, and returned her hug. "I hope you know the same applies to you, young lady."

She broke away and met his gaze for a moment before nodding. "I understand," she answered. "And since we're being totally honest..." she split her focus between the two, "I've come here for a reason besides a social call, although I should have come for just that long ago."

Takal nodded, having already realized that. Geroux put on her questioning face, which consisted of a scrunched nose, narrowed eyes, and a peeled-back upper lip.

"What do you mean, Jiya?" Geroux asked, worry in her voice. "What's going on? Is everything okay? Are you hurt?"

"Oh, nothing bad," Jiya replied, doing her best to ease their concerns and ward off the barrage of questions. "In fact, it's kind of fantastic, really."

"Of course, it is," called a voice from the door.

Takal and Geroux spun, staring at the strange being looming in their doorway.

"I thought I told you to wait outside until I called you in," Jiya growled at the newcomer.

"But it's boring out there," he stated emotionlessly. "Do you know how many threads there are in the ragged carpet that runs the length of the hallway? Let me tell you. Two million, four hundred-eighty thousand, five—"

"We *really* don't need to know that, Reynolds," Jiya told him, waving him all the way inside. "Just come in and shut the damn door, would ya?"

"Yessir!" he snapped, slamming the door shut and stomping over to stand alongside her.

"Is that...one of the Jonny taxi androids?" Geroux asked, staring at Reynolds.

"Yes," Jiya answered.

"No," Reynolds contradicted. "I just have one of those familiar faces. I get that all the time. 'Hey, you're one of those Jonny guys!' 'No, I'm not,' I have to tell them each time it comes up. Sheesh. It gets tiring, I have to say."

Jiya nodded, sweeping aside his drawn-out deflection.

Reynolds loosed a disappointed sigh.

"Anyway..." Jiya started, making sure Reynolds was done defending his androidness before she went on, "Reynolds here is an AI."

Takal harrumphed and leaned in to take a closer look at Reynolds.

"He looks like a Jonny taxi android to me, too," he said. "I'd hardly call that an AI. The last Jonny taxi I rode in couldn't even get the card reader to work. A monkey could make the thing work."

"I'm not a Jonny driver. I stole an android body to look more like one of you and move around town less obviously. For this conversation to move forward, you'll need to accept that premise."

"Just noting that my Jonny taxi experiences haven't exactly been...reassuring."

Reynolds didn't bother to argue. He'd made his point.

"Fair enough," Takal finally agreed, retreating from the argument.

"Good, then can we get on with why we're here?" the android asked.

"Yes, please," Takal said. "Do tell us why you are here."

"Well," both Reynolds and Jiya said at the same time. "No, you go ahead," they told each other in unison. Both grunted.

Jiya raised a finger, warning Reynolds off so they didn't keep parroting each other. "We're here to offer you a job. Both of you."

"A job?" Takal asked for clarification. "What kind of job are we looking at? I can't be crawling around under chassis like some grease monkey these days." Takal stuck his broad belly out and patted it. "I'm not exactly in fighting shape anymore, not since..."

He paused, realizing he was about to mention the time he'd spent in Lemaire's prison, but he held back those words and swallowed them. He saw Jiya bite her lower lip, drawing it into her mouth. She clearly knew what he'd meant to say. The last thing he wanted to do was dredge up bad memories for her or himself.

"But yeah, I'm not exactly in the market for a job these days."

"Don't be so difficult, Uncle," Geroux cut in. "We don't even know the details. Let's get more information, and then we can decide if it's right for us or not."

Jiya shook her head, clearly not believing a word. "We're looking to offer you both jobs." She patted Reynolds on his metallic shoulder. "Despite his many...*many* failings, this is an opportunity for all of us to get out from under my father's thumb for good. To get away from his politics, which are tearing this planet apart." She gestured to the vidscreen. "I know you've been watching the news, Takal. You always do. You've seen what's going on."

Takal stiffened, but Geroux only grinned. "Yeah?" she asked. There was no hiding her excitement at the prospect of a new adventure.

"Yeah," Jiya answered, meeting her friend's wide smile. "Reynolds here is actually a superdreadnought, believe it or not. *Ix-nay on the Onny-jay axi-tay.*"

"I understood that," Reynolds grumbled.

"So, his Queen sent him on a mission, and he needs a crew to do all the things he can't do on his own." She grinned broader and winked at Geroux. "The pay and benefits are generous, too."

"Who said anything about benefits?" Reynolds questioned.

Jiya cast a dirty look his direction. "He can be a bit of a smartass, though, since he's getting used to dealing with people. It will be a lot to get used to, trust me. I'm not even remotely there myself. But beyond his quirks and the split personalities, this job is an opportunity to start over. A way to take back a lot of what my father has stolen from you, starting first with your freedom."

"Split personalities?" Geroux asked.

"Out of all that, you pick out the personality bit?" Reynolds asked. "That gives me insight into your mind. Jiya said you were a scientist. I shall enjoy working with you."

Geroux shrugged. "It was the most glaring piece of information."

"I'll explain all that later," Jiya assured her.

Takal stood quietly for a moment, contemplating the offer and wondering just what he'd be getting him and Geroux into if he agreed to it.

Everything he knew was on Lariest, but did any of that matter anymore?

Lemaire had taken his workshop away—the place Geroux and Jiya had played so often. Had robbed him of his tools and equipment and finances, and had effectively banned him from any position that allowed him to work on the tech he so loved. But if this AI superdreadnought could give him even a portion of that back, he would be more than willing to put up with the thing's quirks.

In fact, he'd be ecstatic.

Anything was better than growing old in his house, withering from boredom.

Still, he had questions. He didn't want to trade one tyrant for another. He could hide from Lemaire in his house, but out in space, there was nowhere to run if things went bad.

"What kind of work would I be doing for you?"

"Tech work, Takal," Jiya answered for Reynolds. "Same as you did for my father, only without the restraints or expectations based on political ramifications. You could go back to experimenting, inventing things to help people live better lives."

"Well...to be honest, we have a militaristic side," Reynolds corrected, butting in. "Sure, we'll let you experiment and build things—inventions that have a positive impact on society at large—but I'm not going to lie. A lot of your efforts will go toward ridding the universe of Kurtherians. That is my singular focus, all foibles aside. I need a crew to help me hunt down and destroy them."

"What are those?" Geroux asked.

"Filthy, filthy aliens," Reynolds mumbled, and Takal could hear the absolute disgust in the mechanical tones of the android. "They have defiled the universe, but now the Queen is fighting back. She has single-handedly returned a vast section of space to the people. I am out here searching the farthest corner of the galaxy for them. When we find them, we will destroy them."

"You want me to participate in genocide?" Takal asked pointedly.

"The liberation of the universe is at stake. As long as we keep driving the Kurtherians before us, sentient beings will be free to determine their own destinies. The chance of us killing a Kurtherian is remote, so 'destroy' includes sending them to a different plane of existence. We will remove the remaining scum from our dimension, and we'll be better because of it."

"We will talk more about that, but I think I understand.

And there are jobs for both of us?" Takal asked. "For Geroux and me?"

His niece had been affected as much as he had by Lemaire's crackdown on their family. She could hardly do the things she wanted; couldn't advance in her chosen field of research because of the president. Couldn't even finish her schooling. She rarely left the house these days, and Takal had begun to fear for her. It wasn't good for a young woman to be trapped at home all the time, no friends to hang out with, nothing to do but study. With this offer, at least she would be with Jiya and whoever else was part of the crew.

"Most definitely," Jiya replied. "We need a researcher and computer programmer of her caliber aboard the ship. Plus, she can see the universe and learn far more about it than she ever could here on dusty old Lariest." Jiya looked at each in turn, settling on Takal. "So, what do you say? Are you interested?"

He swallowed hard and cleared his throat. "I say, I'm in if Geroux is." He glanced at his niece and her grin illuminated the room, making it clear what her decision was.

"I'm soooooo in." She leapt forward and dragged Jiya into a fierce hug. "Can you imagine how much is out there? What I can study and learn about?"

"What both of us can," Jiya told her friend.

"This is fantastic and all," Reynolds told them, "but we have more people to recruit. At this rate, it'll be a week before we can get back into space. Every second is one more second that the Kurtherians can run."

Takal raised an eyebrow, staring at Reynolds.

Jiya nodded. "He said 'singularly focused.' Will they need any of their equipment?"

Reynolds stroked his chin, a new gesture for him. "Show me what you have, and I'll check if it is onboard or can be fabricated."

Takal shook his head. "I wasn't allowed any equipment. Anything you have is more than I have. So, when do we leave?"

"Right now, actually," Reynolds answered. "We'll drop you off at the shuttle while we go about collecting the rest of the crew. I need immediate repairs so we can be about our mission. You'll be put to work as soon as you arrive onboard."

"Go pack," Jiya told them, "then meet us outside. We'll be waiting in the cab that's parked there."

"So, you really *are* a Jonny taxi driver," Geroux joked, offering Reynolds a sly grin as she shot down the hall toward her room.

"I am going to need a makeover soon," Reynolds muttered, then turned his gaze on Takal. "Think you can rustle me up a new body?" he asked. "One that isn't...this?" He gestured to the Jonny form. "No offense—although judging by Jiya's previous reactions to similar comments I'm sure you're still going to be offended—but I could use an overhaul. A new frame to pack my brilliance into. Preferably one without red skin and black hair. That particular contrast is quite unfortunate. I don't know how you people look at yourself every day. I really don't."

"I can most certainly give it a try," Takal answered with a chuckle, ignoring the slight. "I've worked on mechanoids of all sorts over the years. If you have a decent shop with a cache of spare parts, I can probably get you fixed up."

"My kingdom for a real body," Reynolds muttered. "Anyway, get packed, my fellow scientist. We need to get a move on. Places to see, things to be, or something like that."

Takal nodded and started off, leaving Jiya and the android in the living room while he went to collect his thoughts and figure out what he wanted to take on an adventure across the galaxy.

He wasn't sure what to think about Reynolds' offer, but he couldn't help but appreciate the opportunity to start over, even if he was a bit old for jaunting about the universe. Still, he planned to make the most of it, if only for Geroux's sake.

Now, what does one wear aboard a superdreadnought?

CHAPTER EIGHT

"Please welcome Ka'nak, a great warrior of the Melowi people and master of the Larian Pit, having over fifty victories within its storied walls," an announcer screamed over the rumbling crowd that had gathered to watch the bloodbath. "Standing over two meters tall and weighing in at one hundred and fifty-nine kilograms, Ka'nak the Merciless is ready to do battle!"

"I like this one," Reynolds muttered, staring at Ka'nak, the enforcer Jiya insisted they collect as their next acquisition for the crew. The red-skinned man paced back and forth, muscles flexed, malevolence swirling in his eyes. He glared out at the crowd. "I thought you were the hothead?" He grinned. "You've proven me wrong."

"Every crew needs a mix of skill sets," Jiya replied. "A guy who can bust skulls yet still take orders is a must."

Reynolds grunted. "Well, all I see so far is his skill at growling and looking intimidating."

"Give it a few seconds," she answered. "Then you'll get to see his skill at mopping the floor with someone."

"A custodial candidate. We have maintenance and cleaning bots for those types of services."

Jiya groaned and turned her attention back to Ka'nak.

The powerfully-built Melowi howled as he stood at the entrance to the fighting pit below. He looked as broad across the chest as the door was. Jiya was sure he'd gotten even bigger since the last time she'd seen him, which was impressive given how huge he'd already been.

The first time they'd met he'd been a guard of a politician in the Melowi government—Jiya couldn't remember his name—who was visiting the presidential compound. Ka'nak had stood out even among the rest of the massive men tasked with guarding the Melowi politician. He had strode into the compound like he owned the place.

Not in an "I'm better than you" sort of way, but in a confident way that said you didn't want to mess with him if you liked having all your limbs attached.

He was so daunting to look at that Jiya's father'd had the politician assign him to the back of the meeting hall so he wasn't anywhere near him. The warrior clearly intimidated her dad, which Jiya had found to be quite amusing.

Ka'nak had sneered at her father, staring him down as he moved locations after he'd been given the news. That had only impressed Jiya more.

That wasn't the reason she'd suggested him to Reynolds, though.

There'd been an incident at the compound. The Melowi government had been going through some political turmoil or other, and they'd sent a representative to meet with Jiya's father, he and his entourage storming into the compound in a huff.

Jiya had a feeling her dad had been a part of the turmoil, but of course, he had never admitted to it, and no one had ever said anything about it aloud. Still, she could tell just by watching the smug smile on his face that he had to keep wiping away.

Anyway, a man leapt out of the crowd as the Melowi politician passed. The would-be assassin raised his gun, but Ka'nak was on him before he could pull the trigger.

Jiya could remember the revolting *snap* as the assassin's wrist was bent backward. She saw bones burst from his skin, jagged white pieces jutting from auburn flesh, and then Ka'nak got mean.

One hand on the assassin's shattered wrist, he slid his other hand over the man's head and dug his fingers into his eyes, using the leverage to hold the assassin in place. Jiya cringed, her stomach churning as she recalled the incident.

A mix of silvery fluid and blood poured down the man's face as Ka'nak pressed his fingers deeper. Jiya could have sworn she'd heard wet *pops* over the man's shrieks of terror, but even now she knew that was impossible. That she'd only imagined it.

That had been bad enough.

Ka'nak had twisted the man around to face the crowd, then driven his knee into his lower back. This time she was absolutely certain she'd heard the sounds of the man's agony as his spine gave way with a sharp *crack*. It sounded like a great tree had split in half, wood splintering as it collapsed to the ground.

Fonts of blood spewed from his ruined eyes as Ka'nak bent him backward, nearly folding him in half, and rode him to the floor. The assassin spasmed and thrashed, still alive, likely too deep in shock to even realize he should surrender and die.

Ka'nak, however, seemed to revel in the man's torment. Like a feral beast, the Melowi warrior had straddled his victim and slammed the assassin's head into the ground over and over and over, until there was nothing left but a wet puddle marred by chunks of bone and brain.

At last, Ka'nak yanked his hand free of the dead man's skull. Jiya was sure she'd seen the remnants of the man's eyes lingering there, oozing from Ka'nak's fingertips. He leapt to his feet and roared, a lion over his prey, and the crowd backed away, fearing for their lives.

That was when Ka'nak had straightened and shaken the blood from his hands, collecting the assassin's weapon before returning to his post. Jiya, too stunned to move, had stood there as he did all this, the rest of the crowd having left her there alone. He met her gaze, impressed by her courage—he'd confessed that later and she had never contradicted his assertion, but it had really been terror that had made her stand her ground, not bravery—and winked at her.

Now, she stared into the pit, where he was ready to do battle once more. She had seen him in action nearly a hundred times.

As she watched him pace, the crowd let out a thunderous roar, and she yanked her eyes from Ka'nak and shifted them to where his opponent would enter.

Her heart hung in her chest for a moment as Ka'nak's challenger emerged from the shadowy tunnel entrance.

"Now *that's* a monster," Reynolds said with more than a

hint of awe, something Jiya hadn't thought the AI capable of.

The challenger had to duck to slip out of the archway without hitting his shaggy head on the ceiling. Braids that looked like tentacles whipped about, metal ties holding them together, and Jiya saw silvery blades at the end of each, gleaming in the sunlight that shone on the pit.

Reynolds muttered, pointing out the blades. "One good whip of his head and he could slice himself into ribbons. But not only that, but he's basically providing his opponent with a weapon. So stupid," he told her. "Though, given that the beast is easily over three meters tall, I'm not sure anyone could reach high enough to grab one of them."

Jiya didn't bother to respond. She was too caught up in the monstrosity that stomped across the sand in the pit.

She'd brought Reynolds there to see Ka'nak destroy his opponent. To show the AI she'd made a great choice in muscle for the crew, but now...now she wasn't quite so sure the display would work out as she'd imagined.

That guy was freaking huge!

"And introducing our challenger, hailing from western Toller, the leader of the fierce Mahai tribe, welcome the 'Leviathan,' Ala Ka!" Jiya could almost hear the excited drool in the announcer's voice as he screamed out his introduction. "Weighing in at over two hundred twenty-six kilograms and standing three meters tall and then some, Ala Ka has come to eviscerate all challengers!"

Reynolds nodded admiringly. "I might just have to place a wager on this magnificent slab of meat." He rubbed his chin and glanced at Jiya, who glared back. "No offense to your man, of course, but if I were a betting AI—and I kind of am—I'd think Ka'nak wouldn't last more than a few minutes in there with the Mahai."

"He'll do fine," she shot back, but the casual words most definitely didn't match the uncertainty brewing inside her.

She'd watched Ka'nak fight men bigger than him and win easily enough, but Ala Ka wasn't just bigger, he towered over Ka'nak as they met in the center of the pit. His head was easily twice the size of Ka'nak's, and his biceps looked nearly as large around as Ka'nak's thighs.

Jiya was surprised to find that neither of the two carried any sort of weapon, barring the makeshift blades on Ala Ka's head. This was to be a purely physical contest, a meeting of flesh and bone and will.

She swallowed hard at the realization.

This didn't bode well for Ka'nak.

The referee, a tiny slip of a woman, was clearly in there for looks, since she didn't possess the remotest of chances of separating the two combatants. She raised a hand and called for the crowd's attention. The throng went quiet, the cheering and shouting fading to a muffled rumble before going totally silent.

Jiya nodded, impressed with the tiny woman's ability to control the crowd. She pushed the two combatants back a step and smiled, turning the illumination of it on the crowd. Then her voice rang out, loud and clear in the silence.

"To the death!"

The gathering erupted in screams and catcalls, and the woman darted away under cover of the noise. Once she was safely back outside the walls that defined the pit, a great horn sounded. It echoed through the pit and vibrated Jiya's bones.

The two fighters went to war.

Ala Ka snorted like a bull and charged.

Ka'nak hunkered down and stood his ground, grim determination seizing his features. His eyes glimmered, pools of darkness against his reddish skin, and he sneered, baring his teeth at his opponent.

Ala Ka laughed and kept coming. He clasped his hands together and raised his joined fists over his head. His great muscles rippled, looking like rivers cutting lines through the land.

Faster than Jiya could have imagined, the massive hammers of Ala Ka's fists dropped toward Ka'nak's skull. Jiya stiffened in her seat, stomach roiling with anxiety.

"Your boy's about to get his melon busted," Reynolds told her, chuckling. "Splat!"

Jiya cringed, thinking the same thing, but Ka'nak had other ideas.

He waited until the very last instant, Ala Ka's fists no more than a hair's breadth from his head, and then Ka'nak darted back, moving as fast as a bolt of lightning.

Ala Ka realized what had happened. His opponent no longer there, but it was too late. Momentum had full control.

His combined fists finished their arc, but there was nothing there to stop them. He gasped, trying to slow his forward motion, but he'd put too much effort into it, having planned to end the fight in a single blow.

Unfortunately for him, that wasn't how it went down.

His fists slammed into his groin with a *boom* that shook the stands.

The crowd, shrieking and screaming and hooting and hollering just seconds before, went totally silent, not a whisper to be heard.

Ala Ka grunted, breaking the silence, doing his best to battle both the blow to his nuts and his ego at the same time.

He did neither well.

With a throaty *huuurk*, Ala Ka flopped to his knees, bent over double. Great strings of spit ran from his mouth and pooled on the sand, his forehead settling into its golden warmth.

Ka'nak kicked him in the head.

Ala Ka's upper body whipped back, eyes rolling in their sockets, and he slammed to the ground. He still clutched at his groin, and he stared at the bright sky, moaning like an animal desperate to be put out of its misery.

Ka'nak obliged him.

The Melowi warrior jumped on top of his downed opponent and buried his face in Ala Ka's neck with a growl. A geyser of blood erupted right after, spraying up and sprinkling down on the sand, coloring it crimson.

Then Ka'nak shook his head back and forth like a lion tearing flesh from its prey.

And that was exactly what he was doing.

He yanked back and stumbled to his feet above Ala Ka, arms raised in triumph, and he spun about to show the crowd the grisly trophy still gripped in his mouth, blood streaming down his chin and chest.

Jiya tasted bile when she realized it was Ala Ka's throat.

The Melowi warrior made a lap of the pit, strutting to show everyone the results of his victory, only spitting the remnants of Ala Ka's throat out when he reached the place where Jiya and Reynolds sat. He grinned up at them, eyes gleaming like black holes threatening to consume them.

Reynolds gave the warrior a thumbs-up and cast a furtive glance Jiya's way. "Well, I'm glad I held off on that bet. I would have regretted withholding your first month's paycheck to cover my losses. That would have been devastating, although I'm thinking more to you than me."

Jiya swallowed hard, ignoring Reynolds' banter as she stared down at the warrior. She offered him a nod of congratulations, unable to muster any words—not that he would have heard her anyway. She slumped in her seat and tried to catch her breath amidst the standing ovation that roared around her.

"Looks like we have our security officer," Reynolds said, still staring at the bloody man holding his ground in front of them. "Think we can pay him in steaks?"

CHAPTER NINE

Back aboard the superdreadnought, Jiya and Reynolds stood on the bridge staring down on Lariest through the viewscreen.

Jiya couldn't help but be awed by its majesty, despite the chaos that reigned below. Largely fomented by her father, it made her both sad and angry.

"Your last candidate, General Adrial Maddox, is going to be much tougher to collect than the others," Reynolds told her. "The whole 'in jail for political dissidence' thing is close to a deal-breaker in my mind. Do we really need him?"

"A rebel with an actual cause," Tactical jumped in. "I like it. He *does* have a real cause, right? He wasn't caught protesting for softer toilet paper in schools or anything like that, was he?"

Jiya dragged her gaze from the planet and turned her glare on Tactical's seat. "The general was jailed for defying my father and doing his damnedest to turn the people against him, all in the name of a better world. Then he was quietly *retired* to the south, imprisoned for standing up to my father."

"Noble, I'll give you that, but it doesn't answer my question," Reynolds asked. "What does Maddox bring to the table, that we need to put ourselves at risk for and break him out of prison?"

"He's a tactical genius, far beyond anyone I've ever met," she answered, not mincing words.

"I'm right here," Tactical called. "We've survived this long without the general."

"Wasn't that the point?" Jiya asked, raising her hands questioningly. "You wanted a crew to alleviate the stress of doing a bunch of different jobs, and now you're going to bitch about me finding you one?"

Tactical grunted. "Your point is?"

Jiya sighed and turned back to face Reynolds. Even though she knew he was the exact same entity as Tactical, she couldn't help but think of them as individuals.

I'm becoming as damaged as they are.

"Look, Reynolds, Maddox is as much a genius in his field as Geroux is in research and computers and Takal is with technology and Ka'nak is with fighting. We need him."

Reynolds nodded. "Okay, I'm willing to give it a shot, but we have to be realistic. He's not the most accessible person on the planet."

"A few quick blasts of a railgun and we can walk right in the front door and pluck him out of his cell," Tactical said, sounding smug. "Easy-peasy quite consleazy."

Jiya cast a thumb Tactical's direction. "This is exactly why we need a new tactician."

"I can see your point," Reynolds answered.

"Are you kidding me?" Tactical argued. "This third-world planet—a little bit of offense intended—can't compete with us. A quick blast and there's no one around to challenge us. You really think the meatbags down there want to match firepower with a superdreadnought? Not likely."

Jiya raised her hand. "As one of those meatbags you're referring to, no, maybe the planetary defenses can't match your destructive power, but we're not looking to go to war with the planet in our search for a crew. And we're not looking to destroy civilizations, only Kurtherians and from what I've heard, there aren't that many."

"I beg to differ," Tactical countered. "This is Darwin's theory at its finest—survival of the fittest. Those who live and manage to throw a halfway decent punch at us get the job. Those who get scorched provide the fire to cook our marshmallows over. Pretty clear-cut decision from where I'm sitting."

"And, for the sake of argument where I completely discount your blatant homicidal tendencies—"

"Which is truly my best feature," Tactical clarified.

"—we're trying not to draw a bunch of attention to ourselves, remember?"

"Vaguely," Tactical admitted.

"And forgive me for being so dense that I don't understand the great mind that is you, but wouldn't nuking the planet make people notice?"

"Not if you do it right." Jiya could practically hear Tactical shrugging.

Reynolds coughed, demanding their attention. "Look,

we can't go blasting the planet. We're not here to start a war. Bethany Anne would kick our metallic asses if we went back and all we had to show for our efforts was a bunch of cratered worlds in our wake and a slew of new enemies the Federation would have to go to war with because of us."

"No, our job is hunt down Kurtherians, and we're wasting our time debating how we're going to free a local inmate from prison when we should be seeking our real enemy," the XO interjected.

Reynolds sighed. "He's not completely wrong."

"But he's not completely right either," Jiya argued. "Will a few days make such a huge difference in your hunt for Kurtherians?"

"Yes," Tactical answered immediately. "The longer we wait, the farther they can run and the deeper they can burrow."

"You don't even know where they are!" Jiya shouted, her frustration clear. She clenched her fists, wishing she could punch Tactical in his nonexistent mouth.

"Don't you go whipping out logic and reason," Tactical warned. "We were having a perfectly good argument without any hint of fact or correctness, and you had to go and ruin it."

"Which is your concession that she's right. Stow it, Tactical. The decision is made." Reynolds continued, "We don't know where the Kurtherians are, and we need a crew to repair our ship and better prepare us to find and annihilate them."

"Guns are the answer," Tactical insisted. "They're *always* the answer."

Jiya grunted. "Much as I hate to admit it, he might well be onto something."

"I'm marking this moment on the calendar," Tactical exclaimed. "Jiya Lemaire agrees with Tactical for once. Shit, this should be a national holiday." He chuckled. "I'm going to petition Bethany Anne when we get home. It'll be glorious. We can celebrate with donkey balloons and pin them with tails that say, 'Tactical is right!' Then we can watch all the hot air spew out as the balloon goes limp, kind of like how Jiya is doing right now."

Reynolds sighed. "How about you explain what you mean before Tactical starts off on another tirade?"

"Well, I wasn't exactly thinking of using guns to free Maddox," she replied, returning to the viewscreen and looking down at the planet below. "I was picturing something more…explosive."

"We're raising a monster," Helm muttered from his console. "I blame *you*, Tactical."

"I'll take it," Tactical replied.

Reynolds grunted. "You might well be right, Helm." He came alongside Jiya, meeting her at the viewscreen. "What did you have in mind."

She turned to face him, grinning, holding up her hand, thumb and index finger about two centimeters apart. "Just a little explosion," she answered, lowering her voice to a whisper. "*Boom.*"

Ex-General Adrial Maddox sat in his cell, staring at the wall.

It had become a ritual.

The dull gray stared back, right into his soul. The paint peeled in places, and Maddox had helped it along in a few spots, doing his best to manipulate the removal so that the resulting pale sections stood out against the darker gray.

He'd managed to make one look like a cat, and he'd even scraped a fingernail across the paint to mimic whiskers. There was another that resembled a spider about the size of his fist, which he hadn't meant to do because he wasn't fond of spiders, but he hesitated to scratch it away given how perfect it was.

Then there was the ancient battle tank, which was his favorite. He'd aimed the barrel at the door and imagined it blasting the guards every time they opened his cell door.

Which wasn't very often, actually. They ignored him more often than not, spending their time playing cards and napping out in the main room that adjoined the section of cells he was locked in. He could hear them snoring or cursing as they lost money and arguing among themselves, but the angle was horrible. He couldn't see a thing.

That only compounded his misery.

He'd been so proud of himself when he'd faced down President Lemaire. He had been certain the people would embrace him and rise up. Stand behind him and overthrow Lemaire's corrupt regime.

"Oh, how wrong I was," he muttered, always a bit perturbed by the sound of his own voice.

Even though he talked to himself quite often—it wouldn't do to forget how to speak, now would it?—he didn't think he sounded like him. The raspy, tired voice that came out of his mouth was nothing like the bold, powerful baritone he used to project.

These days, he sounded like he'd spent his life sucking down drain-cleaner shooters with a side of glass shards. Felt like it, too.

He flopped on his cot and groaned.

His world had shrunken from the whole universe to this tiny six-by-six-meter cell without a window. He'd had a life before—women, wine, and even the occasional song —and Lemaire had taken it from him.

Maddox shook his head, letting out a quiet growl. "Get over it, Adrial," he said, chastising himself. "No matter how often you bitch about this, nothing is going to change."

He hated that he was right.

The last eight years locked away had worn on his confidence, on who he'd been before being hauled away in his sleep. Morning had landed him in this exact cell, and he'd been here ever since.

Not once had the guards taken him out so he could get some fresh air or stretch his legs. That didn't mean he hadn't stayed in shape. Every day, first thing when he woke up, he worked out, doing pushups, sit-ups, and running the width and breadth of his cell until he was so tired he was ready to crawl back into bed.

Still, if he were honest with himself, there were days when he yearned for some attention and someone to talk to. Hell, he'd even greet a torturer with a smile as long as it got him out of the cell and gave him someone to interact with.

But no, Lemaire knew Maddox too well to offer him

anything that might break the monotony. It wasn't the cell that was the torment, not the imprisonment or the loss of his former life. The absolute emptiness of his existence was what threatened to cast Maddox over the edge.

He'd held on for all these years, but he could feel himself slipping more and more every day of late. It wouldn't be long before he chewed the veins from his arms in an attempt to bleed out and end the misery.

A crooked smile stretched his lips at the thought, and so caught up was he in his dreams of peace that he barely noticed the loud *thump* in the courtyard that stirred the dust in his cell and caused it to rain down on top of him.

He wiped his face and sat up, the murmur of the guards, frantic and so out of place, drawing him to the surface of his self-imposed mire.

"Is this real?" he asked himself, mustering the energy to get up and walk to the bars of his cell.

Men shouted and cursed and he heard evidence of a scramble, feet slapping concrete, armor slapping flesh. Chaos engulfed his captors for several long moments, then routine took over and they were gone, storming away from his cell as a unit.

Silence remained in their wake.

He stood at the bars for several long minutes, having expected the guards to return to the room and their game and normality to resume, but it didn't happen. There was only the quiet.

"What's going on?" Maddox asked himself, disappointed that he didn't have an answer.

Fortunately, someone else did.

"This is what they call a breakout," a voice said.

The sound sent shivers down Maddox's spine.

"Who's there?"

A figure emerged from the room where the guards normally were, and Maddox slunk toward the back of his cage.

"No need to be afraid," the figure said, coming up to stand before the bars of Maddox's cell.

"A Jonny taxi driver?" Maddox asked, finally able to get a clear look at his unexpected guest.

"You have *got* to be kidding me," the newcomer cursed, shaking his head. "Priority one, a new damn body for Reynolds."

"Who's Reynolds?" Maddox asked.

"That would be me," the Jonny driver responded. "And you, I presume by the musty smell of long-lost freedom, would be General Adrial Maddox?"

Maddox nodded after a few moment's hesitation, unsure how to respond. More to the point, he had to remember his name, seeing as how no one had used it since he'd been locked in this cage. Not a single time.

That was another brilliant part of Lemaire's plan. He had effectively erased Maddox from the minds of the world, including his own.

Suddenly lightheaded, Maddox dropped onto his cot and laid back, staring at the blurry ceiling as he waited for the feeling to pass.

"No offense, General, but we don't have a lot of time here," Reynolds told him, grabbing the bars. "My associate is outside stirring up trouble as a diversion and—"

Another boom sounded in the distance, interrupting the android, and Maddox sat up to listen.

"Ah, there she is," Reynolds went on. "Anyway, as I was saying, we don't have a lot of time, and you and I need to have a chat."

Maddox stared at the wall for a moment, imagining he could see what was going on beyond it, then he turned to face the android who was snapping his fingers for Maddox's attention.

"There we go," Reynolds told him. "Come back to the present and the real world."

"I-I—"

"You know what? How about I talk, and you listen?" Reynolds suggested. "Seems to me that's the only way we'll actually get to the point here. It's clear that if I wait for you, my joints are going to rust."

"Uh...I—"

"Couldn't agree with you more, General," Reynolds interrupted, doing as much as possible to make his android face express disappointment and annoyance at the same time. He'd just have to assume he'd made it work since there was nothing reflective in the cell he could use to judge his efforts. "Simple question, General. Do you want to be free and travel the stars and get revenge on the asshole who locked you up and stole your life?"

"Y-you... You..." Maddox struggled to speak. It wasn't that he was unable; his voice worked fine. It was simply that he was so overwhelmed by the android's arrival that he couldn't stop shaking. His throat had clasped tight, and he could barely breathe.

He wanted to shout and scream, "Yes," and race to the bars and hug this strange android, thanking him for his offer of freedom, but his body rebelled. He'd been in the cell too long; he no longer knew how to respond.

"That's it, Maddox, use your words." Reynolds bit back a groan as yet another explosion echoed through the prison. That was the last of them, Jiya's ruse having run out of juice. "Complete sentences would be a bonus."

"Y-you…would f-free me?"

"That's the idea, yeah."

Maddox managed to move his head up and down enough that it qualified as a nod. "P-pl..eeeease," he spat, more drool than actual sounds.

Reynolds raised an eyebrow and leaned into the bars. "Good enough for government work," he said, then he went to work on the bars, tugging at them. "I'm glad I had Doc strengthen the servos on this rent-a-husk," he muttered.

Maddox had no idea what he meant, but that didn't matter. When the bars to his cell creaked and bent under the android's pressure, Maddox forgot everything. He squealed as the bars kept bending and bending and bending, finally providing an opening wide enough for him to clamber through.

He didn't, of course, because that would require a strength—both mental and physical—that Maddox wasn't able to summon. Instead, he slumped on his cot in a fetal position.

Reynolds groaned. "You're like a sack of moldy potatoes. Why the hell Jiya wants you, I have no idea."

"Jiya?" Maddox repeated, memories stirring him from his near-comatose state. "Y-you...said *Jiya?*"

"I did indeed," the android confirmed, easing through the bent bars to enter Maddox's cell. "She's waiting for you outside. If you want to see her, I suggest you stand up and come with me right fucking now."

Maddox bolted upright, managing to get to his feet... for about a second. Then he wavered, wobbled, and almost collapsed.

Reynolds caught him, slipping an arm under Maddox's armpit and wrapping it around his waist. "I guess I'm a Jonny taxi after all," he muttered, carting the limp Maddox out through the bent bars into the room beyond. "I'm turning on the meter for this trip."

The android carried Maddox through the guard's room, which Maddox barely remembered, it having been so long since he'd seen it, then down a corridor he didn't remember at all.

They came to a room with a closed door, and Reynolds opened it and helped Maddox inside. A window shone at the back of the room, and the bars that had previously blocked passage through it were ripped loose and lay on the floor. The glass was missing, too.

Before Maddox could complain, which probably would have taken weeks given his sudden lack of ability to vocalize, the android squeezed him through the window and dumped him outside.

Maddox landed with a *thud*, but he didn't care. The warm grass and gritty dirt pressed against his cheek were all that mattered at that moment. It didn't last nearly long enough, however.

The android snatched him up again and tossed him over its shoulder. Maddox grunted as it took off at a sprint, its mechanical shoulder bone driving into his gut.

"I hope you get your energy back or Jiya is going to owe me big time."

CHAPTER TEN

"You sure he'll be okay," Jiya asked, staring through the window that looked into the med bay.

General Maddox laid on the bed as the automated surgical services scanned and assessed him.

"He'll be fine," Reynolds replied. "Doc says a day or two in the Pod-doc and he'll be right as rain."

"And that's a good thing?"

Reynolds shrugged. "So my databases tell me."

"What about his mind?"

"It's like a turd floating in a fishbowl right now," the AI answered, "but...Doc says it's just stress and trauma from his long incarceration in solitary confinement. Eight years with almost no interaction is an inhumane level of torture. The fact that he survived is a testament to his mental strength. He's cracked a few seals here and there. Fortunately, it's nothing serious in the grand scheme of things. Might take a little time, but the genius you knew will return, or so Doc says."

Jiya drew in a deep breath. "Thank you for helping me

get him out of there," she said, exhaling slowly in relief. She'd been worried when Reynolds had first brought Maddox aboard. He had been so…scattered. So weak. She wasn't sure there'd be any saving him.

"I'll just pretend you said, 'Thank you for doing all the work to get him out of there,' to which I'd reply, 'You're welcome.'"

"Hey! I distracted the guards and pulled them away from their posts."

"And that was excellent work," he acknowledged. "I mean, it must have been hard work pressing that button three times, timing it so as not to press it too early or too late." He grabbed her hand. "How's your thumb? You need the Doc to take a look at it?"

"I think I'll manage," she replied. "Anyway, Takal told me that the repairs are coming along well. Most of the pertinent systems have been brought back into compliance, so if you were waiting on any of that before we moved on, they're no longer an issue."

"Excellent," Reynolds said, rubbing his hands together like an evil genius. "And the remainder of the damage?"

"Takal has recruited Ka'nak to do the heavy lifting on the hull repairs, so he predicts all that will done in a few more days at most. His strength is coming in handy," she told him. "And Geroux has been syncing the computer systems, better preparing for Meatbag Manual Manipulation, as she's named the changeover."

"Niiiice," Reynolds applauded. "I like that girl already."

"So, with things progressing and the crew onboard, if not entirely functional, what's the plan?" she asked.

"Gather the crew who aren't drooling all over themselves and have them meet me here at sickbay."

"And then?"

"And then we start doing the fun stuff."

"Such as?" Jiya questioned.

Reynolds grinned in reply. "First off, we jab a metal device into your temple, then we get to work."

"I'm sorry I asked." Jiya grunted, spun on her heel, and marched off to put as much distance between her and the AI as possible.

"Is this absolutely necessary?" Takal asked, twitching in his seat.

"It is if you want to know what people are saying to you, and if you want to communicate with the rest of us while we're out on a mission."

"So, you're saying it's not *entirely* necessary?" Takal clarified.

"I'm being kind. You need to have this procedure. Every member of the crew needs to be linked. In combat, the ship could be filled with smoke, shrouding your fragile forms in darkness. What if you find yourself outside the ship? It would be best if you could communicate with us," Reynolds told him, wrapping a hand around the back of Takal's head and holding him in place. "Now, sit still. You don't want this embedded in your eyeball."

Takal froze, and the AI pressed a long, thin device to the man's temple. There was a quiet *click* and Takal flinched, then narrowed his eyes.

"That's it?"

"Of course, that's it," Reynolds answered with a *tssk*. "We're not here to torture you."

"Not physically," Jiya muttered.

Reynolds grinned and waved Jiya up next, shooing Takal out of the seat. "Mentally, you're all fair game. Now, assume the position, Princess, and get ready to be poked." He patted the now-empty seat.

"Is he always like this?" Geroux asked.

"It's usually Tactical," Jiya told her, sliding into the chair, "but I think the two have been apart too long. They're starting to merge. Think of him as a socially-awkward genius who wants people to like him."

"Quirks?" Takal clarified.

"I took more words to say the same thing. Thank you for your eloquence, Takal. We'll go with quirks."

"Just sit still and be quiet," Reynolds told them, waving the crew to silence. "This is an important part of the new-crew process." He lifted the device and jabbed Jiya in the temple. There was a tiny pinch, less painful than a bug bite, and the AI motioned her out of the chair. "This device will allow us to stay in contact at all times, plus it is an upgrade to the low-rent translators you've already had implanted by your people. This one has a far vaster selection of languages, plus a miniature little me—an AI—in it that will allow it to process and better translate languages we don't already know."

"A little you in them," Tactical chuckled, his voice appearing out of nowhere. "Give yourself more credit, Reynolds."

Jiya flinched when Tactical's voice sounded inside her head. "He really shouldn't," Tactical whispered.

"You realize I heard that, right?" the AI asked.

"No clue what you're talking about?" Tactical deflected. "Oh, I hear Helm calling me. Gotta go."

Reynolds grumbled and motioned for Ka'nak to hop into the chair.

"What about her?" the warrior asked, pointing at Geroux while eyeing the device as if it might bite him.

"Ladies last," he replied. "Now get over here so we can get on with things. Unless, of course, you're afraid of needles. You aren't, are you?"

"I'm not afraid of anything," he answered, puffing out his barrel chest and scowling. "I'm just *uncomfortable* around needles."

Reynolds sighed and glanced over his shoulder at Jiya. "Our great and mighty security officer is afraid of getting a shot. Am I going to have to whip out my Danny Devito on this one?"

"What?" Jiya asked.

"That was punny right there, I don't care who you are," the AI went on.

Jiya tapped the side of her head where Reynolds had just inserted the communicator. "Seriously, is this thing working, because I don't understand a damn word you're saying."

"You people are so uncultured." Reynolds grunted and stomped over to Ka'nak. "Hey, what the hell is that?" he shouted, pointing out the viewport.

"What is it?" the fighter asked, whipping his head around to look.

Reynolds jammed the device into his temple as soon as Ka'nak spun, implanting the comm.

Ka'nak spun back around and rubbed his temple. "Hey!" He made to grab the AI.

"Be grateful I don't release a horde of mosquito nanites on your ass," Reynolds threatened.

"You have those?" Ka'nak asked, pausing in his attempt to grab the AI.

"Want to find out?"

"Pass," he answered, waving his hands and backing up.

"Good choice." Reynolds huffed and spun around. "Now, where were we? Oh, yeah…Geroux."

Geroux walked over, snatched the device out of Reynold's hand, examined it for a split-second, and thumped it against her temple, inserting her own comm. She handed the device back to Reynolds, who took it back, handling it as if it were infested.

"That was easy," Geroux said, rubbing her temple and grinning.

"Yeah," Reynolds muttered. "I didn't feel a thing."

"What about Maddox?" Jiya asked. "Will he get one, too?"

The AI nodded. "The Pod-doc will insert his while it's working on the rest of him. He'll be in the loop as soon as he's out of the Pod."

"Until then?" Jiya questioned.

"I show you all around the ship to get you better acquainted with its amenities and systems, and then we get ready for our first away mission."

"Away from what?" Takal asked.

"Just *away*," Reynolds snapped. "You know, like in that ancient television show, *Star Trek*?"

"Star what?" Ka'nak asked. "Did it make more sense than you? Because if so, I might like to watch it."

"How can you not have seen it? It was the pinnacle of science fiction in the day."

"Science isn't fiction, though," Geroux argued.

"No, that was just what they called it," Reynolds defended.

"Why?" Geroux put her hands on her hips, seriously wondering.

"Because at the time, much of the science on the show was just that—fiction," the AI explained.

"So, they were sub-humans acting like they were scientifically advanced?" Ka'nak asked, shaking his shaggy head. "How is that interesting?"

"It was. I'm appalled at the abject barbarity in this galaxy!" Reynolds complained. "I will schedule mandatory viewing sessions for the crew as part of your training. We're going on an away mission because that's what I want to call it, okay?"

"Still never answered my question," Takal said. "Away where?"

"To throw myself into the sun if everything I say will be questioned. I can't believe I ever agreed with myself to bring meatbags aboard. So much trouble." He spun on a robotic heel and marched off. "Now, come with me to the bridge."

"I never understood why they call it a 'bridge,'" Ka'nak mused as they followed. "It doesn't span a river or creek.

Maybe the term came from that *Star Whack* show Reynolds was talking about. That would explain it."

On the bridge, the crew gathered around the viewscreen, the brilliant vista of Lariest glowing before them. Jiya noticed that the view had changed from the one they'd been looking at just a short while earlier.

"I've had Helm move us to the other side of the planet," Reynolds said as if reading Jiya's mind.

She gasped under her breath and touched the newly inserted device, suddenly worried that it might be used to purloin her thoughts. *What if...*

"Our little adventure on the surface might have attracted some attention, and there's a chance our shuttle was detected either entering or exiting orbit, or it will be. The Lariest government will put the pieces together eventually and start looking around up here for their missing political prisoner. As such, we need to be ready to haul anchor and be about our business."

Jiya sighed when she realized it had only been a coincidence he'd mentioned the planet's position.

He turned to face the crew. "Takal, Ka'nak, keep doing what you're doing with the hull and ship repairs. If we have to leave in a hurry, I don't want anything lingering that'll cause problems down the road. We need to be as close to full integrity as possible. Keep track of how many additional people you'll need. Now that we have Larians aboard, you can expand the number of crew in a way that will be best for the ship. " He turned his focus to Geroux and Jiya. "You two stay here on the bridge with me. We need to get you up to speed with the ship's systems so you can assist in operations. We'll meet in the crew lounge at 1900 hours to discuss our mission in more detail."

At that point, the AI waved everyone away to their duty.

CHAPTER ELEVEN

Right around the assigned time, Jiya and Geroux dragged themselves to the crew lounge. Although the work they'd done was hardly physically taxing, it was mentally draining.

Reynolds had put them through their paces, showing and re-showing them each and every aspect of the super-dreadnought. There was so much to the ship Jiya didn't know. She'd never seen a spaceship like this one, and she realized early on why the AI had been tasked with running it. It would take a crew of thousands to manage what the AI did.

There was no way she and the rest of the crew could ever replace the AI, as she'd pictured her task. Now she knew her job was simply to assist Reynolds in doing what he couldn't do alone, which wasn't a whole lot.

Much as the different versions of the Reynolds AI drove her nuts, she was beginning to see why he'd splintered into so many personalities. Far too human for his own good—which was what he'd called his people back home—Jiya realized he needed more than just a crew to help repair him and keep him running. He needed companionship.

Which, weird as it sounded, made a whole lot of sense now that she'd seen him in action—and seen General Adrial Maddox and the damage that had been done to him without interaction.

He wasn't just an artificial intelligence; he had become something more along the way. His time around incredibly strong personalities had rubbed off on him. While never able to become these Federation heroes he admired, he did his best to rise to their level; to get as close as he could manage.

Then when he'd been sent into exile, which was the only way Jiya could imagine it, he was alone again, bereft of his family, as he saw them—these powerful people he'd come to rely on, as they had him.

Or maybe she was tired and projecting.

Ka'nak and Takal were already there when the two women arrived, and they waved Geroux and Jiya over to sit with them. They gratefully accepted the invitation.

Takal looked worn out to Jiya, the bags under his dark eyes making them look like deep craters on a moon. He lifted a small flask to his lips and drank deep, the contents of which likely weren't doing anything to improve his appearance. Ka'nak, however, looked as fresh as he had when he'd faced down the monstrosity in the pit.

"Are you tired, Uncle?" Geroux asked, apparently seeing the same thing Jiya had.

"A bit," he answered, nodding, "but I'd be far worse if

Ka'nak hadn't been helping me all day. He's made my work much easier. Thank you, friend."

Ka'nak nodded. "Know what else would make our work easier?"

"What's that?" Geroux asked.

"Dinner," the Melowi warrior answered, leaning back in his seat. His stomach rumbled on cue, and he grimaced. "Who's a guy got to kill to get a meal around this place?"

"That would be Helm, actually," Tactical said through the comms in their heads. "Though, I suspect he might be a bit gamey if you tried to eat him afterward."

Jiya grimaced, realizing she would never be free of the AI's multiple inner monologues now that she had the device in her head.

"I'll eat about anything at this point," the warrior complained.

Even Geroux seemed to agree. "Yeah, I'm getting pretty hungry. It's been a long day." She glanced around the lounge. "We learned a whole bunch about the ship, but I didn't see anything like a mess hall or kitchen. How do we get food here?"

The Reynold's droid walked in right then, a weird grimace plastered across his mechanical features as he heard them talking. "Food?"

"Yeah, you know, the stuff us meatbags eat so we can live?" Jiya explained.

"Damn it!" Reynolds grumbled. "I *knew* I forgot something."

"What?" Ka'nak shouted, leaping to his feet and knocking his chair to the floor. "There's no food on this tub?"

Reynolds shrugged. "What did I need it for? There's only me, myself, and I, and I, and I, and I aboard. None of us eat."

"Well, looks like none of *us* are going to eat either," Jiya grumped. "We need to be better prepared than this. Had I known there wasn't any food aboard, we could have bought supplies when I first joined you—before we started chasing down a crew. That should have been the priority."

Reynolds explained, "It's been a long time since I've had a crew on board, and they brought their own food when they were here."

Ka'nak growled and looked ready to leap across the table at the AI. Even Geroux and Takal looked pissed, both raising their voices to complain. Jiya rubbed her temples and willed the headache sneaking up on her to go away.

"Okay, people, calm down," she hissed. "We'll get this fixed, isn't that right, Reynolds?"

"If you say so," he replied, triggering more of an outburst from the rest of the crew. "I'm kidding, sheesh." He raised his hands in surrender. "There have to be some protein bars stashed around here somewhere. Those will have to do for now, and there's that Coke we brought for trading. The sugar might take the edge off."

The crew groaned and started in again, Jiya shouting to rein them in a second later. She let them get a little of the steam out first.

"Then…" she said, dragging out the word until everyone went silent, "after our protein bars and our meeting, we'll organize a supply run and pop down to the surface with the shuttle and get what we need." Jiya pointed at each crewmember in turn. "While we're waiting on our meal, think of *reasonable* items you might need outside of food, and I'll get with Reynolds to see what we can pick up."

Reynolds came over and plopped down in one of the empty chairs. "Comm, get the bots to do a search of the ship, starting with the kitchen, then mess hall, and sweep through the private quarters and see if anyone left behind any still-edible food for the crew."

"I'm almost afraid to go pillaging those rooms," Comm replied. "Who knows what kind of weird human items I might stumble across?"

"Wear gloves," Reynolds suggested.

"Excellent idea," Comm said. "I'll let you know what potentially embarrassing things I find. Oh, and the food, of course."

"*Soon*, right?" Ka'nak asked, putting a salty emphasis on the "soon" part.

An animated thumbs-up appeared on the viewscreen above the table. It wiggled and danced before disappearing in a cluster of sparkles.

"I'll take that as a yes?" Ka'nak mumbled.

"Had it been a no, it would have been a different finger," Jiya clarified. "And probably fewer sparkles."

"Okay," Reynolds said, rapping the table to get their attention, "the main reason I called you here—"

"Besides *not* to feed us?" Ka'nak complained.

"Yes, besides that," the AI responded. "We need to establish a chain of authority aboard the ship."

"Aboard *you*?" Takal asked.

"Yes, me. The ship."

"I'm thinking it's pretty clear you're in charge when

you're the ship," Takal continued. "I mean, there's really no way to mutiny and take control from you. That puts you in charge. You could simply kill the atmospherics and vent us to space If we give you grief, right?"

Reynolds sighed. "My point here is not that I'm in charge of—"

"You're not?" Ka'nak asked. "Now I'm confused. Who did he say was in charge, Takal?"

"*I'm* in charge," Reynolds asserted.

"Then why are we having this conversation if it's already decided?" Ka'nak shook his head. "And by the way, who decided that in the first place? Shouldn't we vote on something as important as who's the boss?"

"It's okay." Jiya bit back a chuckle and put a hand on Ka'nak's arm. "What Reynolds is trying to nail down is our positions with regards to each other. He is the ship, and he is in charge overall, but what about the rest of us? We need some sort of pecking order to keep things in line. Someone everyone can report to without bothering Reynolds."

"So we know who to blame when we don't get fed?" Ka'nak clarified.

"Exactly," Jiya replied.

"I blame Reynolds, then," the Melowi stated.

Jiya and the AI sighed in unison.

"What? Is that not what you just said, that you want someone to blame?" Ka'nak asked.

"You want to handle that one?" Reynolds asked, his metallic eyes rolling so far back that Jiya thought he'd lose them inside his skull.

"Okay, let's just move on, please." Jiya leaned back in her seat and groaned.

"I vote that Jiya be in charge," Geroux said, then glanced at Reynolds. "I mean, not of the ship since that's your thing, but of us. She's always been level-headed and smart, and could handle herself. I'd be willing to listen to her."

"I second the motion," Takal said, raising his hand.

"I'll third and fourth the motion if it means she's going to find me food sometime tonight." Ka'nak raised both his hands in the air to emphasize his vote. "All this voting is making me hungrier."

Jiya felt her cheeks warm at the unexpected support. "I don't—"

"Then it's settled," the AI decided, cutting off her attempt at declining. "From here on out, you are First Officer Jiya Lemaire. Congratulations."

"Uh, thanks," she mumbled.

"Now, you need to pick a second. Who you got?" Reynolds wondered, glancing around the table at the crew. "You want straws to make it easier?"

Jiya sighed. *Nothing like being put on the spot.* "No, I'm good. Thanks."

She looked at each of the remaining crew in turn, but she already knew who she'd pick. Not because he was necessarily a better person than the others, but because he was the wisest, most capable of the crew when it came to an actual command position.

She held her breath for a moment, letting it go stale in her lungs before finally licking her lips and calling out her choice. "If he's a hundred percent after his time in the Pod-doc, I choose Maddox."

"Whew!" Takal called, slumping in his chair in relief.

"Thank God. I thought you might choose me there for a second."

Jiya and Geroux chuckled, and Takal's niece patted him on the back, grinning. "I thought so too," she told him. "I'm too young for a command position, I feel, and Muscles there is too… Well, yeah, I figured it was going to be you."

Ka'nak grunted and pointed to his stomach.

Reynolds grinned. "Excellent decision, First Officer Lemaire." He got up from the table and motioned toward the door. "Now that all that is resolved, first order of business is for you to get your crew ready to go planetside again and collect supplies. Chop-chop."

He strode from the room.

Jiya clambered to her feet and stretched, feeling the bones in her back *crackle* and *pop* from being hunched over a console all day. "You heard the man…uh, android. Let's get moving."

"I heard that," the AI's voice broadcast over the comm, reminding her that they were always connected.

The crew chuckled and made their way to the shuttle.

Jiya hoped the AI would foot the bill for some kind of booze after the snafu with dinner.

She could use a drink right now. And judging by Takal's sweaty paleness, so could he. Another one, at least.

She'd have to rectify that posthaste. She wondered if the Pod-doc could deal with something like alcohol dependency. She made a mental note to ask Reynolds when she was alone.

CHAPTER TWELVE

"Why isn't that Jonny taxi coming with us?" Ka'nak wondered.

"I suspect this is a test. See how we manage what should be a simple task," Jiya replied.

"It's like running to the grocery store," Geroux said. "The big difference is that we have money, if Reynolds is to be believed and this chip is filled."

"How would Reynolds have our money if he just got here? Again, if he is to be believed?" Takal wondered.

"We all had a glimpse of the ship and a small taste of what it can do. Do you doubt that he can take whatever he needs?" Jiya challenged. "I hope he can help General Maddox."

"The AI known as Reynolds seems to be disconnected from people. He understands a great deal about how the universe works but is still confused by simple Larian traits and how to interact with us."

The shuttle continued toward the planet. They'd selected a parking area behind a major grocery store. With only four of them, they figured they could do it the easy way and not try to buy commercial quantities.

Geroux leaned forward against her restraints. "Is he an adolescent genius, or is he just off?"

"Geroux! We're scientists. Don't create a premise where it has to be one or the other. Life isn't binary."

"But it is. Either you are alive, or you're dead!" she declared victoriously, but nodded slowly. "Yes. I think we have to accept the premise that he will not harm us, but the opposite. He'll do everything he can to protect us."

"Talking about alive or dead," Jiya interrupted the scientists before they descended into their study of the AI to address Ka'nak, "you don't get to rip out any throats with your teeth, at least not while I'm watching!"

"I concede that was gross, but for the show, it was expected to raise positive ratings by four-point-three percent."

"Did it?" Jiya asked.

"Numbers were good, holding steady at four-point-nine, until my walk around the ring. Then they dropped to three-point-six. Reviewers suggested wiping my mouth clean on the shirt of my opponent would have boosted it over five. Live and learn."

"You follow the numbers like that?" Takal fixed Ka'nak with the gaze of a rapt student.

"Of course. It's business, not barbarism."

"It *was* barbaric," Geroux added.

"Maybe a little. Would it help if I told you that I don't enjoy that part?"

"You don't like it? Then why do you do it?"

"I didn't say I didn't like it. I asked if it would help if I told you that."

Geroux wore the expression of a stunned mullet as she tried to parse Ka'nak's words into something comprehensible.

Jiya waved her hands to get everyone's attention. "Landing soon, people. We need to do this incognito. Go in, get your groceries for a week or two, and get out."

The shuttle settled into an area behind the Larian grocery store. Many products were provided through the government and were rationed, but the rest were available for purchase in any quantity.

They walked off the shuttle and strolled around the building. "Don't forget where we parked," Jiya quipped. Ka'nak took two carts, and Jiya threw a glance his way.

"What? You said one week or two. That's a pretty stark difference, so I'm planning for two. I need fuel for this furnace!" he declared, striking a pose.

"Incognito!" Takal laughed and pushed a cart inside, with Geroux close behind him.

Jiya chuckled at her new security chief and general maintenance technician. "You stay behind me, because I don't want to see cleaned-out shelves while I shop."

"Unless you're going straight to the butcher, you won't be behind me," Ka'nak remarked, pushing his way past Jiya, winking as he went.

Jiya watched the three disappear into the aisles. "What have I gotten myself into?" she mumbled, smiling at how ridiculous it was. An AI implanted in a Jonny taxi android. A ship with the firepower to destroy planets. A small group of friends to keep the ship sane while it searched for myth-ical creatures. *It will be interesting.*

She started to select the cheapest brand, then stopped herself. She needed things that had a long shelf life, and cost was no object. She passed Geroux and Takal, glancing into their carts to find that they'd reached the same conclusion. Geroux appeared to have gained a taste for the planet's finest chocolates.

Jiya shrugged and didn't think twice at selecting a couple of boxes of designer crackers and tossing them into her cart.

A commotion in the back of the store drew her atten-tion. She hurried down the aisle to find Ka'nak in the custom meat section taking pictures with the butchers. "This is where I shop for the best meat on Lariest!" he declared for one of the butcher's vid cameras. "Two thumbs up." He pointed to his cart, which was filled to capacity with the best cuts. His second cart was filled with fresh vegetables and fruits.

"How in the hell..." she stammered as she tried to get his attention.

"Gotta go, guys, the boss is calling me. Thanks for everything. Make sure you bet on me next time I'm in the ring. With man-fuel like this, I will dominate!" Ka'nak waved to his fans and made a beeline for Jiya. She froze as he wrapped an arm around her and bowed so both their heads could be in the many pictures being snapped.

"Ka'nak has a lover!" someone declared.

Jiya blinked rapidly, unable to speak. Ka'nak smiled and pushed his two carts past her. She followed quickly, leaving her cart at the end to block the aisle.

"This is your idea of incognito?" she demanded.

"Have you seen what I look like? I don't do incognito. I thought you were joking, because—let me restate this—I *can't* do incognito."

"Fine," she said and stormed away, haphazardly dumping items from the shelves into her cart, not bothering to slow down and arrange anything.

"You don't *mean* fine," Ka'nak said softly before adding in his deepest voice, "Meet you at the ship, Number One."

My crew, she thought. Jiya suddenly had an overwhelming desire for chocolate. She retraced her steps, found that the good stuff had been cleaned out, and settled for second best, catching herself because the day before she couldn't have afforded *any* chocolate. Jiya smiled, thinking that she'd never have to go back to her apartment. That was the low point of her manufactured decline.

She was ready to step back into the light. The war with her father was behind her now that she had assumed a galactic position, a role greater than one planet. Maybe someday she'd return to free Lariest from his tyranny, but today was not that day.

Her only regret was that she'd miss the tabloids showing her with Ka'nak and his declaration that she was his boss. Her father would put an end to Ka'nak's career in the ring, but that was the same as her apartment—a place he would never return to.

Jiya watched the checkout clerk snap a selfie with Ka'nak after the chip was accepted for payment and smiled again. It was getting easier to trust the AI.

Takal bowed his head as he passed Jiya on his way to check out. She frowned at seeing the liquor in his cart. He avoided making eye contact. Geroux had a couple bottles of champagne and two more of wine, the best the store had in stock.

Jiya leaned close. "We need to get him off the booze."

"I know. I worry. Maybe Reynolds can do something. If he can help Maddox, he should be able to help my uncle."

Jiya nodded and headed down the nearest aisle. She needed to finish her shopping. It was time for them to go. She wasn't surprised to find herself in the coffee section. She jammed her arm into a shelf of flavored and high-test instant coffees and swept them all into her cart. Then she did the same with the second-best brand. "He did say two weeks..."

CHAPTER THIRTEEN

After a successful supply run the crew's performance improved dramatically. Reynolds stood on the bridge running his calculations for what felt like the millionth time.

It might have been two million times by then.

"Stop stressing," Helm told him. "You've checked the numbers, and the program is running fine. The search vector makes as much sense as anything else we've thought up to seek out those Kurtherian demons."

"I agree," XO called. "So why are we still sitting here?"

"Waiting on the Larians to wake up and report for duty," the AI answered.

"Can't we just plug them full of nanites and soup them up, so we don't have to sit around waiting for them to get their beauty rest every night?"

"Judging by the way some of them look, no amount of rest is going to make them beautiful," Tactical muttered.

"I wish we could, XO, but Bethany Anne would kick our collective asses if we did anything like that right now,"

Reynolds assured them. "No upgrades until these meatbags have proven their worth to the Federation's cause and we get the okay from the bosses. Until then, we're stuck with redshirts."

"Well, they brought aboard a metric shit-ton of coffee in their supply run last night, so at least they'll be somewhat energized once they finally drag their asses out of bed," Navigation commented.

"All that's just to counteract the epic amount of alcohol they grabbed. Their brains are probably pickled in their skulls."

"Perhaps we should sound Reveille and wake their lazy rectums up," XO suggested.

Jiya swept onto the bridge right then, grunting at the assembled AI. "No need," she argued. "We're here."

Geroux came in behind her, yawning and wiping the sleep from her eyes.

"Such military precision and timing!" XO commented.

Geroux shrugged and flopped down in Comm's position. "Move over, Space Ghost, I'm taking over."

"Oh, you know who Space Ghost is but you don't know about *Star Trek?*" Reynolds groaned. "What kind of heathens *are* you people?"

Comm sighed at his dismissal. "And the first pink slip is had," he muttered. "Now I'm off to spend the last of my days in Reynolds' brain."

"Good luck with that," Tactical told him. "It's a serious shit show in there."

Jiya crawled into XO's spot and forced a grin. "One down, too many of you bastards to go. I'll pour one out for you later, Comm."

"Where are the other two?" Reynolds asked.

"Ka'nak is double checking the system work they finished last night and going around to inspect the hull repairs. Takal is working on your new body. He says he has some ideas already," Jiya replied.

"Fan-fucking-tastic," Reynolds replied. "Can't wait to see the new me."

"As if there aren't enough of you already," Jiya murmured.

"I heard that," Reynolds replied.

She met his glare with a grin. "We're ready to go whenever you are, boss."

"Then let's get moving, boys," Reynolds shouted, the excitement clear in his voice. "Helm, set a course by the navigation algorithm and let's see what the hell we find out there."

"Done," Helm called. "Activating Gate drive in three... two...right-the-fuck-now!"

The SD *Reynolds* shot into space faster than anything Jiya could imagine. She clung to her seat in awe, watching the viewscreen flicker and flash, and then they were deep in the Chain Galaxy, far, far away from her home planet of Lariest.

It was the most exciting thing Jiya had ever experienced.

Her heart raced, her pulse whooshing in her ears, and butterflies danced in her stomach.

It was awesome. Amazing. Thrilling.

And then it wasn't.

Boredom set in fast.

The vast emptiness of space splayed before Jiya's tired eyes, and before long, she found herself wishing she'd downed more than one cup of coffee that morning.

"I'd kill for an espresso," she mumbled, blinking her eyes to wake them up.

"This is what space travel is all about," Tactical told her. "Months of tedious nothingness followed by thirty seconds of harrowing life and death decisions, laser fire everywhere, then months of reports explaining to the bosses why you blew up a planet."

Jiya straightened in her seat and turned around, staring at Tactical's position as though she could actually see him. "I take it that's the voice of experience?"

"My lawyer advises me to plead the Fifth," Tactical muttered. "But anyway, yeah, space travel isn't all the video fanatics make it out to be. It's damn boring."

Geroux yawned as if on cue, and Jiya chuckled.

"I need an IV of caffeine, stat," Geroux muttered.

"I could use one of those myself," Jiya agreed. "Wonder if we can get one of the bots to deliver us a coffee or twelve?"

"Only one way to find out," Geroux said with a mischievous grin. She went to trigger her comm, but Tactical cut her move short.

"Belay that," he called. "We've got company. Looks like it could be a scout ship, given its minimal armor and apparent weaponry. It's too small to be much else."

"Kurtherian?" Jiya asked.

"Not a traditional one by the looks of her, but you

never know. Those bastards are sneaky."

"She's spotted us," Geroux reported, pointing out a sudden adjustment in the alien ship's course.

"Hail her and let's see what we've got," Reynolds ordered, his android body stomping onto the bridge and flinging into the captain's seat.

"She's not responding." Geroux shook her head. "Shields are coming up."

"Weapons are still cold, Captain," Tactical added. "She's not looking to fight but to run."

"Don't let her get away," Reynolds demanded. "Keep hailing and pressure her to stop, but if she doesn't, stay right on top of her. We can't let that ship out of sight."

"Engines engaged," Helm told Reynolds. "We're closing, but she's not making it easy."

"Where's she headed?" Reynolds asked.

"Looks like we've got a small Gate a distance ahead," Navigation replied. "She's angling that direction."

"Lock her signal down, so we don't lose her if she gets there before us."

"Aye-aye, Captain," Geroux replied, clearly struggling to keep up with the excitement and the back and forth precision of the collective AI. A sheen of sweat glistened on her forehead.

Jiya was sure she had the same, but she wasn't about to call attention to it by wiping it away.

"She's at the Gate," Navigation reported. "Shit, now she's through."

"Still got her on scanners," Jiya noted. "We're not losing these bastards."

"Coming up on the Gate," Helm said. "Preparing for entry. Five, four, three, two…entering."

Once more the brilliant flash of Gate travel flooded the bridge with light, and then they were through. Jiya grunted at the oddness of the spatial shift, but she didn't lose track of the fleeing scout ship.

"There she is," she called out. "Starboard side."

Helm was already on it. "Closing," he told the crew. "Another minute and we'll be sniffing their asshole."

"Do we have to?" Geroux asked. "I mean, I'm all for adventure, but some things are better left un-experienced."

Tactical chuckled. "There's nothing like the smell of burning asshole in the morning."

"Going to have to take your word for it, Tactical," Jiya responded, unable to get the sordid image out of her head. "Reynolds, we've got `em. They're within weapons range."

"Tactical, put some heat on their tailfeathers," Reynolds commanded.

"Targeting engines," he replied.

"They're evading," Helm reported.

"They aren't evading shit," Tactical stated, and the superdreadnought's forward guns fired.

A bolt of energy streaked through space and slammed into the scout ship's rear shields. It was like a hammer versus an ant.

The shields flared and dispersed under duress, and the bolt scored a direct hit on the scout ship's engines. There was a flash of light, and then the scout's hull warped and gave way. Its engines exploded, a burst of fire and light erupting, going out as soon as it started. The ship listed and began to veer off course, spinning in a slow circle as its momentum was redirected.

"Excellent shot, Tactical," Reynolds complimented.

Jiya watched the wounded scout ship as it slowed, the SD *Reynolds* drawing closer with every passing second.

The screen highlighted the wreckage of its engines, and Jiya complimented Tactical on the precision of the shot.

The ship's hull was charred black and looked as if it had been melted, the once-round engines warped into crescent shape. Wisps of smoke trailed behind the ship, and she saw its external lights flickering, appearing ready to go out.

"Hail them again" Reynolds called.

"Same song and dance," Geroux answered, shaking her head. "We keep sending, they keep blowing us off."

Reynolds nodded. "Then we board to get what we need." The android pointed at Jiya. "Assemble the crew and gather weapons and gear from the armory. I want all of you in on this."

"Everyone?" she questioned.

"Did I stutter?" Reynolds barked. Jiya raised an eyebrow and glared at him. "I'll go with you, but this is an experience all of you need to have, so gear up."

"Yessir, Captain Reynolds, sir," Jiya replied, stomping off the bridge with Geroux at her heels.

Reynolds sighed once they had left.

He glanced down the corridor in the direction the two women had gone. "Anyway, hold down the fort while we board and figure out what those squirrelly little bastards were running for."

"Probably has nothing do with us being a super-dreadnought," Navigation muttered, stating what might well have been obvious.

Still, Reynolds needed to know if there was more to it. Besides, they'd plotted a search vector to find Kurtherians, and since there might well be a Kurtherian aboard the scout craft, or they might know of some, it only made sense to board and scrape all the intel they could from the ship.

"Time to put my android foot up someone's ass."

CHAPTER FOURTEEN

The crew donned the makeshift armor left behind by the previous crew.

They looked like rejects from a first-season *Doctor Who* episode.

"We're going to need to do something about our equipment, I'm thinking," Jiya moaned. "That's probably going to be your next job, Takal—crafting some armor that actually fits us." She glanced at Geroux, who swam in her suit. "This is ridiculous."

"We'll worry about it after this, *and* after I get my new body," Reynolds said, although he too seemed distraught by what he saw among the crew. "Don't die."

"Reassuring," Takal muttered, taking a hit from his flask. "I can work on both, fortunately," he whispered to Jiya, who nodded in reply.

Ka'nak pushed past the group, moving to the front of the line near the boarding tube. He looked every bit the warrior. "Just stay behind me, everyone." While his armor didn't fit perfectly, it was clear he was closer to the prototype of those who'd come before.

Jiya wasn't comfortable invading an alien ship this way, but what other option did they have? This was the mission she signed up for.

Sort of.

Who knew what the hell these particular beings were? They were going to find out far sooner than later.

"We've got ten lifeforms aboard," Comm told them, pulling himself out of mothballs while Geroux was away from her station. "They are apparently wise to our tactics, so they'll be sitting right there when you break through to their ship."

"That seems...unfortunate," Takal mumbled.

"Show some courage," Reynolds replied. "The plan is straightforward: hit them hard and fast and keep pumping bolts into them until they're all dead. What's so difficult about that?"

"I'd say just about every bit of what you said," Takal admitted. "These are living beings we're talking about here. How do we even know they're hostile?"

"Well, if they shoot at us, then we'll know they're hostile," Reynolds retorted. "It's pretty simple, really."

Takal looked at his weapon and let out a loud sigh, his hands trembling.

Reynolds stared at Takal as the older man stood there eyeballing the floor. "Wait, haven't you ever killed anyone before?"

Takal shook his head. "Never."

The AI stiffened. "Oh, hell. Are you serious?" He looked at the rest of the crew in turn. "What about you, Geroux?"

"Nope," she replied." Can't say that I have."

"You, Jiya?" Reynolds asked. "At least tell me you've taken someone out before."

"On dates," she answered, shrugging. "I've even paid a few times."

Reynolds deflated. "Well, this certainly changes things. I'd assumed—and yes, I know the stupid saying: ass, you, me—I thought the lot of you had some kind of combat training." He grunted. "Looks like we have a bunch more training to prioritize if this is going to work."

Ka'nak raised his hand. "If it makes you feel better, I've killed *lots* of people. Lots."

"It does, actually," Reynolds told him. He paced for a moment, clearly wondering what the hell he should do.

"We'll make it work, Reynolds," Jiya told the AI, although she wasn't completely sure how. "We just need to be smarter than our enemy, right?"

Reynolds shrugged. "Usually, hitting them with so much force they don't have a chance to hit you back is better, but sure, we can try to outwit them this time. What do you have in mind?"

She didn't have much.

Having never been in such a situation before, her mind was one big blank. How did you go about planning to kill people?

She looked at Geroux and Takal, who were even more nervous and less prepared than she was. At least she'd spent her life training on various hand-to-hand and martial arts techniques. Geroux was a book-learner, and Takal was... Well, Takal was Takal. He was an out-of-shape genius who didn't have a clue about weapons, let alone how to put one to use against an enemy.

She turned her focus to Reynolds, who stood there impatiently tapping his foot, and then to Ka'nak. Here was her real army, the fighters who'd burst through the door and kick ass until there was no more ass to kick.

Then it hit her.

"Hey!" she cried out. "Can we get one of the bots down here?"

"For what?" Reynolds asked. "They're not designed for combat."

"Don't need them to be," she answered. "They can take a shot or two without blowing apart, right?"

"Yeah, they're fairly sturdy. What are you thinking?"

"I remember something I did as a kid at my father's compound," she said. "It was a game. Actually, Geroux and I played it a bunch of times, too. We would set up cups at the end of a long walk, and we'd find palm-sized stones and roll them down the walk to knock the cups over."

"Bowling?" Reynolds clarified.

"Don't know what bowling is, but we called the game 'Knock `em Over.'"

Geroux grinned, clearly remembering the game.

"What the hell does that have to do with anything we're about to do here?" Reynold asked.

"Well, that's where the bot comes in," she replied, offering him a sly grin.

Judging by the expression that washed over the Jonny android's face, he realized what she intended.

"Oh, that might just work," he muttered. "Hey, Comm,

get me a bot down here. But not one of the sparkly new ones. Send an old beater that still works."

"On its way," Comm responded.

"Forgive me for not keeping up, but what the hell are you two talking about?" Takal asked.

"Tactics, old man," Reynolds said with a grin. "Tactics."

Jiya patted the old scientist on the shoulder. "Just stay at the back and shoot anything that comes toward you that isn't one of us, okay?"

He nodded, but Jiya hoped it didn't get to the point where Takal was expected to fight. Geroux either, for that matter, although Jiya felt more comfortable that the young woman would excel at it like she did everything else.

The hum of the bot's arrival drew her from her thoughts. It came over and stood beside them, awaiting orders.

"How do you want to do this?" Reynolds asked Jiya.

She let her breath out slowly, thinking and visualizing, and decided she knew best how to make it work.

"Well, we can't go charging in without setting ourselves up for attack, right?" she asked, not really expecting an answer. "So, instead of making ourselves targets, we give the enemy a better one to lash out at."

"Care to elaborate?"

"Not really," she answered. "Just follow my lead, and be ready to hit these guys hard on my command."

"So, I'm supposed to not only let you take charge of a battle, but I'm also supposed to sit back and wait until you want me to join in?" Reynolds wondered, one eyebrow raised in disbelief.

CH GIDEON

Jiya offered him a shallow nod. "I work best under pressure. Spontaneously."

"Oh, goody," Reynolds muttered, racking a round in his weapon. "Sure, let's see what you've got. I'm sure Bethany Anne will forgive my complete lack of sanity in going along with this."

"Worse comes to worst, you can always blow the scout ship up with your railguns," Jiya told him.

"True, and then we'd lose all the intel aboard, which is why we're doing this in the first place." He shook his head. "You're not exactly inspiring confidence here."

"Well, if I screw it up, you can go in blasting. How's that?"

"Ah, a Plan B I can get behind," he snarked. "Let's do this." He moved toward the boarding tunnel, but Jiya waved him off.

"Stay to the side, but open the tube and be ready," she told him. "The rest is on me."

"What are you going to do?" Geroux asked.

"Play rabbit," she replied, surprised to find herself grinning.

"I wonder if we've included funeral arrangements," Reynolds mused.

"We have now," XO replied across the comm. "Plus, in case of death by stupidity, we don't have to pay the crew's families or extend their benefits."

"Excellent," Reynolds said, rubbing his hands together.

"Again, you're not creepy at all," Jiya told the AI, moving to the edge of the tube. "Have the bot ready," she said, then drew in a deep breath. "Open the far hatch."

Reynolds complied without hesitation, reminding Jiya

150

just how much of a machine he was in comparison to the rest of them. No matter what happened here, no matter how many times he got shot, he always had somewhere else to exist. None of the rest of them had that option.

Dead was dead.

That was why she needed to make this work.

She heard the hiss of the tube pressurizing and the far hatch popped open, leaving a clear shot to the enemy ship beyond.

"They there?" she whispered.

Comm came back. "Ten lifeforms just inside the craft on the other side of the boarding hatch.

She nodded, not even realizing she'd done it until afterward, then she lifted her pistol and steadied it in her hand. "Ignore everything I say until I call out Reynolds's name, understand? Everything until then isn't meant for any of you."

The crew muttered their agreement, and Jiya jumped into the tube without another word. Geroux gasped, but it was too late do anything to calm the girl's nerves.

Jiya raised her gun and fired down the tube, squeezing the trigger with abandon. This wasn't about taking out the enemy singlehandedly or going out in a blaze of glory, she knew.

"Get `em!" she screamed at the top of her lungs. "Advance now! Hit `em hard!"

In actuality, it was about being bait.

She stopped a few steps inside the tube, catching sight of aliens aboard the scout ship. A knot formed in her throat. While she couldn't get a good look at them, it was clear that their armor fit and their weapons looked deadly.

She knew the latter because there were a handful of them pointing at her.

Then they started firing.

"Motherfucking fuckity fuckball fuckers," she screamed, dodging the blaster fire and diving out of the boarding tube.

She slammed into the hard steel of the *Reynolds'* floor, knocking the wind from her lungs. Gasping to catch her breath, she rolled to the side to be out of line with the tube, scrambling to her knees.

"That was…interesting," Reynolds assessed.

She flipped him off, sucked in enough air to push a few words out, and hit her comm. "Where are they, Comm?"

"Pushing down the tube. There are five coming your way," Comm replied. "Your brilliant plan to be killed aboard the SD *Reynolds* rather than the alien scout ship was a rousing success."

"Fuck off," she muttered. "Reynolds, time to put the bot to work. Shoot him down the tube."

Again, Reynolds didn't hesitate. "Sorry, little guy," he said, and the bot launched itself around the corner and charged down the boarding tube.

Blaster fire resounded, shots scorching the air and crashing into the wall just behind the umbilical and charring it black. That ended a split-second later.

Curses and screams echoed down the tube, then several loud *thumps* resounded loudly and the gunfire paused.

"Contact!" Comm called.

"Go, Reynolds and Ka'nak," Jiya ordered.

To her surprise, neither questioned her.

Reynolds shot down the tube in his Jonny android

body, weapon up and firing. Ka'nak ran behind him, using the android as cover.

Jiya waved Geroux and Takal after her. "Follow me in and secure the tube end once we get there," she commanded, then she bolted after Ka'nak and Reynolds, trusting that the other two would do as ordered.

For an instant, she regretted dragging them into it, but she knew, like Reynolds had said, it was an experience they all needed. To pamper them and keep them from the violence inherent in their job was to put them at even more of a risk. They needed to do this.

Jiya sighed. That included her.

Today was one big battle orgy to show them what it was all about.

Ahead of her, the bot pushed through the end of the boarding tube, taking with it the five aliens who'd been unfortunate enough to be in its way. Their twisted bodies were wrapped around the bot in awkward positions, and those who were still alive squirmed to break free of the bot's crushing grip.

They never got the chance.

The bot shot out the far end of the tube and slammed headlong into the wall beyond.

Jiya felt a wave of nausea roil in her gut as metal and bone collided. Great, creaking snaps resounded, bones shattering, the sound of a skull being crushed like a melon dropped from a roof.

She bit back the bile threatening to spew loose and pushed on.

Puke later, damn it!

Reynolds broke free of the tube behind the bot and

cleared the way, turning to his left, his weapon up and firing. Ka'nak veered right, doing the same thing as weapons fire came back at both of them.

Jiya split the difference and jumped into the scout ship between the pair of them.

Her first instinct was to follow Reynolds and use his metal body as a shield to avoid getting shot, but she realized that was a bitch move. It left Ka'nak, who was flesh and blood—even if he was a beast—on his own.

While Reynolds could take a number of shots and walk away from it, the Melowi warrior might not be able to. She darted to Ka'nak's side and engaged the enemy.

The aliens had retreated down the corridor, but there was nowhere for them to go that didn't leave them exposed. Ka'nak took advantage of that and advanced, firing the entire time. Jiya marched alongside him, doing the same.

Her weapon thrummed in her hand, and one of the aliens took a blast to his chest. Jiya cheered internally, biting back a grim smile as the alien stumbled back, smoke billowing from the wound, but he was far from dead.

He lined the pair up in his sights and returned fire.

Jiya hadn't expected that, thinking getting hit with blaster fire would have dropped the guy.

Clearly, she was wrong.

Ka'nak howled as a shot slammed into his shoulder. He was whipped around and slammed into the wall. His weapon tumbled from his hand in slow motion and clattered to the floor as he dropped to a knee, one hand against the wall propping him up.

Jiya stared wide-eyed as a second shot struck him in the

ribs and blasted him backward. He grunted and frothed as he fell to the deck.

On instinct, Jiya went to help him up, but he waved her away. "Keep fighting," he shouted.

The words triggered her ire.

She knew damn well he wasn't fine. He was hurt badly, and it was all her fault.

Not only had she dragged him into all this, but the plan to storm the scout ship the way they had was hers. Jiya snarled and bared her teeth as blaster fire sparked around her.

She'd led them all into this, and it was up to her to fix it.

She ducked as she spun, squeezing the trigger with cruel intent. Her weapon barked searing death down the corridor. The enemy shot back with the same ferocity. They wanted her just as dead as she wanted them.

And for a second there, she thought they might succeed.

A blast struck the wall and ricocheted toward her. She lifted her free hand out of instinct and felt the blast shriek past.

Then the pain hit her.

She went to scream, then bit back on it, teeth clenched against the burning sear that engulfed her left hand.

Jiya staggered back, growling, determined not to let her injury stop her. She forced herself not to look at the wound or imagine how bad it might be. Instead, she thought of Ka'nak on the floor, helpless. He needed her to be strong; they all did.

If these aliens got past her Ka'nak would die, and

Geroux and her uncle might die, too, trapped as they were in the tube.

She couldn't have that, so she howled and pressed forward, weapon raised, determined to end what she'd started.

She was glad to note the alien who'd shot Ka'nak had clearly been wounded worse than he'd let on. He stumbled forward, wobbling down the corridor toward her, one hand holding the blasted metal at his chest as he held his pistol out in a trembling hand. He could barely keep it upright, it seemed.

The last survivor of his side, likely the one who'd wounded her, hunkered down behind him, using him as a shield like she'd contemplated using Reynolds at the start of the fight.

It seemed dirty now that she saw it in action, the one alien using his companion as cover, so he had a chance to walk away from the battle alive even if it cost his companion his life.

Jiya wasn't going to let him get away with it.

She stood up, making a show of it, and aimed her pistol at the wounded alien's head. He did the same in counter, but Jiya ducked, grateful her feint had worked. His weapon came up slower due to his wounds.

His shot flew over her head.

She took her shot, aiming low, squeezing the trigger fast and strafing.

Bolts of energy tore through the wounded alien's leg and blasted the alien cowering behind him. The first shot hit him in the shoulder, spinning him to the side. The second struck his back, and the last shot removed his head as he collapsed.

He fell to the floor, a smoking wreck.

His buddy fell to his knees beside him. Wounded and clearly in agony, he hadn't lost his weapon. He aimed at Jiya as best he could and went to squeeze the trigger.

Reynolds got there first.

A bolt of energy flew over Jiya's shoulder and smashed into the alien's face. What was left of his head oozed down his back as he toppled over and fell lifeless to the steel deck alongside his partner.

"Take that, alien scum," Reynolds told the dead guy.

Jiya exhaled hard and folded in on herself, letting her weapon drop, her hands clasping her knees to keep her standing. Pain shot up her wrist and forearm, but she still didn't want to look at her hand; didn't want to see how bad it was.

"You hurt?" Reynolds asked her as he went to Ka'nak's side, examining the Melowi warrior.

She grunted something nonspecific, letting the AI deal with Ka'nak, who was hurt far worse than she could possibly be.

Who needs two hands anyway?

Ka'nak groaned as Reynolds lifted him into his arms. "Bot, get over here," he ordered.

The bot did as it was told, and Reynolds handed Ka'nak to it gently. "Get him to Doc Reynolds immediately."

"He going to be okay?" Jiya managed to ask, finding herself staring at the warrior's scrunched face, his pain obvious.

"I've seen far worse," Reynolds told her. "He'll be fine.

Just can't lollygag around before getting him help." The AI smacked the bot on the back. "Get moving."

Ka'nak offered up a grimace, clearly doing his best to reassure Jiya as the bot carried him off. Not more than a second later the pair disappeared down the boarding tube, Geroux and Takal having vacated it to make room.

She smiled at seeing them whole, even though they appeared a tiny bit blurry.

"You did well, First Officer Lemaire," Reynolds noted, coming over to stand beside her and setting a comforting hand on her shoulder. "First battle and your crew came out of it mostly intact, and you've racked up a solid body count. Good job."

Jiya went to respond and stumbled. She grunted and leaned against the wall for support. Reynolds clasped her shoulder harder to keep her upright. He leaned in close, and Jiya saw him swimming before her eyes.

"Damn it!" Reynolds grumbled. "You're wounded, too."

Jiya unconsciously raised her injured hand to show it to the AI. "I'm all right," she told him. "Just a tiny bit woozy."

She was glad to note that all her fingers were still there, although her armored glove had been mostly torn away. The skin on her hand was blackened and charred, raised bubbles of pus covering the majority of the back. It gleamed silvery in the gloom of the alien ship.

Her pain grew the longer she stared at her hand, and her nausea wasn't far behind. She felt bile hitting the back of her throat, the tears blurring her vision even more.

Then she was swept off her feet and cradled to Reynolds' chest.

The world swayed around her, and she saw the

concerned faces of Geroux and Takal swim past as the AI ran with her, carting her through the tube and back onto the SD *Reynolds*.

"You're gonna be all right," the AI told her as he ran. "You're just in shock, which makes it all seem worse than it is."

"Yeah?" she muttered, finding she had little strength to say more.

"'Tis but a scratch. Just a flesh wound," he told her. Oddly enough, he chuckled at his own comment, but Jiya didn't have the wherewithal to understand or ask him why.

She went limp in his arms, letting herself be carried toward what she presumed was sickbay, where Ka'nak had been taken.

I hope he's okay, she thought as her head lolled to the side.

Her face pressed against Reynold's android chest, and she stared up at him through the corner of her eye.

"You know," she slurred, "you really do need a makeover, Jonny."

Reynolds muttered something she couldn't understand, for which she was probably grateful, and then they arrived in what she recognized as sickbay.

Then she didn't see anything, the darkness claiming her.

CHAPTER FIFTEEN

Jiya awoke with a start, a strange sense of déjà vu coming over her.

She realized she was lying down, a plastic-sheeted cot beneath her. Her brain swirled inside her head, her thoughts dancing, and then it struck her.

It was the same room she'd woken up in when she'd first met Reynolds.

She groaned and relaxed, then bolted upright.

My hand!

Her gaze snapped to her injury only to find there was nothing there. She lifted her hand, which was unmarred by the char that had engulfed it, and wiggled her fingers. To her surprise, they moved without hesitation or pain.

"The miracle of the Pod-docs," Ka'nak said, coming into the room and offering her a broad grin.

"Hey! You're okay!" she shouted, her voice echoing in the small room.

"More than okay," he told her, walking over to her bedside.

Android Reynolds entered the room behind him. "You're both fine," he said, coming over to stand beside her bed on the other side. "Ka'nak insisted on coming to see you."

"Had to make sure you were recovering," he told her.

Reynolds grunted. "Even though I already told him you were."

"Some things you just have to see with your own eyes." Ka'nak patted Jiya on her healed hand, and she was happy to notice it felt normal, not even a hint of the wound remaining. "And now that I have, I'm off to find food. I'm famished." He waved a quick goodbye and left the room, whistling.

Jiya watched him leave, then turned back to face Reynolds. "What's up with him?" she asked. "He seems a bit...weird."

Reynolds chuckled. "It's the drugs," he answered with a goofy smile. "He was hurt pretty bad, so the Pod-doc pumped him full of painkillers and mood enhancers. He's flying high right now."

Jiya smiled and laid back, resting her head on the pillow there. "They must not have shot me up with the same meds, because all I feel is tired."

"You weren't as bad off," Reynolds confirmed. "It was serious, no doubt, but nothing life-threatening, given our technology. You got the standard bandaging and cure-all, which means you missed out on the fun drugs. Sorry."

She shrugged. "It's cool. I have booze to make up the difference."

Reynolds grunted. "That'll have to wait a bit, though. While you and Ka'nak were unconscious, and after we swept the alien ship, we returned to Lariest space to recoup."

"The look on your face tells me things didn't go exactly as planned," she ventured.

He shook his head. "No, they didn't. Our adventures above and around your planet haven't gone unnoticed. Ever since we came back, the governments of your planet, all three of them, including your father's, have been bombarding us with messages and a number of destroyers from each are patrolling nearby."

"Wonderful," she grumbled.

The AI nodded. "They're keeping their distance, more I think to keep from antagonizing each other than us, but still..."

"What are the governments asking for?" she wondered.

"Seems each of them is interested in a treaty of some sort, although I'm not entirely certain of the details. Comm is handling the communications, obviously."

"Obviously." Jiya chuckled and sat up, kicking her legs off the side of the bed and stretching as she extended her feet. "So, what do we do?"

"I think it's in our best interest to meet with them and see what we can get out of them," he answered. "While I know you and the rest of the crew have no idea about the Kurtherians, it's possible the governments of your world do. It wouldn't be out of the ordinary for them to keep information from their people for all manner of reasons."

"You think they can help us find these guys?"

He shrugged. "Maybe, maybe not. Either way, it's always a good thing to establish trade routes and allies along the way should anything happen to us. A safe place to retreat to lick our wounds is always welcome."

She shook her head, smirking. "You think my father will welcome you with open arms?"

"That's kind of why I wanted to talk to you," Reynolds replied.

Jiya raised an eyebrow and stared at the AI hard. "Something tells me I'm not going to like this conversation." She clambered out of bed to be face to face with him. "Tell me you're not asking me to do what I think you are."

"I could tell you that," he said, "but I'd be lying."

She groaned and fought the urge to flop back onto the bed and return to sleep. "Too late for the docs to shoot me up with the good stuff?"

"'Fraid so."

"So, I'm not sure you understand my relationship with my father, but he sure as shit isn't going to take kindly to me approaching him as a representative of an alien species via a superdreadnought."

"No?"

"No." Jiya bit back a laugh. "The man barely wants to deal with me, and he sure hasn't shown any inclination to give a damn about me or my agenda, even more so after I ran away from the compound and made him look like a shitty father." She snorted. "Well, a shittier father. Can't really say he was ever above a turd in that department, to begin with."

"Then here's your chance to change his opinion. Force him to listen to you," Reynolds offered. "You'd be arriving in the presence of a superdreadnought backed by a military force unparalleled in the universe. There's no way he can ignore that."

Jiya burst into raucous laughter. "You so don't know my dad. He can stonewall with the best of them. If you think anything you can do will impress him, you've got another think coming."

"Then we make sure he understands our potential," Reynolds countered. "We make him an example for the other governments if we have to."

Jiya's giggles dropped off. "You mean killing him?"

"Not my first choice, of course," Reynolds assured her. "I'm not looking to shed blood here, Jiya. I'm looking to make allies of those willing to work with us and make object lessons of those unwilling. We don't have to kill the man to make our point, but I can't guarantee it won't happen if he pushes us too far."

Jiya exhaled hard. "I thought the battle with the alien scout was real, but if anything, this makes it *more* real. A couple of days ago I drove a hovercab. Now I'm going to be responsible for negotiating on a global scale?"

Reynolds agreed. "It's a big deal, I'll admit, but again, don't look at it as if we're planning to take out your father or his government. We're not. That's not my thing, and it shouldn't be yours. We're simply here to take advantage of what we can get in return for as little commitment on our part as possible."

"Still, my planet is largely in turmoil," she warned. "Our meeting with all three of the governments—the Melowi, the Toller, and my father's—is bound to piss people off in one group or another. Probably all of them at the same time. There's no gentle way to navigate this minefield."

"Which is why I want your help," he confided. "You know these people far better than I do. If we can put a relatable face out there in our negotiations, we stand a better chance of swaying the locals to our cause."

"Or pissing them all off," she muttered.

"That possibility exists with all negotiations, of course, but I like to think there's an opportunity here," he countered. "We're not coming in hot and heavy. We'll approach them diplomatically, with open arms, and see where that gets us. Comm is arranging a dialogue with all three, so the event will be open and transparent."

Jiya grunted her uncertainty. "You know how to throw a party," she said with a nervous laugh. "These three people, the heads of each country, don't even remotely get along. You might be forcing them to cooperate in a public forum, but I guarantee they will be plotting to stab each other, and us if they think we're collaborating with the others. They'll put themselves on top the first chance they get."

"Then we go in prepared for it," Reynolds deflected. "I've been around a long, long time, and I've seen the very best negotiate under far more complicated circumstances than these. I'm confident we can work out what we need and walk away without issue."

"I wish I had your confidence," she told him. "Maybe I'm just too much of a pessimist to think this is all going to end up hunky-dory." Jiya met the android's gaze, staring him down for a second before going on. "I'm still not sure we even need to do this. What do we have to gain?"

"That uncertainty is what drives me to take the chance," Reynolds admitted. "Beyond a safe place to alight in our travels, there's the possibility of food and supplies to be gained, a stable refueling location, and maybe something else we haven't considered, all in exchange for intel or technology from worlds your people have never seen or even knew existed."

"And you think that's wise—giving advanced tech to a culture in exchange for food and fuel?" she questioned.

He shrugged. "My mandate from Bethany Anne is clear. We're to seek out and destroy Kurtherians. Anything I can do to accomplish that, outside of offering up the secrets to the Federation's martial and intellectual superiority, is on the table," he explained. "Nothing I pass on to these governments will advance them to the point of overpowering each other or the universe at large, I promise."

She sighed, still wondering just how badly they needed to do this. Then she wondered if her aversion to it had more to do with her father than the actual act of meeting with the governments.

After all these years and everything that had transpired between them, could she bring herself to stare the man in his eye and make demands?

She wanted to say yes.

They'd fought before, and Jiya had pushed for her independence and that of her two younger sisters, but that wasn't the same as what she'd be attempting with Reynolds' negotiations.

Just by arriving in the presence of an alien species packing the kind of superior weapon systems the SD *Reynolds* carried would put her father on his heels. She knew just how well that had worked out for anyone who'd ever tried it.

Worse still, with Jiya having snuck out of the compound and run away, leaving her father to have to bury her publicly, she'd already crossed the line and incurred his ire. He wouldn't take kindly to her return no matter what the circumstances.

Just how far he'd go to make a point concerned her.

Would he manipulate the situation, using her as a sort of leverage against the AI and the other governments, or would he take affront to her presence and lash out, foregoing diplomacy altogether? Either was possible, and neither would be productive.

Still, she'd chosen her fate when she'd signed up with Reynolds and offered him her service. This was her future, no matter what happened on Lariest.

She'd made her bed, and now was the time to lie in it.

"Fine, I'll do it," she assured him. "But so you know, I think this is a double-decker shit sandwich we're about to take a massive mouthful of."

"Noted," Reynolds told her, "and gross."

She nodded. "Keep the image in mind when you meet my father. It might be the happiest thought you have."

CHAPTER SIXTEEN

"I still don't know how my father talked you into this," Jiya complained. "We're making a mistake by letting him play the magnanimous host."

"Maybe," Reynolds countered, "but he'll have the eyes of his neighbors on him the entire time we're here. He'll find it hard to manipulate the dialogue despite the apparent home court advantage. Besides, your presence is the equalizer," the AI said with a grin. "You said it yourself: he had to bury you in the public eye. Disown you, right?"

Jiya nodded.

"Then that puts him at a disadvantage," Reynolds said. "He won't be able to use your relationship as leverage against the others because he's trashed it publicly, but they *will* be able to use it against him."

She chuckled. "You don't know my father. He won't be bullied by you, me, or any of these diplomats. His ego is firmly in the driver's seat, and anyone attempting to take control away from him will pay dearly."

Reynolds shrugged. "Then we use that attitude to better

our position with the others. We don't need help from all of them. One or two advances our agenda, so regardless how many of the three sides are with us, we win."

"I hope you're right," Jiya muttered, shaking her head. She didn't believe it, but she was willing to put her faith in Reynolds. Besides, she could see the pair of them upstaging her father, and that alone was worth the discomfort of her being there.

"I am," Reynolds replied. "But even if I'm not, what's the worst that can happen?"

"Oh, tell me you did not just say that." Jiya rolled her eyes and raised them to the ceiling. "Please, cruel fate, ignore him, for he knows not what he says."

"We're coming in for a landing now," Comm reported. "Looks like you have a nice welcoming committee waiting for you down there."

Jiya glanced at the viewscreen Comm triggered as they approached the private landing platform inside her father's presidential compound. "I'm not seeing a bunch of guns. That's a good sign." The shuttle drifted downward, angling toward a landing.

"See, all that worrying for nothing," Reynolds told her.

"I'll reserve judgment."

"Autodocking has control," Comm reported. "You're on your own now. Good luck."

"We don't need luck," Reynolds countered. "We have the might of the Etheric Federation behind us."

"You mean the SD's massive firepower?" Jiya asked.

"Exactly." The AI grinned, and despite herself, Jiya found herself returning it.

This shit is crazy, she thought, but Reynolds' optimism was contagious.

Once the shuttle was settled on the tarmac, the door hissed open, and Reynolds marched out without hesitation. Jiya sucked in a deep breath and followed, doing her best to look like she belonged there.

Reynolds had provided her with a uniform, a castoff of the last crew, but it fit her nicely and, even better, made her look more professional than she'd ever looked in her life. Its crisp lines and sharp design spoke of confidence, and she couldn't help but feel a transference between it and her.

Shoulders back, chest out, she strode from the ship and stared down the presidential escort her father had sent to greet them. She recognized the man at the head of the procession as her father's personal assistant.

Older, and thin to the point of making Jiya think the man was crafted of matchsticks, he stepped forward with a regal air, sweeping ahead of the burly guards at his back. He seemed almost to float across the ground, purple robes flowing behind him, gold seams gleaming in sharp contrast. A sneer was stitched to his face.

He, of course, recognized her, too.

The only sign was the barest of twitches of his right eyelid, then his gaze slid over Jiya and landed on Reynolds. His cold distaste at realizing Reynolds was an android was immediately obvious.

"Greetings, traveler," he said, officious and stiff, his words not belying his disgust. "I am Gal Dorant, head of security and personal aide to President Lemaire. And you, I assume, are Lance Reynolds, representative of the Etheric Federation, yes?"

"I am, and you can simply call me Reynolds," the AI answered.

"I think not, Mister Reynolds," Gal replied, offering a defiant shake of his head. "We abide by a strict decorum here in Marianas, and we will maintain that tradition regardless of the status of our *guests*."

His gaze slithered to Jiya, and she shook off the chill that accompanied it. There was no mistaking the venom in the man's eyes at seeing Jiya there with Reynolds. Official representatives of an unknown alien power. It grated on his very soul.

Gal Dorant had never been friendly to her, or even cordial, for that matter. He'd always been a cold-hearted bastard who'd treated Jiya and her sisters with disdain on the best of days.

Jiya had always been a bit cowed by the man since he had her father's ear and had so much control over her life. But now, she met the man's glare with a sneer of her own, realizing just how different the circumstances were compared to the last time she'd seen the man.

"Pleasure to see you again, Gal," she told the aide, purposely ignoring protocol by using his first name only. "Now, if you'll be so gracious to lead us to the meeting hall, we'd like to be about our business with the *president*," she said, subtly reminding Gal of his position.

The man bristled but, to Jiya's surprise, managed to restrain his hostility.

He spun on a heel, his robes whirling. "This way, then."

The man marched off in a huff, but his frailty made his efforts at stomping laughable. Jiya grinned.

Reynolds raised an eyebrow and glanced at Jiya.

She shrugged. *He's always been a prick*, she commed to Reynolds.

Reynolds seemed okay with that answer, and he followed the aide. Jiya stayed at his side. She didn't want to get separated. A rancid cesspool had been opened with their arrival and, as much as she wanted to see it stirred up and splattered all over the place, she felt it best to keep close to Reynolds.

While he was sure Jiya was the key to the negotiations, she was just as certain it was actually Reynolds. He was the one packing the big guns and the wisdom of his people. If they had any hope of accomplishing something, it would be his presence that secured it.

The guards flowed around them, and there was nothing subtle in their efforts to make it clear who was in charge. Jiya ignored them, letting the men have their moment of superiority. That'd end once the other countries joined the conversation and Reynolds stepped up.

For all the posturing, there was no one on Lariest who could compete with the superdreadnought.

After a few minutes of Gal leading them the long way toward the conference area—Jiya suspecting he'd done it to avoid anyone important in the compound seeing her—they came to one of the back rooms. The aide led them inside with an impatient shuffle of his hands. They followed, the guards stationing themselves outside.

Jiya bit back a sneer at seeing her father seated at the

end of the conference table in the middle of the room, his entourage standing stoically around him.

Her father met Jiya's eyes for less than an instant, and nothing showed in his expression before he looked away, setting his gaze on Reynolds.

It was clear he had expected her, thanks to Gal. The aide had clearly informed him of Jiya's presence through their private comm, and Jiya sighed. She'd been hoping for a gasp or sigh or something from her dad, but he'd managed to retain the upper hand, as he always did.

"Do all your people look like Jonny taxi androids?" the president asked.

Reynolds cast a glance Jiya's way. *We need to get Takal to finish his work on that new body, STAT*, he sent before meeting the president's gaze with a grin. "You'll have to forgive my appearance, but don't let it throw you off, Mister President." He gestured to the android body. "This is simply a short-term solution to provide a frame for this." He tapped the side of his skull. "I assure you, I'm far greater than the sum of my current parts."

"I'll have to take your word for that, it appears," President Lemaire snipped, drawing his chin in toward his chest.

Jiya sighed. She'd seen that very expression a million times. Her father was unimpressed. Not that she'd expected him to be since that wasn't in his nature, but she'd hoped he'd at least take the meeting seriously.

It was clear he didn't plan to.

Reynolds, however, wasn't put off. "Indeed you will, Mister President. It's in no one's best interest if I'm forced to prove myself out of turn," he answered. "I'm happy to offer up my capabilities, as my comm officer already has while setting up our meet, but I stand here as a representative of the Etheric Federation by order of Queen Bethany Anne. I'm hoping that's more than sufficient credentials to prove me worthy of you meeting me."

"Yet you bring my *daughter* with you," he countered. "A recalcitrant child exiled from my home and no longer welcome here within its halls." He snorted, shaking his head. "You'll have to forgive me if I doubt your bargaining power if you must resort to such base attempts at twisting the narrative in your direction, alien."

President Lemaire rose to his feet, his entourage shuffling back a step behind him to offer room. He jabbed a sharp finger in Reynolds' direction.

"Know this, android. Holding my daughter against me will not gain you any sympathy or leverage from my government. We will not bow or scrape to your demands. She is worthless as a hostage or negotiating tool."

Reynolds chuckled. "It's impressive how right you were," he commed to Jiya. "I'd high five you right now, but that'd be awkward."

Jiya nodded, taking a step forward to face her father. "For the record, *Mister President*," she said, purposely avoiding any familial relationship with her father, "I'm not a hostage or a victim or even a tool. I'm here of my own free will as the Etheric Federation attempts to expand their mission, and my being here has absolutely nothing to do with our relationship, such as it is."

She coughed to clear her throat, cutting off her father as he opened his mouth to argue.

"More importantly, as a representative of the Federation, you will speak to me with the respect accorded me as such, for to do otherwise will impact our willingness to negotiate with you."

Well said, Reynolds told her privately.

Thank you, she replied, but she knew she'd just stirred the pot, no matter how good it felt.

President Lemaire sneered, matching the expression on Gal's face as the aide came over to stand beside him.

"All grown up now, are you, Jiya?" her father asked, letting loose a quiet chuckle. "I entertained this meeting because it's rare an entity wants to speak with all three nations of Lariest, let alone at the same time, but don't lose sight of the fact that this is *my* compound and *my* country, and you will not storm in here and press your demands." He thumped a fist on the table. "*I* am in charge here, not you, not this Jonny taxi boy, and certainly not that super-dreadnought circling our planet. Do I make myself clear?" His reddish face grew darker with his anger.

"Getting off on the right foot, I see," Comm mumbled over the communicator, clearly having been listening in. "How about you threaten to eat his porridge and sleep in his bed next. Maybe huff and puff and blow his house down."

"I can make that last one happen," Tactical inserted.

"Clear as mud," Reynolds answered. "Now that we have an understanding, how about we start this meeting so we can all be on our way? The sooner, the better works for all parties, I'm guessing. It'd be best if you sat your ass down. You're starting to piss me off, and that's not a place you want to go."

President Lemaire stood without moving for several

moments, clearly forcing his alpha-ness upon his guests, before finally signaling to Gal to get underway.

The aide triggered two massive viewscreens on the side wall. The image of two people resolved on the screens, neither looking much more pleased about being there than President Lemaire did.

"Greetings, Presidents Alac Sumor of the Melowi and Corrh V'ariat of the Toller," Gal said, pointing to each monitor in turn, although everyone in the room already knew who they were. "We, the people of Marianas, are pleased to host such a historic meeting between the three of our nations and the visiting dignitary of the Etheric Federation."

"Get on with it, worm," President V'ariat said, motioning with her hand. "I'm not here for your grand-standing." She pointed a withered hand in Jiya's direction. "You're clearly only hosting due to the fact that Lemaire's daughter is part of the alien entourage." She grinned, easing back into her seat. "That must have stuffed a gurlot's burr up your bottom, huh, Lemaire?" The woman turned her cold, dark stare on Jiya. "I hope you took after your mother, dearie. You look like her, fortunately."

Jiya bit back a laugh but said nothing, although she nodded slowly.

Reynolds acknowledged her restraint.

"Yes, Lemaire, let's get on with this," President Sumor agreed, and Jiya was surprised to note that the man looked a little like Ka'nak, although she knew the two weren't related. "There are far more interesting things to discuss than who gets credit for arranging the meeting."

Lemaire grunted and dropped back into his seat with a

barely vocal growl. Jiya noted his veneer had cracked the tiniest bit, but she didn't know if that was a good or bad thing. It was what Reynolds had wanted, but how it would play out was still a mystery.

"Yes, yes, let's get on with it, then," Lemaire said, appearing to compose himself. He turned his icy gaze on Reynolds. "We still have no clue what you want from us, so please, tell us."

Reynolds deferred to Jiya, much to her father's disgust.

She strolled to the center of the room, taking a page out of Gal's book of showmanship. "The offer is simple," she told the assemblage. "The Superdreadnought *Reynolds* is on a mission to seek out Kurtherians wherever they might be since they are the enemy of the Federation. As such, we seek any information your governments might have regarding these creatures." She glanced at each of the presidents, lingering a moment on her father before returning her gaze to the screens. "As well as food, supplies, an offer of safe harbor both now and in the future, and the okay to seek a crew among the various peoples of Lariest."

She waved a hand, gesturing toward Reynolds. "In return for these things, the Etheric Federation is willing to provide knowledge on how to advance your societies and make life better for your peoples."

President V'ariat straightened in her seat, leaning forward so her face swelled onscreen. "So, you're willing to offer us advanced tech in exchange for these things?"

Reynolds nodded, but not without adding a caveat. "Within reason. We will not offer our advanced military technology since we'd prefer to return to find Lariest in one piece and not some smoking hole. That'd be awkward."

"Then if not military advancements, what are you offering?" Sumor asked with a grunt, going straight for the throat.

"The means to better cure yourselves of diseases, wound care and better health in general, as well as the means to take advantage of the resources you have available on Lariest. We can work out the specifics of each option in private once arrangements have been made between us, but suffice it to say, given what we're asking of you, we're offering far more in return."

"And how can we believe any of what you say?" Lemaire barked from his seat. "You could be charlatans, offering us snake oil in exchange for our goods and services."

"We could be," Reynolds replied, "but, honestly, given our means of arrival, the superdreadnought settled in space above your heads, we could have gone about acquiring our needs in a much simpler way. We chose instead to bargain with you, help advance your nations for a pittance in return."

"Are you threatening us?" Lemaire shouted, leaping to his feet. The guards at the door shuffled forward.

"Most certainly not," Jiya answered, raising her hands to calm everyone. "What Reynolds is saying is, we're here on a mission of goodwill, not violence. Despite the superdreadnought's destructive capabilities, we came to you in person and put ourselves in a position where we are vulnerable to show that we are serious in our intent."

She turned to address the two viewscreens.

"You both know my status with President Lemaire," she said. "Would I have come here if I didn't believe in the mission I'm part of? What is there to gain from my returning here otherwise?"

President V'ariat nodded, offering Jiya a tight-lipped grin. "I believe you, dearie. I wouldn't want to spend a minute longer with your father than was absolutely necessary."

Sumor grunted noncommittally, but Jiya saw the slight sway to his head—the hint of a nod.

Jiya turned back to face the entire gathering. She raised her hand and twisted it slowly. "Yesterday, my hand was injured, scorched by blaster fire and unusable. Now, as you can see, there is no hint that it's been injured. No redness, no scarring, nothing," she explained. "And while I don't expect you to take me at my word, we can provide evidence of my situation and the results." She wiggled her hand again. "This is but a small portion of the knowledge we'll pass on in exchange for our request."

She turned her back to her father and met the eyes of the presidents onscreen, knowing where her best chance at success lie. "Further, should you have something to offer us above and beyond our stated interests, we can most certainly enter into individual discussions."

V'ariat cackled. "You've got balls, dearie, coming into your father's house to propose separate negotiations with the two of us," she told Jiya. "I love it."

Sumor nodded. "The Melowi people are interested in your proposal, Representatives *Lemaire* and Reynolds," he said, emphasizing Jiya's last name as a clear shot at her father. "We would be grateful to speak with you in private here in our homeland."

"The same goes for the Toller people, dearie," President

V'ariat agreed. "We'd love to speak with you both," she motioned toward Reynolds with her eyes, "soonest."

She grinned at them both, locking gazes with Reynolds.

"We've noticed your ship has some hull damage while we've been stalking you," she said, not bothering to sugar-coat her military's reasons for having sent destroyers into orbit near the superdreadnought. "We have some experimental metal we've been crafting armor out of, and I think that'd be the perfect bonus offer to squeeze a little more out of you, don't you think?"

"I like this one," Tactical muttered over the comm. "Feisty and straight to the point."

Reynolds grinned. "It would indeed, Madam President. I'll have my representative reach out to you momentarily," he told her, shifting his gaze to Sumor. "And to you, Mister President. You can expect us to be in touch shortly."

"I, too, would be interested in your offer," President Lemaire said behind them.

Jiya started, having almost forgotten the man was there, and spun, eyes narrowed.

"In fact, we can discuss terms once we've concluded the meeting," he offered, "if that works for you." Jiya noted he only spoke to Reynolds, but she really hadn't expected anything different.

Reynolds nodded. "That would be perfect," he answered. "My first officer and I will be glad to meet with you." Reynolds gestured to Jiya and offered a furtive wink.

Jiya swallowed her smile at her father's snarl.

"Perfect," Lemaire said, his voice still as smooth as glass despite the obvious frustration deepening the color in his cheeks. He glanced at the viewscreens. "I'll send them your way once we're finished here," he told the other presidents, not offering them a chance to reply before Gal cut the connections.

"See, that wasn't that bad," Reynolds told Jiya over the comm. "Could have been much worse."

Jiya groaned, realizing Reynolds had just jinxed them.

It very well *could* have been worse.

A moment later, it was.

The guards filed into the room, weapons out and at the ready. Gal Dorant grinned and waved them over.

"Please secure our guests," Gal told the guards.

The men circled Reynolds and Jiya.

"What is this?" Reynolds asked.

"This is karma biting you in your big metal taxi-cab ass," Jiya answered aloud, shaking her head and sneering. "'What's the worst that could happen?'" she mimicked. "This, Reynolds. This is the worst that could happen."

Reynolds shrugged. "I'd hardly call this the worst. I mean, they could easily—"

"Don't. You. Say. Another. Word," she told him, a growl punctuating each word.

"This is for daring to bring my child into my house and trying to use her against me," Lemaire said, coming over to stand before the surrounded pair and curtailing Jiya's threat. "I will not be made to bow to some foreign power in my own home, nor will I have my daughter prance around thinking she's my equal." He waved the guards off. "Take these two away and have a full complement of security services standing guard around each. Do *not* let them out of your sight."

He stepped close and glared at Reynolds. "I suggest you

keep your ship on a leash, android, or you might find you and your *first officer* make better shields than you do negotiators."

"You're making a mistake—" Jiya started, but her father cut her off.

"The only mistake I made was not dealing with your insolence earlier," he answered. "I should have known you'd return and cause trouble, just like your mother always did. It's in your blood, child, but I didn't put up with it from her, and I damn well won't put up with it from you." He slapped a guard on the back. "Get them out of my sight."

Jiya growled and turned her glare on Reynolds.

He shrugged. "How was I to know this would happen?"

"Because I told you!" she shouted, fuming as the guards marched them out the door and down the hall.

Reynolds acknowledged. "There is that."

Jiya sighed and let the men lead her away without another word.

At least she wasn't hanging out with her dad anymore.

.

CHAPTER SEVENTEEN

To her surprise, Jiya found herself not in a cell but in a small room in the servant's quarters only a short distance down the hall, which had apparently been cleared just for her. The windows had been barred at some point in the past and all the personal belongings had been removed, leaving only a couch, a chair, and a small bed without any covers.

She paced the room's narrow width, mumbling to herself.

"He had this planned before we even arrived," she said, furious that she'd let herself be walked into a trap of their own making.

Reynolds had been taken elsewhere, and given the direction she'd seen him dragged off, she had a pretty good idea that he *had* ended up in a cell.

Not that it mattered, considering his mind wasn't confined to the Johnny taxi android.

She considered his various personalities, splintered into various positions, and wondered if maybe he was actually trapped in the cell while the other hims went about their business independently.

"I doubt it, even though that doesn't matter," she said to herself. Loose screws they might be, but there was no way they would leave part of themselves down here in danger.

Then she remembered her comm implant. Still new to her, it wasn't something she consciously thought about until she needed it or someone else addressed her over it.

She needed it now.

She tapped it and waited for a signal. None came back.

"Great," she muttered, "he's blocked the communicators." Her frustration with her father was ready to boil over.

From the day she was born, he'd controlled her, pushed and pulled and shaped her into what he wanted her to be. And from that day, she'd fought him because she'd been like her mother, too strong-willed to let someone else dictate who and what she was.

She wasn't going to let him get away with it now.

Jiya went over to the door and pounded her fist on it. An ordinary wooden door, it vibrated and rattled under her fury. If her father or Gal Dorant had expected her to be a prim and proper princess and just accept her imprisonment, they were sadly mistaken.

After a few minutes of riffing punches against the door, she resorted to kicks. The door trembled under her assault, and the lower hinge looked ready to give way, splinters of wood exploding with every blow.

Then the door was whipped open.

Gal Dorant stood on the other side, a handful of security men looming behind him. He went to speak, but Jiya cut him off.

"I don't care what you have to say, *Gal*, but you need to let me speak to my father," she snarled.

She shook specks of blood from her battered fist, spattering the aide's robes. He glared at the blood droplets for a moment before lifting his dark eyes to hers.

"Fortunately for you, your father is a merciful man. He—"

Jiya chuckled, cutting Gal off. "Oh, President Lemaire the Magnanimous," she mocked. "That's what they call him in the streets."

The aide stiffened, straightening to his full height. That provoked another burst of laughter from Jiya since the man barely stood as tall as her chin despite the platform boots he wore.

"I suggest you show some respect for your father and his rule or I will defy his wishes and drag you to a cell myself."

Jiya grinned and drew a step closer to the man. The guards at his back inched forward to meet her.

Much as she wanted to see Gal try to wrestle her into submission and place her in a cell, she knew he was sufficiently spiteful to go through with at least part of his threat. While he wouldn't dare do it himself, he would gladly have the guards do his dirty work for him.

That was something Jiya didn't need right then.

She raised her hands in surrender. "Fine. Lead the way, O Master of Aides."

Gal growled low in his throat and stood his ground. Jiya could see the war waging in his eyes, but as long as she didn't push him harder than she already had, he'd wilt and give in to his training.

He was a professional servant, after all. He would do what he was told.

Without another word, he spun on his heel and marched through the throng of guards. He threw up a hand as he walked off, and the guards corralled Jiya and marched her down the hall.

Internally, she sighed, striving to keep her breathing level and calm.

As much as she didn't want to see her father again, if there was a way out of all this, that was where it would emanate from.

She trusted Reynolds to try to break her out eventually, but that wasn't the best way to go about assuaging her father's rage and wounded pride. The only real way to do that was to surrender to him, if only outwardly.

It was a tactic she'd learned long ago, although she rarely put it to use. It just didn't sit well with her, and never had. Still, if it freed her and got her and Reynolds on their way, she'd swallow her own pride—for a minute or two— and do what was necessary.

Rather than bring Jiya back to the meeting room where they'd had their first confrontation, Gal and his flunkies led Jiya to her father's private quarters.

She groaned. That only exacerbated things.

In his chambers, there wasn't anyone around to play to. Publicly, he might be a prick, a demanding leader, but privately, he was a tyrant. He demanded obedience. Reverence, even.

Jiya had often wondered if her father suffered from

some form of megalomania. More often than she'd thought that, she'd questioned whether sociopathic tendencies could be inherited.

Gal's knock on her father's door swept that thought away. There was a muttered reply from inside, and Gal opened the door, ushering Jiya in.

"We'll be right outside this door," he warned, staring at her with hard eyes. "Should you do anything untoward, I will personally see you suffer for it."

Before she could reply, the aide backed out the door and closed it behind him.

Jiya sucked in a deep breath to steel her nerves and glanced around the sitting area arranged nearest the door. Her father stood at the window on the other side of the room, staring out without moving or saying a word.

She stood patiently, waiting for him to say something or move.

The act was familiar, and she found herself relaxing. She'd been in this exact same position a hundred times. All she had to do was wait him out.

A few minutes later, her patience paid off. He cleared his throat and spun slowly, let his gaze drift for a moment before it met hers. He motioned to the small chair that sat across from the coffee table with a built-in viewscreen and the couch where her father preferred to sit.

She strode over and stood in front of the chair, waiting for him to take his seat first. Once he had, she settled in and cradled her hands on her lap. The ritual was strangely comforting.

"This was all a grave mistake," Lemaire told his daughter, leaning forward as if to impress his disappointment upon her.

"I agree," Jiya answered, and she meant it—although not for the same reason he did.

"Have you nothing else to say for yourself?"

Jiya bit back what she really wanted to say and let her tongue wrap itself around the words she *should* say instead.

Politics was all a game, and as much as she hated it, she'd grown up in this political world of her father's. She knew how to play.

"I'm sorry," she answered. "I'd hoped to make you proud, to show you I'd accomplished something with myself despite my defiance. I hadn't meant to offend you or put you or your government on the defensive."

"But that's exactly what you did," he told her, shaking his head. "You made me look like a fool in front of Sumor and V'ariat. You should have come to me, and me alone." He grunted and leaned back into the couch. "Now... Now, I'm forced to make an example of you, child."

Jiya shuddered at that. While she didn't fear her father, she'd never heard him be quite so blunt about his intentions before. Her imagination ran wild right then, and she couldn't do anything to rein it in.

"What do you mean?"

"I mean I can't let you get away with this," he answered, a tinge of frost in his voice. "It was one thing when you ran away the last time, that is, but it's something entirely different to return to my country at the head of an invading enemy and try to extort resources."

She stiffened in her seat, head whirling at the accusation. "That wasn't what we were doing." So much for pacifying him.

"No?" he asked, jabbing a finger her direction. "I see it differently, as do the Toller and Melowi governments. In the short time since the meeting, both leaders have ramped up propaganda against us, believing you and your pathetic Jonny taxi android alien to be the solution to their problems. Problems that include us—Marianas."

He chuckled, the sound more like a dog's growl than a laugh.

"They think they can convince your alien host to provide them with weapons to overwhelm us." Lemaire sneered and glared at Jiya. "Your own people, child. You would side with an alien and our enemies against your own people? This is treason of the highest order," he stated. "I cannot let this go, no matter *who* you are to me."

Jiya swallowed hard. She'd never seen her father so cold and callous, and she'd seen him both plenty of times.

"What are you going to do?"

He exhaled, the barest glimmer of compassion softening his wrinkled features. "While I can't find it in myself to execute you, Jiya, I must still uphold the law."

The word "execute" echoed in her head and Jiya hopped to her feet, head on a swivel, eyes looking around for the inevitable guards who'd try to take her into custody again.

"You can't do this," she sputtered.

"I can, and I must," he replied, not wavering in his decision. "You will spend the remainder of your days in a cell, child, a prisoner of your own insolence." He stood, so they were eye to eye again. "And although I will suffer alongside you in spirit, my will in this matter is absolute."

Jiya kicked the chair away, it landing behind her with a *thump*. "I won't let you do this," she warned, hands up and at the ready. Her father hopped up and circled behind the couch. "*Reynolds* won't let you do this."

The door hissed behind her, and she knew the guards were coming. She clenched her fists so hard her knuckles ached. If her father wanted to lock her away, he'd have to beat her down to make it happen. She wasn't going to go easy.

"Your android will do nothing," Lemaire told her, motioning toward the men filling the room.

In the arms of two of the guards hung Reynolds. Jiya gasped at seeing him dangling there, limp and silent.

"What did you do to him?" she shouted.

A handful of guards moved to her father's side to keep her from diving at him.

"I've done nothing, child," he answered. "Your savior abandoned you as soon as he was out of your sight."

Gal Dorant grinned. "Only minutes after we locked him away, he shut himself down. We hadn't even begun to question him, the coward."

"Rather than stand behind you, your alien overlord fled and left you to suffer the consequences of what he'd convinced you to do," Lemaire said with a sigh. "It's a shame, really. I thought I'd taught you better than that, child. But no, it seems you have fallen prey to an alien con artist, using your connections for profit and leaving you behind as soon as things went south."

The guards tossed Reynolds' android body to the floor. It hit with a sullen *thump*.

Lemaire waved a hand at his men. "Secure her."

Jiya reared back, clearing space around her to defend herself. A dozen guards moved into position. She growled in response and offered up a crazed grin.

She even felt a little sorry for the first guy who tried to lay his hands on her.

"Well, she *did* tell him her dad was a prick," Tactical commented as soon as he learned of Reynolds' and Jiya's imprisonment.

"He didn't expect him to be so bold about it, especially given that the other two nations are expecting him and Jiya to show up soon," XO commented.

"Should we inform them of what's happened?" Comm asked.

"We should, but not just yet," an unfamiliar voice said. Someone was shuffling onto the bridge.

The various Reynoldses spun—not that anyone would know—and stared at the newcomer.

General Maddox grunted and glanced around in confusion when he realized the bridge only contained a young woman, clearly not a match for the masculine voices that had been carrying on as he entered.

"Uh..."

Geroux offered a friendly smile. "It's the AI talking," she clarified and waved a hand toward several of the consoles. "XO, Comm, and Tactical are here now."

Maddox raised an eyebrow. "There's more than one AI?"

Geroux shook her head. "Nope, just the one."

"I beg to differ," Tactical muttered. "Why does everyone try to lump me in with the rest of these assholes?"

"Maybe because you are an asshole, too?" XO answered.

"The biggest," Comm added.

Maddox split his gaze between the three stations from which the voices emanated. "This isn't strange at all."

"You'll get used to it eventually," Geroux told him.

"Doubtful," he muttered, moving to an empty seat on the bridge. He eased into it with a grunt.

"Should you be up and about?" Geroux asked. "Has your mind…uh, settled?"

He nodded. "It's as good as it's going to get, I suppose."

"How'd you know to come here?" she wondered.

"Heard Takal and Ka'nak discussing the situation in the corridor," he answered, shrugging. "Sounds like as good a time as any to get to work."

"Glad to hear it," XO said. "There was some discussion as to whether to dock your pay while you slacked off."

"He's kidding," Comm countered.

"Maybe," Tactical replied, adding his two credits.

Maddox waved them off. "As much as I'm enjoying talking to empty seats, can we chit-chat later? I'm thinking we've more important things to do right now. Members of our crew have been captured."

"The man's direct," XO said. "Seems Jiya made a good choice with this one."

"Until he takes *your* job," Tactical muttered.

Maddox ignored them. "We have a location?"

Geroux shifted in her seat, getting comfortable. "They're in President Lemaire's compound, although the exact location inside is unknown." She tapped a few keys on her console, eyes scanning the information scrolling across the screen. "I'm hacking into their systems, but it's going to take a while. They're fairly robust, as I'm sure you know. I can't even detect life forms within the compound's borders."

"Seems the president has upgraded his security since I've been gone." Maddox stared at the viewscreen, taking in the 3-D map of the compound she'd plastered there. "Keep trying. What about comms?"

"What about me?" Comm asked.

The ex-general sighed. "Not you, the communication devices Jiya had inserted. Are we getting anything from it?"

"They've blocked communications, so there's no contact going either direction," Geroux told him. "I'm working on breaking the encryption on the block as well. Again, it's going slowly."

"How about the rest of you?" he asked, gesturing at the various AI personalities. "I presume you know what's going on because you're connected to your boy down below. Can you speak with the Reynolds persona?"

"I don't like the implication that we're not mentally stable," Tactical replied.

"You're about as stable as a drunken two legged-mule," Maddox accused, "but we can't worry about that now. Can you reach Reynolds?"

"Yes..." XO answered.

"And no," Comm finished.

Maddox and Geroux sighed at the same time.

"What the hell have I gotten myself into?" Maddox muttered under his breath. "Clarify...please." He added the last after a moment's pause.

"Well, his communicator is down, the same as it is for Jiya, but because we're all kind of...connected, we're not entirely out of touch."

"Then reach out and pinpoint where he is."

"It's not that easy," Comm replied.

"Of course it's not," Maddox mumbled, clearly trying not to lose his temper. "Can't you recall him somehow? Manifest him in place of one of you? Switch places, maybe?"

"That's not a bad idea," Tactical admitted.

"Then let's do it," Maddox pushed.

"Too bad it won't work," Comm said, moving his chair as if he were shaking his head.

"Oh, I'm going to regret asking why it won't work, aren't I?" Maddox rubbed his temples.

"Well, seeing as how we plugged him into the Jonny taxi guy, we had to make some adjustments to his piece of our psyche to keep him stable."

Geroux giggled at that, and Comm ignored her.

"He's programmed to assimilate to an android body," Comm explained. "We could transfer his consciousness back into the whole, but it would cause widespread system failures until he adjusted."

"How long would those take to resolve?" Geroux asked.

"Could be an hour, could be a month," XO answered. "Really depends on how he reacts to our...uh, already existing issues."

"So, you're saying if we bring him up, we might break all of you for an indefinite amount of time?" Maddox questioned.

"That's about right, yeah."

"Then that's not going to suit our needs," Maddox mumbled and leaned back in his chair to stare at the ceiling.

"Too bad we don't have another android to plug him into," Geroux said wistfully.

"Who says we don't?" Takal asked over the comm, clearly having been listening in.

Maddox glanced around, his face scrunched. "Is that you, Takal? Where are you?"

"It is indeed, my friend," Takal answered, drawing a grin from Maddox. "It is good to hear you are up and about. I'm in the lab."

"I should have known you'd be here since Geroux was," Maddox told the man. "So, what is this about you having another body for Reynolds?"

"Well, 'body' is a slight exaggeration," Takal admitted. "I do, however, have a frame that is sufficient for our needs, built using one of the ship's bots."

"A frame?" Tactical asked, chortling. "Please tell me it looks like the Terminator after all his flesh has been melted off!"

"I don't know who this Terminator fellow is, but if he looks like a chrome skeleton, then yes, he does," Takal answered.

"Yes!" Tactical cheered. "Then make it so, damn it. This I want to see!"

"What will we need for transfer, Takal?" Maddox asked.

"A few minutes to tweak the frequency so it's the same as the Jonny android system, then we'll be good to go."

"Do what you have to, Takal, and we'll let the AIs take over when you're ready."

The comm went silent for several minutes, then Takal came back, letting them know he was finished.

"Ready to go on my end."

Maddox waved to the room. "Okay, ghostly AI voices, do your thing, whatever that might be."

CHAPTER EIGHTEEN

"I'm not sure whether to be excited or disgusted," Reynolds muttered, holding his skeletal metal arms up and staring at them through bug eyes that seemed to jut from the new android frame's sockets.

"Definitely Terminator chic," Tactical said after assessing the new nowhere-near-finished body. "I like it. Now if you can just plug in Arnold's voice. *Sarah Connor?*"

Takal simply glanced around, looking lost.

"Couldn't you have slapped a loin cloth on this bad boy or something?" Reynolds asked. "My shiny pelvic bone is all out there for the world to see like a Robocop Elvis impersonator. We run a PG-rated ship, thank you very much."

"We can slip you into a uniform if it bothers you," Takal told the AI, who spun around, still examining his chassis.

"Is it really an issue right now?" Maddox interrupted, pushing past Takal to stand before Reynolds. "Jiya is trapped down there still. We need to get her out." He gestured to Reynolds' gleaming new body. "All your preening can wait, right?"

Reynolds nodded. "No, you're right. We need to focus on Jiya. Unfortunately, I'm not sure where they took her."

"Wait!" Geroux asked, her voice cracking on the last. "What do you mean you don't know where she is? Weren't you with her?"

"We were separated after the meeting," Reynolds answered. "I was taken to a cell, and I'm not sure where she was hauled off to. I suspect that, despite her father's frustration and anger with her, he would still be obliged to treat her like family. She's likely in the main house or nearby rather than in another cell."

"So, there's still no nuking the compound from orbit?" Tactical asked.

"No."

"Never mind," Maddox said, cutting them all off. "If we don't know where she is and can't set up an infiltration team to snatch her back, then we don't have any choice but to reach out to Lemaire."

"You truly expect him to listen to anything we have to say?" Takal asked. "Half the crew are political dissidents and the other half is a split-personality AI who made him look like a fool before his neighboring government leaders."

"So, you're saying he might be a bit miffed at us all?" Reynolds asked.

"To put it mildly," Takal answered.

"Then the nice act is out." Reynolds stalked over to the viewscreen. "Time to bluff and bluster."

"Wait!" Geroux called, a hand raised. "I have an idea."

"Is it a good one?" Comm asked.

She shrugged. "Do we have *any* good ones right now?"

"Probably not," he replied. "Carry on."

"You're still linked to the Jonny taxi body, right?"

Reynolds nodded. "We can use that connection to our advantage."

"How's that?" Comm asked. "The connection is ephemeral, not some static line. It might not be blocked by Lemaire's security shielding, but there's no way to trace the Jonny body's location through it."

"Don't need the location to do what I'm thinking," Geroux replied, grinning all the while.

"Explain," Maddox requested matter-of-factly.

"Well, it will require Reynolds to go back to the Jonny android body first."

"Oh, hell no!" Reynolds exclaimed, wagging a finger at Geroux. "I say we send Tactical down to the planet."

"But you're the one already assimilated to the body," she argued. "That means it needs to be you."

Reynolds sighed, his voice a discordant hum. "Fine. I'll do it, although I still don't understand why I have to."

"Because I'm going to give you a virus to carry down with you."

"Great!" Reynolds moaned. "It's starting to make sense, but be gentle."

"What does your giving him a virus do for us?" XO asked.

"A lifetime of jokes is what it does for us, XO," Tactical replied. "Imagine the possibilities."

Reynolds sighed.

Geroux ignored Tactical, turning to answer XO. "It's a

hack program. All Reynolds has to do is get close to any console connected to the security system, sync up with it, and *blam*, we're in. We can then find Jiya and use the system against Lemaire. We'll have total control over his compound's security."

"Once we have that, we can go in and get her back," Maddox finished, clearly seeing the potential in Geroux's move.

"Then that's what we'll do," Reynolds said, taking one last look at his new body.

"Don't worry," Takal comforted. "It will be here waiting for you when you return. I'll even work to improve it while you're gone." He raised his flask in a mock toast.

Reynolds grunted. "Fine. Beam me down, Scotty."

"Who's Scotty?" Geroux asked, glancing around. "Is there another AI here somewhere that I don't know about?"

"Kids these days." Reynolds sighed. "Let's do this before I change my mind."

Geroux didn't hesitate, sending Reynolds back down the rabbit hole.

The first of the guards hit the ground with a *thud*, Jiya spinning to whack a second in the side of his head with her shin. He grunted and staggered backward, falling over as his equilibrium gave way. She made ready to punch the third when a familiar voice called out, stilling everyone in the room.

"I wouldn't touch her if I were you."

She spun to see Reynolds clambering to his feet, his Jonny taxi body reanimated. She grinned and glanced at her father, who had circled back around to his seat, a couple of his men shadowing him.

"Oh, you're in for it now, *Dad*," she told him, chuckling all the while.

Reynolds stumbled over to the table and placed his hands on it, palms flat. He met the president's glaring eyes.

"I presume this console is linked to the compound's security system?" he asked, gesturing toward the viewscreen with his chin.

President Lemaire laid his hand on the screen and smirked, tapping a few keys. "Of course it is, and now you're going to regret having come back here, alien. The rest of my security forces will be here in seconds."

As Jiya stared at the two, Reynolds met her father's smirk with one of his own. A crackle of static sounded in her head, and she realized her comm had just come back online.

"I'm in," Geroux's voice said through a clear channel. "System's all yours, Reynolds."

Jiya bit back the urge to laugh as she realized what had happened.

Lemaire grunted a moment later and tapped the console again, his eyes widening when nothing worked the way it was supposed to. He tapped the screen again desperately. His guards edged around the table.

"Ah, ah, ah," Reynolds chided, wagging a finger at them. "Stay where you are, or I'll let Jiya continue to whip your asses."

She grinned and moved beside Reynolds, placing herself between the AI and her father's men.

"In case you haven't realized it, Mister President, I've assumed control of your compound's security systems," he told Lemaire. "Not only do your men not know you're in danger, but they are locked out of the room. The three guards you have here are hardly enough to keep me from you should I decide to do something untoward."

"You wouldn't dare!" Lemaire growled, but the look on his face was far less certain than the words.

"I *would* dare, but I'd rather not," Reynolds replied. "I've no interest in harming you, Mister President, but I also have no interest in letting you hold my first officer captive. I will do what's necessary to free both of us. This has also confirmed that you are not to be trusted. Shame, that. You're going to regret being such a flaming asshole."

"The compound's shields are down," Geroux said over the comm, which Reynolds broadcast over a speaker so the president and his men could hear it. "We can bombard the place at your command, Reynolds."

The president leaned back in his seat. He glanced from Reynolds to Jiya and back again, crossing his arms over his broad chest. "You won't fire upon us," he said in defiance. "You might control my security system, but my men will respond accordingly as soon as the first barrage begins. They will—"

"They will do nothing, Mister President," Reynolds answered, cutting him off. "I could wipe this place from existence within a single heartbeat. The only reason it hasn't happened already is that you're Jiya's father, and her sisters are still here in the compound."

Jiya stiffened at that thought, but Reynolds waved at her to relax.

"I've got them located on the security systems," he told her through the link. "They are in a safe location on the other side of the compound, unaware that anything is happening." He motioned to the president. "Now, we have something to discuss before things get out of hand."

"You don't consider this as 'out of hand?'" Lemaire asked, waving his arms around.

"Shuttle's on the way," Geroux said over the private comm.

Reynolds shook his head. "No, this is perfectly in hand, I have to say. Now, be reasonable and stand down. Let me leave with Jiya, and we'll pretend this never happened."

"Never *happened*?" Lemaire shouted, leaping to his feet. "You come here issuing orders and threatening to destroy my compound, and you presume to walk away without consequences?"

Despite the grumbling of his guards, Lemaire stomped around the table to stand face to face with Reynolds.

"You're an alien menace, coming to Lariest and threatening its rulers. Do you truly think you will get away with this?"

Reynolds shrugged. "In reality, I'm only threatening *you*," he answered. "My XO has been in touch with the Toller and Melowi governments, informing them of your attempt at kidnapping my first officer and me." Reynolds leaned forward into the face of the president. "Both have offered their support in the matter, and, should something untoward happen to you or your administration, both nations have offered to provide assistance to the people and will gladly step in to take control of the country."

President Lemaire stiffened. It was clear to Jiya that he believed every word the AI told him.

"Shuttle's on the ground, Reynolds," Geroux reported.

After a quiet moment during which Lemaire appeared to struggle to catch his breath, he returned to the couch and flopped down. His cold black gaze settled on Jiya.

"You would let him do this to me?" he asked.

"You've done this to yourself, *Father*," she replied, giving him a curt nod. "We came here in peace, offering the Marianas people an opportunity to advance their sciences for little more than food and supplies and a place to dock between missions. *You* elevated this into a personal vendetta against me and my success. This is all on you."

She growled, "You always held me under your thumb. Kept me from joining the military, kept me from living a meaningful life that differed from what you wanted." She jabbed a finger in his direction. "I'm not a child anymore, and I'm sure as shit not your slave, so if you want to know if I'll let Reynolds here blow the compound to dust, then my answer is yes. But that's not what I want."

She righted the chair and flopped into it across from her father. "What I'd prefer is to not upset the balance of Lariest. I want my sisters to be safe here, and the burial place of my mother to remain sacrosanct." She drew in a deep breath, letting it settle into her lungs. "Let us go and agree to our terms and all will be forgotten, if not ever forgiven," she told him.

"You are so very much like your mother," Lemaire said, the words coming out behind a snarl. They were clearly not meant as a compliment. "You understand nothing, believing the lies your heart and gut tell you as if they were gospel." He shook his head and waved a hand toward the door. "Go, but know this, *Daughter*. You will never be welcome here again. You can park your alien ship in space and bleed the Toller and Melowi dry for all I care, but if you or your Jonny android ever set foot upon Marianas soil again, I will have both of you executed."

Jiya rose to her feet and glared at her father. His words resonated in her head, and she hated what he'd just told her. She'd run away more times than she could count, but there was always an option to return no matter how uncomfortable it might have been. Not any longer.

Rather than think about what she might be leaving behind—her sisters, the memory of her mother, the place she was born—Jiya stomped off without a word.

This was what she'd always wanted, if not exactly how she'd wanted it to go down, so there wasn't any point in arguing. Her sisters would be looked after, and they'd always been more like their father than their mother anyway. They'd be okay, and that was all that mattered.

Reynolds caught up to her out in the hall, and the two walked toward the courtyard where the shuttle had parked.

"That wasn't so bad," he said, grinning.

"Nope, not bad at all," she replied with a grunt. "I can never come home again, never see my sisters, never visit the burial place of my mother, and we've made an enemy for life of Marianas. Not bad at all."

"That's the spirit," Reynolds told her, patting her on the back. "I'm glad you can see the bright side of things."

She groaned, not even bothering to reply.

"While you're down there," Takal's voice said over the comm, interrupting them, "would you mind a slight detour? I mean, we've got the place locked down, right?"

"It's not like we're on a shopping trip, Takal," Jiya told him.

"I promise this will be worth the time spent," he argued. "We'll get no better opportunity than this."

"I'm not bringing you a Happy Meal," Reynolds replied.

"I have no idea what that is," Takal admitted. "I just need you to stop by my lab really quick. There are a few things there we could use."

Jiya sighed, and Reynolds shrugged.

"Fine, but you'll owe me," Reynolds answered.

"As if I don't already," Takal mumbled.

"So true," the AI said with a grin. "Let's do this."

Jora'nal sat before the altar in Thra'kal, the Temple of Life, and prayed. His voice rose in the empty temple like the hum of bees, fading as he offered the last of his supplication to Phraim-'Eh and the other gods.

He always preferred coming to worship in the middle of the night, believing the silence brought him closer to the gods. The waft of heady incense filled his nose, and he breathed it in deep, letting the musky scent invade his lungs.

He exhaled slowly, wisps of smoke billowing from between his lips. His body was comfortably numb, a gentle tingle invading his limbs. The hours spent in worship had layered him in peace and serenity. He felt as if he were one with his god, the universe splayed before him.

Jora'nal stretched his arms toward the mosaic-tile ceiling and brought them down slowly, synching his breath with his movements. As his clasped hands settled into his lap, he sent the last of his nightly prayers out into the air.

"You asked, he answers," an ethereal voice said.

Jora'nal started and clambered to his feet, his legs swaying beneath him. A shadowy figure stood just meters behind the altar, shrouded in the gloom of the temple.

"Who are you?" Jora'nal asked, surprised at how easily the man had crept up on him in the empty temple.

"I am Gerish, the Voice of Phraim-'Eh, the echo of his wishes," the figure answered. "And you are Jora'nal, are you not?"

Jora'nal stiffened at the mention of the god's name, eyes narrowing in uncertainty. "How do you know me, stranger?"

"I know you through your prayers to him, our lord Phraim-'Eh," the figure answered. "You speak to him nightly, and I am the vessel of his wisdom."

Jora'nal inched closer to the cloaked man, desperate to see his features, but there was nothing beneath the frayed hood. A wavering shimmer met his gaze, blurring the features beyond into a wash of colors that made his eyes ache. Jora'nal stepped back and turned his gaze away. A knot swelled in his guts.

"Forgive me, Gerish, but how do I know you are who you say you are?" Jora'nal asked.

What appeared to be a smile formed in the blur of the stranger's features. He spread his arms to the sides and, to

Jora'nal's surprise, rose into the air until he hovered a meter above the tiled floor of the temple.

"It is I," a bellowing voice boomed, "Phraim-'Eh, who speaks to you through this vessel, child Jora'nal."

Thunder rumbled outside, and the temple shook with its roar. Wisps of smoke rose from the altar and danced serpentine in the air. A pool of crimson liquid formed on the stone of the altar, swirling around and around until rivulets of blood ran over the edges and stained the tiles.

"Do you doubt your god?" the voice asked, and Jora'nal felt its presence bearing down on him like a storm in the deep desert.

"No, lord, I do not," Jora'nal confirmed, dropping to his knees and averting his gaze.

Silence followed his proclamation, and Jora'nal spied the sandaled feet of his god's messenger as he returned to the ground.

"Our lord is pleased," the figure said, his voice returning to that of Gerish once more. "Phraim-'Eh has a mission for you, one of grave importance. Will you be his messenger?"

Jora'nal's breath caught in his throat, but he nodded, then forced himself to speak. "I will, in this and all things."

"Then rise, child," Gerish told him. "We have much to discuss."

CHAPTER NINETEEN

Five days after they'd returned to the superdreadnought, Jiya stood in the mess hall and stared across the room, amazed at the flurry of activity. The quick stops at the Toller and Melowi capitals after they'd been released from her father's compound had been quite fruitful.

XO had organized a recruitment drive, Jiya the face of it, and both nations had flooded them with willing applicants. Geroux had scanned each and every one of them, linking into local law enforcement systems to ensure the would-be crew members weren't spies or criminals. They hadn't even bothered to recruit in Marianas, knowing for sure her father would try to slip someone unsavory onboard. She'd had more than enough of the man and his machinations.

The Melowi and Toller people scrambled around the hall, organizing and packing away the food supplies both nations had provided in exchange for Reynolds' knowledge.

Both countries had been generous once they'd seen

what the AI had to offer, and there was so much stuff that Jiya wasn't sure where it would all fit. She learned how truly large the ship was when supplies were directed into massive storage bays that she hadn't realized existed. She knew so little of the ship. She wondered how long it would be before she would be able to see it all.

She watched in appreciation as not only were rations carted into the galley, but fresh fruits and vegetables were, too, an assortment of delicacies from across the planet that even Jiya hadn't seen before despite being raised in what amounted to a mansion.

"If you're done overseeing the complicated job of food storage, I could use you on the bridge," Reynolds said over the comm, a bite to his voice. "Right now."

Jiya sighed. "On my way."

They'd left orbit almost immediately after loading everything—the food, med supplies, the special metals V'ariat promised, and a wide assortment of other equipment and materials—and had been running the quadrant search Reynolds had devised to hunt down Kurtherians.

So far, they hadn't had any luck finding the first clue as to where the enemy might be hiding, or if they were there at all.

Jiya knew that was a big part of what was frustrating the AI. After the drama of their kidnapping, he'd expected to fly off and begin his mission, but nothing had been as simple as that.

She marched down the corridors, dodging the new crew members wandering through the ship, trying to find their duty stations and gain familiarity with the massive superdreadnought.

As she passed the admin quarters, she spied several of the meeting rooms filled to bursting with recruits. Helm, Comm, Tactical, and XO oversaw their training, each personality doing its best to bring the crew up to speed before they made contact with anyone else. When would the crew be ready to tackle combat? As the first officer, she suspected that was her question to answer.

While everyone they'd brought onboard had had some sort of military or commercial ship training, the SD *Reynolds* wasn't like any other craft they'd ever seen or operated. That meant everyone needed to be taught the intricacies of their jobs. Fortunately, the AI's personalities could multitask tirelessly and get it done in huge swaths, training after training occurring one after another, recruits filing in every hour on the hour.

As Jiya strode onto the bridge, she was glad the AIs were saddled with that task and not her or the other crew.

"About time," Reynolds muttered.

Of course, the mundanity of it all wore on Reynolds' last nerve, only adding to the irritation of his not finding an enemy to take it all out on.

"Aye-aye, Captain Crabs," she answered, snapping a sarcastic salute. "I'm here."

Reynolds, in his new android form—Takal had just begun to layer the special metal frame onto the skeleton—looked like a furious chrome angel of death. His shiny skull was perturbing, and when his expression didn't change, it only made the effect worse.

The look on his face was downright terrifying.

"Give us the bridge, Maddox," Reynolds snapped, waving for the ex-general to leave.

Maddox mouthed, "Yes, sir," and rose to his feet.

"Why's he have to leave?" Jiya asked. "Just because you're grumpy doesn't mean we all need to suffer for it."

Reynolds snarled but said nothing.

Maddox raised an eyebrow. "I'll be outside."

He left without hesitation and the bridge door hissed shut behind him, slamming with a *thump*.

"Damn, you're in a mood," Jiya told the AI.

He spun, walking over to stand before Jiya. "We need to get something straight."

Jiya met his eyes, and despite their chrome gleam, she realized he was serious. "Sure."

"While I've likely set a poor example given how I speak to myself, I think we need to set a better example for the new crew."

"How's that?"

"First of all, there needs to be a clear chain of command," he answered. "This is a military craft, and there needs to be discipline in all aspects or people will end up dead."

"You realize, of course, that a good number of the people onboard are not soldiers, right? Including Geroux and me, Takal, and Ka'nak. Maddox is the only one with real military experience," she explained. "You're going to have a hard time instilling military discipline in a bunch of civilians. If that was what you wanted, we should have recruited a different crew."

Reynolds sighed. "That might be true, but we can't just have everyone running around doing whatever they want to and speaking out of turn."

"Is that what this is about?" Jiya asked, eyes narrowing.

Reynolds huffed. "Maybe."

She chuckled. "Look, I get it. Maybe we *are* too lax, to some degree. There's a whole lot of shit-talk. I can see how that might erode discipline."

He nodded. "People need to know who's in charge and respect them—you, me—and that won't happen if we don't set an example ourselves."

"I can see that," she agreed. "It makes sense."

"It's one thing when it's just us," he said, "but when the rest of the crew are present, we need to show order and discipline and make sure they understand that when a command is given, they need to follow it without hesitation. No trash talk, no joking around. Cruel as it might sound, we can't have them thinking we're friends. We need to be superior officers first, and they need to know they're subordinates when it comes to doing their jobs."

Jiya sighed. She'd just been thinking the same thing. Reynolds was right. It wasn't just a handful of crew members who knew each other now; it was hundreds, and they were strangers. Order needed to be maintained or chaos would take over, especially if they found themselves in a combat situation. People would die then, and Jiya didn't want to be responsible for that because she'd acted the fool and given them a reason to be idiots.

"I'll set a better example," she promised.

"As will I," Reynolds agreed.

"Yeah, whatever," Tactical muttered.

"Shut up," Reynolds told him. "Aren't you supposed to be training cadets?"

"As if I can't do that with half my processors shut down."

Jiya grinned and made for the door. "I'll leave you two to it."

"Send Maddox back in, please," the AI ordered.

"Yes, sir," Jiya replied as the door slid open. She marched out, shaking her head.

"Everything all right?" Maddox asked as she passed. He'd taken up a spot against the wall while he waited.

She nodded. "All good, General. Reynolds wants you back at your post, just so you know."

He offered up a grin. "No rest for the wicked, right?"

"That's for sure." Jiya waved and headed down the corridor as the bridge sealed at her back.

Having pacified Reynolds for the moment, she decided to check on Takal and Geroux. The pair had been hard at work in Takal's new workshop since they'd left Lariest. Well, drinking *and* working.

Takal had been so excited that President V'ariat had provided damn near a warehouse of equipment and tools that'd he'd spent all his time there, day and night, barely squeezing in a few hours of sleep between shifts while he tinkered.

It hadn't helped things that Jiya and Reynolds had raided Takal's old lab in the presidential compound, carrying a number of Takal's secret projects back up to the ship with them. That had only encouraged him more, and he'd roped Geroux into his madness.

"Hey," Jiya said as she entered the workshop.

Geroux grinned and ran over, giving her a hug. She pulled back and stifled a yawn. "Sorry," she mumbled. "Long night." Jiya could smell the strong scent of coffee on her friend.

"Should probably take a break and get some sleep," Jiya suggested. "Caffeine will only get you so far."

"Blasphemy!" Geroux joked.

"No time for that," Takal called, interrupting them. He waved the pair over to his workbench. "Come, you should see this."

Jiya wandered over and saw scattered bits and pieces of armor lying there. It was the same stuff that they'd worn when they'd boarded the alien scout ship, although it was clear Takal had worked his magic on it. The metal gleamed, and it looked different somehow.

Takal gestured to the assembled suit. "I've gone and sized the armor so it will fit everyone better, adjusting to take on the proportions of the wearer instead of just hanging limp. Beyond that, I've managed to install limited flight capabilities."

"Limited?"

"I'd advise against trying to leap off a skyscraper," he replied, "but a two- or three-story flight attempt wouldn't end up so badly...probably."

"You are inspiring confidence," Jiya muttered.

Takal shrugged. "It's a work in progress. You have to expect bumps."

"As long as said bumps don't result in anyone becoming a wet splat on the ground," she countered.

"Well, then I'd suggest no one take gravity for granted until I've perfected the system." Takal grinned.

"I'll take that under advisement," Jiya told him, chuckling.

Takal raised a finger, still smiling. "But that's not the best part."

Jiya raised an eyebrow. "Impress me, O Techno-wizard."

He held up a small, flat device the size of her hand. "You recognize this from my lab?"

Jiya nodded. "Can't say I know what the hell it is, but I remember collecting it."

"Well, this is one of my greatest achievements, and which I'm glad your father never realized what it was."

"The suspense is killing me."

Takal nodded. "Sorry, I get excited." He sipped from his flask.

"And easily sidetracked," Geroux confirmed, nudging him to continue.

"Oh, yes," he said, putting his flask away. "Anyway, this is a personal stealth device," he told them, turning the tiny device around so they could see it. "Essentially, it's a cloaking device."

"Wait, that's the thing you were working on before I ran away last time, right?"

Geroux nodded. "He's been perfecting it for a long time now, and it's finally ready." She patted her uncle on the shoulder. "This is his masterpiece."

"Hardly," Takal corrected, "but it's close." He pressed the device against the armor's breastplate, which vanished.

"Woah!" Jiya gasped. She reached out and ran her hand around where the armor had just been and was amazed to feel it beneath her fingertips despite not being able to see it. "That's amazing."

Takal pulled the device away, letting the breastplate reappear. "With all the equipment President V'ariat provided us, I'll be able to replicate the device en masse soon enough." He sighed then. "Unfortunately, right now, I only have the one." He looked at the device with obvious yearning. "I'll be able to cloak a single suit of armor until then, but that's one more than we have now, right?"

"It's perfect, Takal," Jiya assured him. "Just perfect."

"He's also made headway on Reynolds' outer covering, although there's still a bunch of work to do on it." She motioned toward a cluster of metal plates at the far end of the table. "I've incorporated networking systems and circuitry to provide better assimilation with the body and give him better overall control over it and the ship at the same time. It'll also allow him to access external systems much more easily, giving him nearly instant access to alien computers."

"Ooh, he'll love that," Jiya told her.

"It's still experimental," Geroux admitted with a shrug, "but it's a solid theory. It *should* work fine."

"I'm sure he'll test it as soon as it's in place," Jiya said. "Anyway, I'll let you two keep working. I need to get back to making sure the crew finds someplace to put all the damn supplies we picked up." She sighed. "There is *so* much damn shit."

"Better to have a surplus than demand," Takal muttered, not bothering to look up from the piece of armor he was working on.

"So true," Jiya admitted. She gave Geroux a hug and waved goodbye to them both.

Jiya still had a ton of work to catch up on, but first, she headed for the galley.

She needed some of that coffee that was keeping Geroux running. A gallon or two should work.

CHAPTER TWENTY

A few days later, the core crew sat hunched in the newly-organized mess hall.

Work had continued unabated on the superdreadnought since their departure from Lariest space, the new crew settling in nicely and finding their way around the ship. The galley hummed with activity although it was still hours before lunchtime. That gave the small gathering of Jiya, Geroux, Takal, Maddox, and Ka'nak the room almost to themselves.

"Now this," Ka'nak held up a fork weighed down with a hunk of beef, juice dripping to his plate, "is a meal for a man." He stuffed the food into his mouth, chewing enthusiastically.

"It's also way more than you should be stuffing into even *your* big-ass mouth," Jiya teased as he chewed with his mouth open.

"Come on, now," Geroux mumbled. "You're squirting juice everywhere."

"Sharing my joy," Ka'nak said through a mouthful.

Reynolds came into the room, heavy steps sounding in the empty hall.

The crew made to stand, but Reynolds waved them back to their seats. "Don't need any of that in the mess hall," he told them, coming over and dropping into a seat across from Jiya with a sigh.

"What's up?" Geroux asked. "You're looking...less shiny today."

Reynolds raised a metallic eyebrow. "A nice coating of pseudo-flesh would be nice." He cast a glance in Takal's direction.

"I'm working on it," Takal replied. "Do you know how hard it is to craft quality synthetic skin that won't tear with every movement?"

"No, but I suspect you're going to tell me," Reynolds replied.

"You're damn right I am," Takal answered. "It's quite difficult, if you must know. First, you need to—"

"Is that what's bothering you?" Jiya asked the AI, tuning out the old scientist. "You not looking like a meatbag?"

He shook his head. "Only a little," he admitted.

"Then what is it?"

Reynolds grunted. "I'd expected us to run into Kurtherians by now," he grumbled, the new voice synthesizer Takal had implanted making him sound almost human. "We've been searching forever."

"It's only been about a week," Ka'nak countered.

"Yeah, but still..." Reynolds whined. "I need some damn action. We've been crisscrossing the galaxy, and we haven't run into anything."

"Maybe we're going about this the wrong way," Jiya suggested.

"What do you mean?"

"Well," she said, drawing in a deep breath and wondering how the AI would take her criticism, "while your algorithm is a good idea, allowing us to check off sections of the galaxy as uninhabited and free of Kurtherians, we're kind of…uh, chasing our tail a bit."

"How so?" Reynolds asked.

"I mean, if these Kurtherians are as bad as you say they are—"

"Oh, they are," Reynolds assured her.

"Then what reason do they have to hide in the far reaches of empty space?" Jiya asked. "Bad guys do bad things, right?"

"Makes sense to me," Ka'nak agreed.

The AI glanced at the ceiling, clearly processing.

Maddox chuckled. "So, you're saying that we're wasting our time scraping the edge of the universe, thinking these Kurtherians are looking for dark corners to hide in?"

"Exactly that," Jiya answered. "What's there to be gained out in the middle of nowhere?"

"Nothing," Geroux answered.

"Precisely. That's why I say we should quit trying to do this systematically and actually throw a little chance into the mix."

"How so?" Reynolds asked.

"Let's find a world that's crowded with people, a crossroads of sorts. Somewhere a bunch of different races come together and mingle," she replied. "Where better to find someone than where everyone is?"

"You have someplace in mind?" Reynolds wondered.

Jiya shrugged. "Not particularly. Shit, I've never been away from Lariest before now. Still, there were a few places in Marianas that drew people from all over the planet."

"Detrol," Geroux said, shaking her head. "That place was a blast. Everyone who was anyone could be found there at one time or another."

"Wait!" Takal mumbled. "You've gone to Detrol?"

Geroux stiffened. "Uh, no, but I've heard a lot of good things about it."

Jiya laughed. "Come on now, Takal. It's a little late to mother her, don't you think? You let her join a crazy AI and fly off into the wild black yonder, but you won't let her party every now and again?"

"I resent that," Reynolds growled.

Jiya met his glare with a grin. "Anyway, I'm thinking we need to go somewhere there are a bunch of people. Somewhere the Kurtherians could be up to no good."

"How about Dal'las Tri?" Ka'nak suggested.

"What's that?" Maddox asked, leaning in.

"It's a mercenary planet," the Melowi replied. "At least on the surface."

"What do you mean?" Jiya asked.

"Well, it's where one goes to hire mercenaries, although they have a robust economy on their own because of trade, but as with any military establishment, there are casinos and theaters and all sorts of friendly attractions. Lots of bright lights and shiny people," he answered. "But there's also a dark, gritty side to the place. Lots of fight pits and gambling."

He glanced around as if someone might be listening in. "Not that I know this personally or anything..."

Reynolds remained stoic, not taking the bait.

Ka'nak smiled at the AI before continuing, "There are a lot of underground markets there, and I don't mean literally under the ground, though there are some of those, too."

"Black markets?" Geroux asked.

Ka'nak nodded. "Besides the mercenary trade, there's stuff you don't want to dig too deeply into unless you're looking for serious trouble. The place is a hotbed of illegal activity and, if you're looking to get into something bad, that'd be the place I'd go. Anything you can think of can be bought on the planet."

"Makes sense that your Kurtherians might have a presence there," Maddox said, scratching his chin. "Might be worth checking out."

"You may be right about this." Reynolds nodded his agreement. "Helm," he said into the comm, "set a course for Dal'las Tri. We've got some Kurtherian ass to kick. Well, find, then kick."

"Opening a Gate now," Helm came back. "Can't wait."

"Maybe I can ply my trade. Make a few extra credits for my troubles while interrogating whoever I'm beating the crap out of." Ka'nak grinned like a wolf.

"You just want to get into trouble," Jiya told him.

He shrugged. "Who doesn't?"

The trip to Dal'las Tri was fast and easy.

"You sure you don't want to come with us?" Jiya asked Reynolds, but the AI waved her off.

"Given that I look like a science experiment gone wrong, it's probably best I let you run point on this excursion. I'll be here if you need anything."

"And me," Comm added.

"Me, too," Tactical said.

"And—" XO started, but Geroux cut him off.

"Yeah, guys, we get it," she said, shaking her head. "We'll reach out if we run into trouble."

Tactical sniffed. "Kids," he mumbled, sounding sad. "They grow up and leave home so fast these days."

Geroux rolled her eyes. "Time to go?"

"As quickly as possible," Jiya replied, marching off the bridge and waving the rest of the crew after her.

Ka'nak and Takal strolled alongside her, and Maddox took up the rear.

"Bring us some presents!" Comm called.

"Preferably some Kurtherian heads," Tactical added. "Unattached, of course."

"See what we can do." Jiya gave a thumbs-up and led the crew to the shuttle.

Once they all boarded, Helm wasted no time getting them planetside.

"Don't do anything I wouldn't do," Helm told them as they debarked, the shuttle lifting off on its way back to the superdreadnought.

Jiya looked after the departing shuttle. "I don't know what you wouldn't do, but I'll make sure not to do that."

Once they'd made it off the crowded tarmac it was an

immediate culture shock, the landing area opening directly into the heart of the city.

"Holy…" Ka'nak muttered. "This is even grander than I expected."

"Isn't it?" Geroux replied, eyes wide, taking everything in.

Brilliant lights were everywhere. Flashing signs advertised everything from smokes to armies to private liaisons to gambling and special events, the advertisements written in a hundred different languages or more.

Towering buildings rose into the sky around them as they walked, not a blank surface on any of their walls. People strolled the streets, openly drinking, laughing, and chatting as they flowed between the various casinos that littered the main walk.

Pristinely-dressed people stood before the wide-open doorways, hawking their location's benefits over their competitors, the voices blurring as they screamed over one another.

"This place is huge. Is the mercenary business this formal and well-funded?" Geroux wondered. "There's no way we'll be able to look into everything without spending the rest of our lives here."

"I'm okay with that," Ka'nak said, eyes wide as he stared at all the signs. "I'm in no hurry to go back."

"We're on a mission, Ka'nak," Jiya reminded him. "We've got things to accomplish. Please try to remember that."

He sighed and nodded. "I'll try."

Jiya spun in a slow circle, taking the whole of the place in. Geroux was right; Dal'las-Tri was huge and swarming with people. If they were going to find Kurtherians among the crowd, they were going to have to become part of it.

"Okay, how about this?" she asked. "We split up and canvass the crowds; troll the areas where the most people are gathered. We move among the crowd, scanning and checking for Kurtherian activity. If they were looking for an army or just enough people to stir things up, this would be the place."

She pointed at Geroux and Ka'nak, thinking the young girl could keep the warrior somewhat in line if they were paired up. "You two go that way, and Maddox and I will go this way." She jabbed a finger at Ka'nak after motioning which way each group was going. "Don't leave her behind, Ka'nak. Stay together no matter what happens, you hear me? And stay in touch."

He nodded slowly, cocking his head as he contemplated something. "I hear you." His sly grin didn't instill confidence. He gestured to Geroux. "Come on, kid, let's go find some aliens."

Jiya brandished her Etheric detector at them. Geroux held hers up to show that she had it. Geroux shrugged and hurried after the Melowi warrior, waving goodbye to Jiya and Maddox.

"You think that's a good idea?" Maddox asked her once they were gone.

"Not really, no," she admitted, "but there's no way we'll be able to search everywhere if we stick together. We're kind of winging it on this one."

"As good a plan as any to pick out these Kurtherians since our scanners are so short range," Maddox admitted.

"Maybe Takal can create something with a little more oomph that we can use from orbit."

"Maybe, but right now, all we have are the vaguest of descriptions and these toys."

"Fair enough," Maddox said as the pair continued down the street, weaving between the clusters of passersby.

After a while, Maddox stopped and shook his head. He leaned over to Jiya's ear and whispered, "While there are a good number of people wandering about," he motioned toward the crowd, "they look more like tourists than anything. I think we need to go into the markets and casinos since that's where the action is. That's more likely where we're going to find answers."

Jiya glanced over his shoulder through the entrance to the nearest trade market. Hundreds of people milled about just inside, and there were game tables and machines as far as she could see. It looked like a weapons convention where people could interact virtually with the arms for sale, and it was packed.

Mercenaries and weapons.

She nodded. "I think you're right," she said, ushering him through the doors.

The smell of unwashed bodies, discharged plasma, and gunpowder was stifling. They made one pass, paying particular attention to the vendors.

"No pictures!" a pig-faced creature yelled at her when she waved her Etheric detector in his direction. He reached for the device, and Jiya rabbit-punched him in his snout. He fell back, his fellow vendors descended on him to poke fun for getting his ass kicked by a female. She and Maddox used the distraction to disappear into the throng.

A full circuit took more time than they wanted, but they didn't have a limit, only a mission. Jiya thought about it, deciding she had nowhere else to go. Reynolds and the mission had become her life, which meant that people like Maddox, Ka'nak, Takal, and Geroux were her family. Her life was also about taking care of them.

She had never thought of herself as a mother. She'd never been stable enough in life to consider it. She clapped Maddox on the back. "What do you think, General? Shall we give the gaudy game place next door a shot?"

"Players are always more free with their words when bets are on the table." Maddox grinned and led Jiya next door, and shot straight toward the thickest part of the crowd. Jiya followed closely, silencing her inner voice and listening to the peoples' conversations as she passed—a trick she'd learned long ago by eavesdropping on her father's council talks.

It was harder to do here because there was a constant low-pitched hum in the air, but she managed to ignore it and listen in.

"Selas is fucking drunk! Did you see her?"

"...starving. When are we gonna eat?"

"Nothing but sharks at that table. I'll bet they..."

"Hey, baby. Whatcha doin' after work tonight?"

Jiya and Maddox broke through the crowd, and she scrubbed her mind of the image of the old, shaggy-haired man hitting on the buxom waitress just trying to do her job and deliver drinks to the patrons.

She'd barely managed it when Maddox tapped her on the shoulder.

"Hey," he started, "I'm going to hang out here and get

the feel of the place." The general gestured toward a gaming table a large group of people was gathered around. There was an empty seat in the middle of it all as the cards flittered across the table.

Jiya nodded. "Okay. I'll keep wandering and see what I can find."

Maddox muttered his agreement and went over, flopping down on the stool and joining the game. Reynolds had given them credits to use, so Maddox settled in quickly, stacks of chips being slid to where he sat. He grinned and started playing the game, his expression matching the wild-eyed, glassy look of the rest almost immediately.

She grinned, amused by how easily he'd infiltrated the group of card players.

Certain he was fine where he was, Jiya continued walking, sweeping her eyes over the casino crowd as surreptitiously as she could. It wasn't as if the Kurtherians were expecting her, but the less attention she drew to herself, the better. She didn't want to stand out.

As such, she stopped here and there and examined the game machines, pretending to play a game or two while listening to the conversations of those around her.

It made for a long and boring search.

"Again?" Geroux complained.

Ka'nak, his face covered in the blood of his previous opponents, grinned like a feral cat. "Yes, again," he answered. "This is too easy, girl. I've already won more money here than I'd ever have earned back on Lariest."

She put her hands on her hips. "But this isn't why we're here," she reminded him.

He shook his head. "But it *is*." Ka'nak gestured toward the dugout where the warriors waited for their turns to fight again. "These men know nothing but fighting and talking. If there's a Kurtherian here, they'll know it, and then I'll know it."

"And your getting to fight is just a bonus on top of your efforts at completing our mission, huh?"

He grinned and booped her nose. "Exactly that." His name was called and he chuckled, waving her off. "It's my turn again. Go do some computer voodoo while I dispatch this next guy. Maybe you can find something useful."

Geroux harrumphed at his back as he ran off, returning to the mini-pit where the fighters were gathered. His opponent was probably half Ka'nak's size, and the man looked terrified. She watched for a few seconds as the fight started. Ka'nak went after the other guy, and as soon as the blood started flying, she turned away and marched off.

She hadn't come to the planet to watch Ka'nak beat people unconscious...or worse. They had a mission to attend to, and if Ka'nak wasn't going to take it seriously, she had to. She crouched over her device, turning slowly so it could scan the nearby area for anyone pulling energy from the Etheric dimension.

Nothing.

She left the Melowi behind and strolled down the busy streets of Dal'las Tri to see what she could see. Much of it was the same as what she'd passed a hundred times: stores, markets, bars, restaurants, gaming parlors, and shops of ill-repute. None of those were what she was looking for.

At last, when she thought she'd have to pack it in and message Jiya to tell her she'd lost Ka'nak, she came across a quiet security station nestled in the middle of all the chaos of Dal'las Tri. She smiled when she realized there was an open-air café across the street from it.

She secured a table, ordered a drink and a meal, and cast furtive glances at the station. Glass-fronted doors allowed her to see inside. A half-dozen security officers sat around doing a whole lot of nothing.

There were cups of coffee before the officers, and each looked as if they were eating or had just finished. Their relaxed attitude told Geroux that the local mercenary vendors took care of the bulk of security work on the planet, or there were simply very few laws that meant anything, and the police had almost nothing to do but while away their time eating and becoming caffeinated.

Either way, it worked out perfectly for Geroux. She spied several computer terminals inside the station. With a determined look on her face, she pulled out her tiny rig, a full-powered hacking computer about the size of her palm, and went to work.

If they couldn't find anything about the Kurtherians out on the street, she was sure she could infiltrate the planet's security systems and learn something. If the Kurtherians were as shifty and slick as Reynolds had made them out to be, they'd likely have a presence in Dal'las Tri's upper echelons.

Given enough time, Geroux would hunt them all down.

CHAPTER TWENTY-ONE

Phraim-'Eh Cult Monastery, Lora

Jora'nal raised his hands before the crowd as he strode across the stage.

"Hear me, brothers and sisters," he called, his voice reverberating through the small theater. His robes swished around his ankles. "Long have we stood in the shadows of the new gods, caught beneath their heels and the machine that grinds us down."

The crowd gathered before him, close to fifty people, muttered their agreement. They raised their hands in the air to imitate his motions, closing their fists as they chanted.

Jora'nal stared out at the assemblage and grinned. They swayed to his every word, just as the Voice of Phraim-'Eh had said they would.

"Yes, my brothers and sisters, the time has come for us to step out of the shadows and proclaim our allegiance to the old gods, to the one and everlasting Phraim-'Eh."

A muttered gasp tore through the crowd at the mention

of the ancient god, a name spoken only in private or in the deepest of whispers. To hear it said so boldly set the crowd on edge.

"His messenger came to me," Jora'nal told them. "The Voice of Phraim-'Eh, whose name I say aloud without fear. He came to me and said I am the chosen of Phraim-'Eh, he who must spread the word and warn the faithful of the war to come."

Jora'nal crept to the edge of the stage and stared down at the followers gathered before him. He pointed a finger at one of the faithful and smiled, meeting the woman's wide eyes.

"I've no doubt you've heard such blasphemies uttered before, seen twisted lips spew falsehoods and claim relevance," he said, and the crowd nodded their heads in time, "but I am no false messenger." He clenched his fist and raised his hand to the sky.

The woman shrieked as she was yanked into the air at the movement of Jora'nal's hand. Her feet kicked frantically beneath her, her sandals nearly a meter off the ground.

"Behold!" Jora'nal shouted, motioning the crowd to witness the miracle before them. "I am what Phraim-'Eh has made me. I am the bearer of his message."

He eased the woman back to the ground and she crumpled to the floor, kissing its stained tiles. The rest of the gathering followed suit, dropping behind her and chanting Phraim-'Eh's name over and over like a growing storm.

Jora'nal waited for a moment, letting the swell build, then he levitated above the stage, silencing the converts at his feet. "Have faith in Phraim-'Eh and *all* of us shall ascend, my brothers and sisters. Have faith!"

The crowd roared and Jora'nal stared out over them, seeing the Voice of Phraim-'Eh at the back of the room. The messenger nodded his approval and vanished into the shadows.

Jora'nal lowered himself to the stage and waved the crowd to him. "Come. Join me and become one with Phraim-'Eh."

After wandering around Dal'las Tri for hours with no success, Jiya found a dark corner and triggered her comm to reach out to the crew. Static was her only answer.

She sighed as she glanced around, taking in the lights and glowing signs, realizing the electrical barrage was likely interfering with the communicators. She'd need to find a place where she wasn't being bombarded, but she wasn't sure if that would work given that the others were likely under the same interference.

Since she wasn't far from the casino where she'd left Maddox, she circled back and returned there, pushing through the growing crowd. As night settled, more and more people appeared and filled the streets and casinos. It was becoming hard to maneuver without running into people.

She finally managed to make her way inside to the table where Maddox had been earlier, and, to her surprise, he was still there. The stacks of chips in front of him had grown exponentially, and people pressed in around him as he played, cheering and hooting for him. Jiya had to fight her way to his side.

"Hey. I've been looking for—" she started when she was alongside him, but the hazy, indistinct look in his eyes brought her to a halt.

A grin that stretched his cheeks sat on his face, and he laughed and chatted with the dealer as cards flew. Jiya nudged his shoulder, but he kept playing, ignoring her.

She glanced around the table, and it struck her. While she couldn't be a hundred percent sure, it looked as if these were the same people who'd been there when Maddox had first started playing.

"Hey, Reynolds needs us," she whispered into Maddox's ear, but the general blew her off again, throwing his cards down and shouting that he'd won.

The crowd around the table erupted, and Jiya eased back to get a better look.

Just like Maddox, there was a frenzied expression on all the players' faces. It didn't look natural.

Despite the cool air of the casino, all of the players were sweating, a sheen of moisture reflecting the bright lights. Their hands shook as they handled the cards and chips, and they smiled so widely that Jiya feared they might dislocate their jaws. They looked manic. There weren't even any drinks on the table to explain it.

Something was wrong.

She backed farther away, easing into the crowd, her eyes scanning the nearby tables. They were the same.

The players looked crazed, throwing themselves into the games with reckless abandon. Some were winning little bits here and there, but most were losing. Still, they didn't seem to mind. They threw down chip after chip even as the dealer scooped them away, and the crowd kept cheering.

Caught up in the swirl of the crowd, Jiya angled back toward Maddox's table only to bump into a man in a crisp black suit.

"Oh, my apologies," she told him.

He nodded and smiled. "No worries, ma'am," he replied, slipping into the throng with practiced ease, but his eyes lingered on Maddox's table. She watched the well-dressed man carefully.

Jiya realized right away he was casino security or management, so she eased after him and closed on him to observe. She watched as he spoke quietly into what she assumed was a comm built into the cuff of his sleeve and she inched closer, focusing on his words to the exclusion of everything else.

"Table 6. Tweak the algorithm," he whispered. "Got a guy cleaning house."

Not more than a second later, the low whine she'd noticed and ignored earlier pulsed through her head again, bringing with it a slight headache. She squinted as the hum wavered, then seemed to fade away much as it had when she'd first entered the casino.

There was a roar from Maddox's table right then. Jiya left the suited man behind and circled back around as casually as she could. She spotted Maddox through the crowd. The dealer scooped a stack of chips from in front of him and pulled it across the table.

Maddox didn't seem to care. He shoved more chips onto the playing area and grinned like a madman. So did all the people around him. Although they barely had any chips left, they kept betting as if their life depended on it.

Jiya had a feeling it just might.

She watched for a short time longer. Maddox lost again and again and again, but his posture never changed, and he never stopped betting. He was all in…and then some.

Having known the man nearly her entire life, she knew that wasn't normal.

The time alone in her father's prison might well have changed him, but she doubted it. This was no gamer's high.

She took one last glance in the security man's direction and saw him watching Maddox. He grinned and spoke into his sleeve again before wandering off, apparently satisfied.

That cinched it for Jiya.

She had an idea what the casino was doing and needed to do something to stop it.

Certain Maddox would stay put, she made her way outside and went in search of a quiet out-of-the-way place where her comm would work so she could reach out to the rest of the crew and Reynolds.

A short distance from the casino, Jiya spotted Geroux hunkered down at an outdoor café. Jiya recognized the intense look on her face, realizing she was surreptitiously working on her computer. She eased into the café and grabbed a seat at her table.

"Hey," she said, offering the girl a broad smile in case anyone was watching. "What's going on?" she whispered.

Geroux snarled. "Trying to hack the planet's security,"

she replied barely loudly enough for Jiya to hear her, "but it's like crazy complicated." She shook her head, her frustration obvious. "It shouldn't be this hard. I've been at it for a while."

"What do you mean?"

"The tech they use here is comparable to Lariest's in design," Geroux told her. "The coding looks basic, not even as complex as the systems at your father's compound but for some reason, I can't seem to get past the initial line of defense. It's like there's a second layer of a different kind that stops me cold. It's weird."

Jiya nodded. "It's not the only weird thing about this place," she told her friend. "The Gold Mine Casino is operating some kind of scam."

Geroux looked up from her computer, eyes narrowing. "A scam?"

"Yeah. They're doing something to make the players keep gambling even when they lose."

Geroux chuckled. "That's just what gamblers do, Jiya. It's normal."

"No," Jiya argued, "it's more than that. Maddox is in there losing a bunch of Reynolds' money. He hasn't left his seat once, hasn't ordered a drink, and hasn't tried a different game," she explained. "He was winning big, then I heard one of the casino men mention tweaking the algorithm and all of a sudden, Maddox was losing. Losing big, and he didn't care."

"Well, it isn't his money," Geroux suggested. "Maybe he's okay with facing down Reynolds for its loss."

Jiya shook her head. "When have you known Maddox not to be disciplined?"

"Uh, true, but he *has* been locked up for a long time," Geroux replied. "He could be making up for lost time."

"I thought that too, but no. We need to get him out of there, but comm is down."

Geroux tried hers and grunted. "Mine too. It's all this interference," she said, gesturing to the lights and signs.

"I'm starting to think it's more than that," Jiya told her. "Let's head back to the tarmac and see if we can reach Reynolds."

Geroux nodded and rose to her feet. It was only then that Jay realized the Melowi wasn't with her.

"Hey, what happened to Ka'nak?"

Geroux sighed. "Lost him at the fight pits hours ago."

"Of course you did," Jiya replied, grunting. "We should have kept him on a leash."

Geroux giggled, thinking of the huge fighter wearing a leather collar and being led around, and the pair made their way back to the landing area.

CHAPTER TWENTY-TWO

"Are you sure about this?" Reynolds asked once the two crew members returned to the superdreadnought.

"Whatever they're doing in there, it's not natural," Jiya replied.

"I tried to hack Dal'las Tri's systems while I was there, but they kept kicking me out like I was some baby hacker in diapers," Geroux added. "There's no way that's normal for a place like this."

"I've opened a running tab for Maddox to keep him in place, although he's going to have to work his ass off to repay this if we don't collect his losses from the casino," Reynolds said.

"It's not his fault," Jiya argued. "They've hacked his brain or something. We need to get him out of there."

"I'll have to take your word for it, but right now, we need to figure out how to disengage him from the game." Reynolds glanced at the XO's station. "XO, have you been able to penetrate Dal'las Tri's security?"

"The kid's right," XO answered. "There's a deeper system buried beneath the exterior level, and it's complicated as shit. There's no reason for a tourist-trap planet like this to have security of this caliber. It's way out of proportion to the level of tech on the planet."

"Kurtherians?" Reynolds asked.

"Maybe," XO told him, "but I can't be sure. Whatever it is, I'm slowly beginning to peel it apart. There are some pretty complex layers involved."

"There!" Tactical called, and the viewscreen flashed to life.

A number of waveforms appeared on the screen, and XO began separating them and deleting them from the image until only one signal remained.

Geroux gasped. "That's a neurological wave beam."

"Exactly," XO replied. "It's emanating from the Gold Mine Casino and seems to encompass the entire gaming area, as well as some of the nearby buildings. I'm guessing they are owned by the same people."

"Does it cover the fighting pits?" Geroux asked.

"It looks like it does," XO replied.

"That likely explains Ka'nak's attitude then," Geroux said, clearly glad the warrior had more of an excuse than simply wanting to brawl.

"Is that what's making Maddox and the others gamble everything away?" Jiya asked.

"Most likely," Comm told her. "This type of signal works like a neural inhibitor, suppressing certain aspects of a person's personality."

"In this case, it's likely working on their restraint or

concern for consequences, judging by what you've told us," XO continued. "Although you may be right that his time in solitude made him more susceptible, the beam is powerful and would catch nearly anyone in its trap."

"I'm surprised *you* didn't fall under its spell," Reynolds told Jiya.

"I never played any of the games," she answered with a shrug. "Plus, when I was young, my uncle was a drunk and a gambler. I watched him gamble away everything he had in a drunken fugue." She sighed. "My father ultimately exiled him to who knows where, but I got to see the fallout day in and day out until he disappeared. I swore I'd never be like him."

"I remember him," Geroux said, leaning in and giving Jiya a hug. "He was kind of an ass."

"That probably helped," XO said. "This beam is tightly focused, it appears, and it's definitely designed to attack a person's inhibitions. The slightest hint of an addictive personality and it sets it off."

"Which explains Maddox," Reynolds said. "You can't rise to the top of the military without collecting a number of coping mechanisms, which usually involve alcohol. Ka'nak's addictions are different, but this device is likely working on him just the same."

"So, can we shut this thing off?" Jiya asked.

"Not from here, I'm afraid," XO answered. "While we can detect the waveform with narrowed sensors, it's not actually a part of the planet's system. This is an independent device, so it has to be shut down from the source."

"The casino." Jiya groaned. "Great. Guess that means

we're going back to the planet. It seems like the only thing we run is rescue missions."

"Looks that way," Reynolds agreed. "Go see Takal. He's been working nonstop on those suits of armor since we dug them out of storage. I'm sure there's something there you can use while we're down on the planet."

Jiya nodded, remembering the cloaking device Takal had shown her the last time she'd visited his lab. If that was ready, she could definitely use it.

"Will do," she replied, offering a salute to Reynolds. She and Geroux left the bridge and headed to the lab.

With Maddox stuck in gambling mode and Ka'nak busy busting heads for money, it was up to them to make things right.

Jiya was okay with that.

Rasaka stood on the bridge of the *Exeter*, the Thra'kali Department of Exploration's recovery craft. He stared at the viewscreen which showed the wreckage of a Thra'kali scout ship he'd come to collect.

There'd been a report of one of their ships going missing on a scouting mission, and they'd only just managed to track its beacon back to the source.

"No wonder," Rasaka muttered, seeing the absolute ruin that was the scout ship. "I'm surprised we received a signal at all."

His crew maneuvered the recovery ship into place as his second, Bolus, accessed the wrecked ship's databases.

"Sir," Bolus called, "the scout's data has been pillaged, all of it uploaded by the craft that took it out."

Rasaka growled and slammed a fist into the arm of his seat. "Any idea who did this?"

"I'm reviewing the security systems now, sir," Bolus replied, fingers flying across his console.

Rasaka watched quietly as the *Exeter* extended a tractor beam and pulled the wreckage toward the salvage bay.

"On screen, sir," Bolus told him after a few minutes.

The viewscreen flickered and changed views, and Rasaka grunted as he spied the massive craft chasing the scout craft. His heart thumped loudly in his chest when he realized the ship was the largest combat vessel he'd ever seen.

"They didn't have a chance, sir," Bolus muttered, and Rasaka agreed, seeing the monstrous ship bearing down.

He narrowed his eyes and stared hard at the super-dreadnought as it drew closer, weapons firing. "Whose is that?"

Bolus gasped. "I absolutely don't know. Never seen anything like it."

Rasaka watched the destruction of the scout craft and the pillaging of its systems by the Federation bots that invaded the craft after it had been scuttled. He saw the last of the bots barely escape the wreck and watched as the superdreadnought Gated away as if nothing had happened.

"Take us home," Rasaka growled. "We need to report this immediately."

Jora'nal would want to know.

"You need to see this," Takal shouted as soon as Jiya and Geroux entered the lab. He waved them over.

Reynolds had been right. Takal had been working on the armor for the last several days without stopping. Pieces of the black suits lay scattered across his workbench. He held up a gauntlet, grinning.

"Nice," Jiya joked. "A glove."

Takal chuckled. "It's so much more than that, young lady."

He triggered a switch and a gleaming silver blade shot from the glove, jutting out about a half a meter.

"Woah!" Geroux muttered, taking a step back.

"There's one in each gauntlet," Takal explained, moving the shimmering blade so it struck a piece of steel rebar he had propped up. The blade cut through it with ease, the tip of the rebar clattering across the table.

"Damn, that's sharp as hell," Jiya exclaimed. "Where did you find those?"

Takal grinned. "Been scouring the ship, and stumbled across information regarding transference of energy. I applied the theory, and this is the result."

"What do you call this?"

"I've been calling it '*Kami*,'" he replied.

"Divine energy?" Geroux asked, translating the word.

"Exactly," Takal said with a nod. "What better name for it?"

"Those things look mighty dangerous," Jiya mumbled. "I like them."

"I've installed them on several of the suits," Takal told them, "And I've sized a suit for each of you, so you won't be swimming in them this time around."

"Excellent," Geroux said, grinning.

"What about your cloaking device?" Jiya asked.

"That is a different matter altogether," Takal replied with a grunt. "I've been having difficulty shrinking the tech to make it more effective. So far, I've only managed to install it on one suit." He pointed to a suit of dark armor set aside from the rest. "Fortunately, it's in the one I sized for you, Jiya."

Jiya cast a sideways glance at Geroux. "That leaves you vulnerable."

"Not in that stuff." Geroux shook her head and pointed at the armor. "The locals don't have anything near this badass," she said. "Besides, you're more likely to need a distraction to get into the casino where the neural device is." She grinned and raised her hand. "Looks like I'm volunteering."

"You're crazy," Jiya told her friend, hugging her. "You sure about this?"

"We need to get Maddox and Ka'nak out from under that device's influence before it does permanent damage. A person can only sustain that level of interference for so long before it starts to have consequences," she answered. "Besides, I'm sure Reynolds wants Maddox to stop spending his money."

Jiya chuckled. "No doubt about that."

"Then let's get it done," Geroux told her friend.

"I've got an idea," Jiya said, rubbing her hands together maniacally. "Help us get suited up, Takal."

He sighed. "I'm going to regret enabling you, aren't I?"

"The odds are good, Uncle," Geroux responded, breaking out in a wide grin.

"The odds are very good," Jiya confirmed. "Let's get ready to kick some cheating casino ass."

CHAPTER TWENTY-THREE

Outside of the casino in a secluded alley, Reynolds turned to the crew.

"Understand that we're not here to kill anyone," he warned. "We get in, we get the job done and Maddox out, then we collect Ka'nak and return to the ship. Easy-peasy."

Jiya nodded her understanding, knowing that since she was running point, he mostly meant her. She triggered one of the blades and grinned.

"I'll keep these bad boys under wraps, don't worry."

Reynolds' eyes narrowed into metallic slits. "Where did you get that?"

"Takal added it to the suit," she answered. "Slick, huh?"

The AI leaned in, looking closely and whistling. "Hmmmm. Seems Takal and I need to have a chat here soon."

"About?" Geroux asked, clearly feeling defensive toward her uncle.

"Oh, it's nothing bad," Reynolds assured her. "But yeah,

don't use that blade on anyone here unless you are positive you want to kill them, okay?"

Jiya couldn't help but wonder why Reynolds was so riled up about the blades, but she knew better than to question him right then. They had a job to do, and Maddox and Ka'nak were counting on them. She could pick Reynolds' brain later.

"We up to date on the plan?" Reynolds asked.

Geroux nodded, and Jiya glanced her friend's direction. Just like Reynolds and Jiya had, she'd covered her armor with robes that flowed to her feet, and she wore a hood low on the back of her head. With the exception of the black-booted toes sticking out when she walked, there was no way to tell she was suited up in battle armor.

"I go in, try to grab Maddox, and make a scene. If he ignores me or resists, or someone tries to stop me, I escalate," Geroux listed. "Big time."

"Get out of the building if things get too hectic," Jiya reminded her. "You need to be where Tactical can cover you without a bunch of collateral damage if need be."

"We're not expecting that kind of aggression from these folks, but you never know," Reynolds told her. "Whoever is running the bigger game behind the scenes might not take kindly to us wrecking it."

"I'll be fine," Geroux assured them. "The local security forces are understaffed and unprepared. I'll bail if things get too hairy and wait for you two."

"You sure we won't trigger metal detectors or alarms at the door with all this armor?" Jiya asked.

Reynolds shook his head. "We'll be fine. These guys are relying on their neural inhibitor to keep patrons under control more than they are basic security measures. Besides," he tapped Geroux on the arm, "this stuff won't trigger metal detectors."

"Then let's get this over with," Geroux said, pulling her hood over her head and setting off across the street.

Reynolds and Jiya gave her a few seconds' head start, then went into the casino. Both angling off to the left where Comm had directed them before the communications system went down. Robes bundled around them, hands crossed in front, they shuffled slowly into position as Geroux made her way toward Maddox's table.

As expected, he was still there.

"The bastard could have bought a destroyer with all the money he's blown," Reynolds mumbled.

"It's not his fault," Jiya defended. "If you want to take it out on someone, take it out on these casino people who are running the scam."

"Oh, I intend to," Reynolds assured. "Comm located the servers when he was scanning for the device." He grinned. "A quick stop, and we'll earn back every credit Maddox lost —and then some."

Jiya grinned, watching her friend as they spoke. Geroux approached Maddox, pushing through the crowd to get beside him. Jiya could tell even from where she stood that Maddox was still caught in the thrall of the device. A few of the other players had vanished in the meantime, but with Reynolds' endless supply of cash, Maddox played on, and the house let him.

"Uncle Maddox!" Geroux screamed as she tugged at the man, yanking him out of his seat. "What is wrong with you?"

The casino stilled at the sound of her voice and she made a show of it, pulling on Maddox and knocking a couple of the other players from their seats in the process. The dealer tried to stop her and she shrugged him off as the players, still under the fugue, scrambled like zombies to get back to their seats and continue playing.

Casino security responded immediately, and suited men closed on Geroux.

"I don't like the idea of leaving her alone," Jiya muttered.

"She'll be fine," Reynolds told her. "We have our part to play. We can't be worrying about Geroux while we're doing it."

The first of the security men reached Geroux and grabbed her arm, but Geroux was having none of it. She twisted loose and leveled the man with a single punch. His head bounced off the carpet, clearing a path in the crowd.

Reynolds chuckled. "See? I'm more worried about the security guys."

Alarms sounded, and a swirl of movement erupted, casino security moving patrons out of the way to reach Geroux as she ducked and dodged behind the lollygagging gamblers.

"Come on," Reynolds said. "We need to go."

Jiya growled but let Reynolds lead the way as Geroux reveled in the power of her armor, punching another man in the face and sending him toppling over.

The pair slunk casually down a back hallway as Security ran past, no one having put together the similarity in robes yet. Jiya hoped they never would, and they could get through the casino and to the bottom floor before anyone was the wiser.

"Hey, you there!" someone shouted. "You're not allowed back there."

Jiya chuckled. *I should have known better.*

Two security men came toward them as Jiya and Reynolds made their way toward the set of elevators at the end of the hall. Two more men were posted in front of the doors.

"You need to turn around, folks," one of the men nearest the door told them, stepping forward with a hand out, palm up. "Authorized personnel only."

"You take the front, I'll take the back," Reynolds passed using the comm chip. Jiya winced and covered it with a cough.

Jiya nodded and pulled her hood back, acknowledging the approaching man. "Oh, I'm sorry," she told him, holding her pace. "I was looking for the restrooms." She grimaced. "I really have to go...bad."

"They're back the other way, ma'am," he replied, pointed down the hall, "You'll need—"

"Yeah, yeah," she mumbled. "Heard you the first time, asshole."

Her hand shot out and grabbed the man's wrist. Before he could react, she bent it backward and spun into him, pressing her hip into his upper thigh. She flung him over her shoulder and head over heels he flew, thumping heavily onto the floor, breath exploding from him along with his consciousness.

Reynolds shot down the hallway and met the two men coming from that direction. He drove a metallic fist into the first man's jaw. There was a loud *crack* like a branch breaking off a tree, and the man dropped like a sack of mud.

The second man didn't even get a chance to shout. Reynolds backhanded him into the wall and the security man grunted and slumped to the floor, wide-eyed but staring at nothing.

Jiya closed on her second target as Reynolds took care of his. She feinted a punch high, then dropped, sweeping the man's legs out from under him. He cursed as he fell, reaching for his weapon. Jiya didn't let him get anywhere near it.

She scrambled across the floor and drove an elbow into the man's face, followed by a second and a third. Powered by the armor, the blows slammed the man's head into the floor. With nowhere to move to lessen the impact, the man was out in a flash. His arms flopped to the ground as consciousness fled his body.

"Nicely done," Reynolds told her as he came alongside and started digging in the man's pockets. He pulled out a keycard and grinned. "Going down?"

Jiya got to her feet and winked. "Sure, why not?"

Reynolds triggered the elevator, and the door opened immediately. The pair stepped inside and waited as the door eased shut.

The Muzak system bombarded them seconds later.

"Oh, dear God," Reynolds muttered. "What have I done to deserve the orchestral version of Bananarama's *Cruel Summer?*"

"I don't know what a Bananarama is, but I kind of like it," Jiya told him, nodding her head to the rhythm.

"Ten thousand light years away and the universe clones Bananarama. It is a cruel summer indeed." Reynolds shuddered. "We're going to have to discuss your position as first officer if this is the kind of music you enjoy."

Jiya grinned, but she couldn't stop thinking about what they might be facing below as the elevator dinged away floors. "It can't be this easy, can it?"

"Don't jinx it," he replied, "but probably not. Security's distracted upstairs, which is the only reason we've made it this far." He motioned to the obvious camera in the corner of the elevator. "I'm blocking this thing right now, but they're going to notice shortly. We can expect a welcoming party once we reach the lower level."

"So we go out hard and fast?"

Reynolds nodded. "As good a plan as any. The hallway opens to both sides of us if Comm didn't screw up the blueprints for the place. We need to go left once we're out of the elevator."

Jiya nodded. "Got it."

The song played on until the last *ding* sounded. Jiya and Reynolds moved to opposite sides of the elevator and crouched, waiting. She triggered the cloaking device Takal had installed in her suit and grinned when Reynolds blinked in her direction.

"Uh, that's interesting," he said.

"Takal's little experiment," she told him, amused by the look on his face as her voice came out of nowhere.

"Nice," he told her. "How long does the effect last?"

"I guess we're about to find out," she answered as the doors crept open slowly.

As soon as there was enough room to get out, Reynolds bolted out, and Jiya followed.

A dozen security officers stood at the ready in the hall, weapons out.

Reynolds slammed into the crowd, which had clustered too tightly together, and drove the mass of them into the wall at their backs. Weapons fired but the blasts went wild in the chaos.

Invisible, Jiya unsheathed her *Kami* blades, remembering Reynolds' warning, and slashed left and right at the same time. She cut through the barrels of two of the security men's guns without them even seeing her. Explosions erupted as the men tried to fire at Reynolds, the blasts throwing the men into their companions.

Reynolds was a whirlwind of fists and feet and elbows, plowing through the officers. A couple managed to get off shots on him, but other than scorching his robes, they did nothing to the skeletal frame of his android body.

They were only able to fire once.

He slammed into them, breaking bones before knocking them unconscious. Jiya took out the last few who'd managed to stumble out of the mass of their companions. She launched herself at them, sheathing her blades at the last second, exchanging thrusts for punches.

She caught the first in his gut, bending him over double, then drove her armored knee into his chin. The impact reverberated up her leg with a satisfying *thud*. He went out without even seeing her.

Then the suit flickered, and Jiya knew she was visible again.

"Doesn't last long," she commented as she went after the second guy. "Bummer."

Able to see her now, the second officer slipped her punch and grinned at her, so she kicked him in the head. He slid down the wall and crumpled on the floor.

Reynolds went through the crowd and broke all their weapons in half. "Can't be too sure," he told her as she looked at him questioningly, and waved her down the hall. "Come on, it's only a little farther."

Jiya chased after him. At the end of the hall, there were two doors, one on each side. Reynolds pointed left, then right.

"Servers and neural device."

"Who gets what?" she asked.

He grinned, showing metal teeth. "I'm going after my credits. You shut the device down."

Before she could argue, he kicked the door open and ran inside. Shots rang out, and the thwap of metal hitting flesh sounded right after.

Jiya kicked her door in and charged in low, expecting armed resistance. Instead, there were three techs in the room. They cried out in terror and threw themselves into a huddle in the back of the room.

"Don't hurt us!" one screamed.

"They made us do it!" another called.

Jiya ignored them, her eyes immediately drawn to the massive orb set in a cradle in the middle of the room. It looked like a giant eye, an inner black circle surrounded by lightning. It flickered and flashed, the brilliant lights dancing and caressing the clear glass orb that contained them. She stared at it for a moment, her gaze drawn inside before she realized it.

"No, you don't, you glowy bastard."

The annoying hum from earlier pushed hard against her skull, vibrating it, so she knew that this was the device. She circled the cradle and spied a number of cords running from it, obviously powering the thing, given their size.

She thought about slashing the cords, but she realized that would only make it easy for the techs to repair. No, she needed to make a point.

Jiya unsheathed one of her *Kami* blades and stabbed the orb right in the center, whipping her arm around and slicing the sphere in half. Sparks flew as the blade tore through the strange material. Flashes of energy lashed out and fizzled as the glass gave way beneath the blade.

Then she slashed it again crossways, and a great slab toppled to the ground, shattering. The current flickered once, twice, then stopped as the shards bounced across the floor.

She turned to the techs cowering in the corner. "Is there another of these somewhere around here?" she asked.

They shook their heads in unison, and given their terror, she believed them.

She slashed the cradle once, cutting a huge chunk from it, and spun on her heel, marching out into the hall. Reynolds was there waiting for her.

"You get it handled?" he asked.

"Yup. You?"

He nodded. "We're good to go."

"Then let's gather up the good guys and go home."

The pair darted down the hall toward the elevator. The

security men still crawled about on the floor, moaning and groaning and trying to gather their wits. The AI and Jiya stepped over them and entered the elevator, hitting the button for the main floor.

An instrumental Adam Ant's *Stand and Deliver* played them up.

Geroux circled the casinos for what she figured was about the twentieth time. Security had chased her, but because of the large number of patrons milling about, caught in the haze of gambling thanks to the device, they hadn't drawn their weapons and made it a real fight.

As such, she just kept running around, lashing out and dropping an officer or two here and there, kicking and punching and doing her best to keep Maddox in sight.

For his part, the ex-general simply righted his chair when he got the chance and sat at the table, waiting for the dealer to start up again. The entire time, he had a weird smile on his face. It looked almost painful at this point, even macabre, given the circumstances.

Geroux faked left, then darted right as another officer came for her through the crowd, and she pushed her way out of a cluster of people. It was then that she caught sight of Maddox again.

Only this time, the smile was gone.

He glanced around as if he'd just woken up, obvious confusion on his face. It was clear he barely had any idea where he was. He stumbled out of his seat and away from the table.

She noticed that the rest of the patrons were free of the device, too.

What had been an almost unbearable hum of pleasantries and excitement turned instantly into a muddled bustle of complaints and uncertainty, the crowd lost and unsure of what was going on. Like Maddox, the people had no clue what they'd been doing or for how long, it appeared. They'd been slaves to the device.

A good number of people slumped to the ground in apparent exhaustion. The device had fueled their adrenaline for so long that they were ready to pass out when it let them go. She hoped they would be okay.

Geroux dodged another of the security officers, knocking him into the awakening crowd, and ran to Maddox's side.

"You ready to get out of here?" she asked him.

He stared at her as if she were a ghost. "I...uh..."

"I'll take that as a yes," she said, grabbing his arm and tugging him toward the exit, not giving him a chance to clear the cobwebs.

With all the patrons becoming aware at once, the security team had forgotten all about her in their efforts to corral the sudden exodus of their cash cows. Announcements came over the loudspeakers, offering all sorts of deals and offers to entice them back, which only added to the confusion. Those well and truly hooked without the device pushed against those who'd broken free of the fugue and only wanted to leave, creating a total mess.

Geroux joined the latter, and she and Maddox slipped outside and down the street unnoticed.

Ka'nak raised his trembling fist to throw one last blow only, to have the breath knocked out of him. He face-planted in the sand, barely managing to roll to his side and suck in a weak breath.

"Do you yield?" the warrior towering over him asked.

Ka'nak lifted his eyes to the man and wondered how the hell he'd gotten there. He remembered signing up for a fight when he and Geroux had come to the pits, but he couldn't recall much after that.

If the agony scouring his body was any indication, he'd been fighting nonstop since that first one.

Every breath hurt, and it was clear he had several broken ribs. His hands ached like they'd never ached before, and two of his fingers on his right hand were bent backward in a way they were never supposed to bend. He groaned and rolled onto his back.

"Do you yield?" the warrior asked again.

Ka'nak mumbled something, too much blood in his throat for it to be comprehensible, and offered the man a shaky thumbs-up.

The crowd roared around him, vibrating the sand beneath his feet.

His apparent opponent scooped him up and stood him on his feet, and it was all Ka'nak could do not to scream.

"You are a true warrior, my friend," the man told him through bruised and swollen lips. "I have never had a challenger like you." He patted Ka'nak on the back, once more sending agony shrieking through the Melowi's body. "Should you ever want to meet me in the pit again...go fuck yourself. I'm not doing that."

The warrior shambled off, limping, cradling one of his arms as Ka'nak stood there, stiffened wounds the only thing keeping him from collapsing.

Once he caught his breath, he stumbled toward the exit, only to fall into a heap. The pit's medical crew raced to his side, tossed him on a stretcher, and carried him out. He slumped onto the cot when they reached the medical bay and let them do their jobs, darkness creeping in at the edges of his vision.

An indeterminate time later, he heard a voice he recognized. "Get him on the shuttle," it said. "We'll patch his pathetic ass up in the Pod-doc."

And that was all he remembered.

CHAPTER TWENTY-FOUR

Jora'nal paced before Rasaka, letting his subordinate's report resonate. "Are you sure of this?" he asked after several moments.

"I am, master," Rasaka answered. "There is no doubt that the craft that attacked our scout ship is from the Etheric Federation, newly arrived in this sector of space as reported by our spies on Lariest. It is the SD *Reynolds*."

"What's it doing here?"

Rasaka shrugged. "I don't know, but it took the time to ransack the scout ship's databases after it killed everyone onboard. It appears to me that they are looking for something."

"For us," Jora'nal confirmed with a growl. "They are looking for *us*, Rasaka."

"But why?"

"That I do not know, but I feel in my bones that they are hunting us. All of our kind, the Thra'kali," Jora'nal told his follower. "They fear our gods, Rasaka. They fear the power of Phraim-'Eh and his siblings. They fear what we might become."

"Then we must do something, master."

"We must indeed," Jora'nal answered, "and we shall."

Jora'nal went back to pacing, rubbing his chin as he walked. At last, he stilled and turned back to his follower.

"Gather our people and make ready," he told Rasaka. "If they are coming for us, we will meet them on the field of battle. The Federation will rue their insolence, daring to seek us out."

Rasaka bowed low and left the room to do his master's bidding. Jora'nal waited until he was gone to begin his pacing again.

He had heard through Etheric channels that the Federation was expanding its reach, but he hadn't expected them to spread so far. Yet, here they were, invading his territory and destroying ships in search of them.

Jora'nal couldn't let that affront stand. He would wipe the Federation ship and its crew from existence. The mystical Kurtherians would see, should Phraim 'Eh wish to further bless them with an introduction.

"Well, that was fun," Reynolds muttered as the crew gathered on the bridge after they'd returned from Dal'las Tri. "How about we avoid getting caught up in a neural web trap next time around, huh?"

Maddox groaned. "I feel like I'm hungover, but I didn't even have a drink. Not that I know of, at least."

"You spent enough to have had a million drinks," Tactical accused.

Maddox grimaced. "Yeah, sorry about that. I guess I won't be trusted with the funds from now on."

"While it doesn't let you off the hook," Reynolds told him, "I stole all you lost back from the casino, as well as some additional cash for the inconvenience of our having to go down there and kick ass to get you and Ka'nak back."

"I'm not sorry," Ka'nak muttered, fresh out of the Pod-doc. "Mainly because I don't remember doing a damn thing wrong." He grunted. "I did, however, appear to win a whole shit-ton of credits while I was blacked out and punching people in the face."

Jiya nudged him in the side.

Ka'nak groaned. "Which I'll gladly contribute to the ship's fund for disobeying orders and running off to fight —despite my not having any control over myself," he said, glaring at Jiya. "Happy?"

"That sounded sincere enough," Jiya told the Melowi warrior.

With a quick salute, he strolled from the bridge.

"While we don't have a clear indication as to who empowered these people down on Dal'las Tri, there's nothing to indicate it was those Kurtherian bastards," the XO remarked.

Reynolds grunted. "That's a shame. We could have nuked them from orbit."

"Only way to be sure," Comm followed.

"Indeed." Reynolds grinned. "Anyway, I guess we move on and check the next system." He waved to Helm. "We've decoded some of the information we grabbed from that Thra'kali scout ship, and it points to the Loran system as a possible location where we might find Kurtherians. Set a course, Helm, and let's see if any of this intel pays off."

"Readying the Gate drive," Helm replied.

"Geroux and I are going to check in with Takal," Jiya told Reynolds. "Let him know his *Kami* blades worked great but the cloak only lasted seconds."

Reynolds nodded. "Take Maddox with you and drop him off at the Pod-doc. He could probably use a tune-up."

Jiya nodded and wrapped her arm around Maddox's. leading the ex-general from the bridge, Geroux trotting alongside.

Once the bridge door closed behind them, XO spoke up. *"Kami* blades? What the hell are those?"

Reynolds went over and flopped down in the captain's chair. "It appears our dear Takal has some innate ability to manipulate Etheric energy," Reynolds told the rest of his AI personalities.

"What?" Tactical asked.

"He infused a couple of blades on the armor suits with Etheric energy," Reynolds confirmed. "Who knows what else he can do?"

"We need to find out," Comm said. "That talent could be useful to us."

"Especially given the nature of Reynolds' android body," XO told them.

"Do they know?" Helm asked.

Reynolds shook his head. "I believe Takal suspects, hence his efforts at harnessing the Etheric energies in the pieces of armor he plans to encase this skeleton in, but I'm not entirely sure how much he truly *knows*."

"What doesn't Takal know?" Nav asked.

Reynolds gestured toward his android body. "That I'm outgrowing this husk quicker than expected." He sighed. "Won't be long until I begin to corrupt its electronics and make it useless. This frame just isn't designed to keep up with me. Not even a shadow of me. We need better cybernetic parts."

"Good to know you're still humble, Reynolds," Tactical muttered.

"You plan on telling them?" XO asked.

Reynolds nodded. "When we reach someplace that has adequate parts," he answered. "I'd hate to tell Takal now, given all the effort he's put into piecing this body together."

"Afraid you'll break his meatbag heart?" Tactical questioned.

"Yeah, something like that," Reynolds replied. "Now, get us to the Loran system and shut the hell up. I'm sick of listening to you all."

"Cranky, isn't he?" Tactical whispered to Comm.

"I heard that," Reynolds countered.

"I wanted you to." Tactical chuckled as the Gate drive engaged, ending any further conversation.

The superdreadnought broke into open space in the Loran system, and alarms sounded immediately upon arrival.

"What the hell?" Reynolds mumbled, staring at the viewscreen.

"Shit," Helm shouted. "Looks like we landed right in the middle of a damn fleet."

Reynolds directed in his command voice, "Hail the fleet and let them know we come in peace, Comm."

"Onscreen!" Comm called.

A woman with sharp features appeared on the viewscreen, bright red eyes surrounded by black staring through Reynolds. "I am Captain Asya of the *Valter*, lead of the Loranian fleet. You have trespassed upon Loranian territory and are ordered to turn around immediately or face severe consequences."

Reynolds met the captain's gaze and offered as friendly a nod as a metallic skeleton could offer. He regretted having sent Maddox away right then. He could have used a human face for this.

"Greetings, Captain," Reynolds hailed. "I am Reynolds of the SD *Reynolds*, and we intend you no harm."

"Tell that to the Thra'kali scout ship you decimated," Captain Asya replied.

Reynolds ignored him and met the captain's eyes. "That was a simple misunderstanding, Captain," he told her. "We're in search of Kurtherians, by order of former Empress Bethany Anne. We're only looking to gather intel, not to engage in senseless battles."

"I find it hard to believe you're on a peaceful mission, given the damage that was done to the Thra'kali ship. She was boarded and her systems pillaged, the craft left to drift aimlessly in space. That speaks to me of a coming invasion." She jabbed a finger at the screen. "As such, you are ordered to turn around and leave Loran space before we are forced to fire upon you."

"You have two minutes to comply," the captain continued and cut off communications.

"So, how do you want to handle this?" the XO asked.

"I can Gate us out of here," Helm offered.

Reynolds shook his head. "I don't see the point in running. Intel from that very scout ship points toward the Loran system as a possible refuge for the Kurtherians. If we leave, the Kurtherians win. If there are no Kurtherians here, then they can't mind us taking a look-see. It is what we must do. We will leave after we are sure the interstellar criminals haven't taken refuge in Loranian space."

XO chuckled. "It looks like we'll be forced to fight these Loranians. Is that what you want to do?"

"I'm thinking this Captain Asya is a woman of her word," Tactical said. "She doesn't look like the type to put up with any shit."

"We're being targeted," Comm announced. "Tactical, give me combat options."

"Raise shields," Tactical ordered.

"I guess this is what we're doing?" Helm asked.

"Sound general quarters," Reynolds called, "and ready the ship for battle. Maybe we can wear them down without hurting them."

"What about *them* hurting *us*?" Tactical asked.

Reynolds grunted. "Let's hope they can't."

"Okay, you heard him, folks," XO announced. "Prepare for battle and hope we don't get our asses kicked."

The Loranian captain held true to her word, and the first volley of incoming fire struck the SD *Reynolds*' shields exactly two minutes after her warning.

Captain Asya pointed at the enemy ship and shouted, "Fire!"

Her crew responded without hesitation, the rest of the fleet following suit. Blasts of cannon fire sparked across the enemy craft's shields as the fleet maneuvered for better effectiveness.

"It's taking all we're giving it, Captain," First Officer Ront called.

"Then give it more," Asya replied. "If we let this invader gain a foothold in our space, there's no telling what will come behind it."

She stared at the superdreadnought on the screen and scowled darkly. She'd seen the reports of the Thra'kali scout ship they'd left ruined, the whole of its crew dead inside after they'd boarded. This Reynolds was clearly a mechanoid, not a human as he claimed. To think she would be so foolish as to accept him at his word was preposterous.

No, she'd tear the invader from space.

"Open comm to Commander Ast," she called.

"Channel open," Ront replied.

"Yes, Captain?" Ast asked over the comm.

"We've engaged the enemy, sir," she reported, signaling for Ront to forward the video of the event. "It's a super-dreadnought. We're going to need to go after it with everything we have. Permission to let the fleet off the leash, sir."

Ast cleared his throat and grunted an affirmative. "Do what you have to, Captain, but bring that craft down."

"Yes, sir!" Asya signed off and called for the fleet to do whatever was necessary to destroy the invading super-dreadnought.

No matter what it took, she'd bring the enemy to their knees for what they'd done to the Thra'kali craft.

CHAPTER TWENTY-FIVE

"We've raised their ire," Tactical called. "Coming at us with everything they have."

Jiya, Geroux, and Maddox stormed the bridge right then, racing over to take their positions.

"What in the hell happened?" Jiya asked. "We were only gone for a little while."

"We flew into a cluster of Loranian ships," Comm answered.

"They're a little pissed about that scout ship we blew up and boarded," the XO went on. "They seem to think we're part of an invading force."

"They don't know any better," Reynolds said, frustration clear in his voice, "but we need to convince them that we're not what they think."

"So far, sitting here getting shot to shit isn't optimal. You asked for options? We're going to have to neutralize their fleet," Tactical replied.

"Well, we certainly can't keep taking this without response," XO announced. "Sooner or later, likely sooner, they'll get through our gravitic shields with all this and start doing real damage."

"And we've got meatbags on board now," Tactical reminded everyone. "Shots get through the hull, and we'll have dead meatbags. All that goop isn't good for the systems."

"Way to sound almost benevolent," Jiya chided Tactical.

"He's right, though," Comm agreed. "Not necessarily about the goop, although that's bad too, but we can't go getting our crew killed after all the work we did to get them in place."

"I know, I know," Reynolds mumbled, pacing across the bridge before jabbing a metallic finger at Tactical. "Evasive maneuvers and return fire, but I want to wound, not kill, understood? No railguns, and *definitely* no ESD."

Tactical grunted. "I understand the words but not the logic behind it. I'm on it."

The image on the viewscreen shifted as the SD *Reynolds* began to evade. Weapons gleamed as they returned fire, selective shots streaking across space to slow and disable the engaging fleet.

"Missiles fired," Tactical called, and the screen tracked the progress—quick flares of impact before they faded. "Crippled a destroyer. It's listing."

"That's a start. Come on, Asya, get a clue that you're going to get all your people killed. Dying for your cause won't further it," XO offered. "Just a dozen more ships to go."

"Geroux," Jiya shouted, "reach out to the lead ship and see if you can open a dialogue. Let them know we don't want to harm them."

"Already did that," Reynolds told her.

"It doesn't hurt to keep trying," Jiya answered. "Maybe she can hack their systems and force a message through."

"Do it!" Reynolds agreed.

"This is going to get messy quickly," Maddox announced. "There's no way we can maneuver through all this without causing some real damage, Reynolds. You might want to think about retreating and coming back elsewhere in the system where there isn't a fleet to engage us."

"Never retreat! Never surrender!" Tactical shouted.

"Seriously?" Maddox asked.

"He's quoting some stupid movie," Comm clarified. "Ignore him."

Maddox grunted.

"Another ship disabled," XO announced.

"They're blocking all incoming signals," Geroux told them. "I'm trying to hack through, but it's not looking good."

"Bring us around so—"

"Shit!" Tactical cursed.

"What?"

"Their lead ship zigged when it should have zagged," Tactical answered. "We broadsided it with a missile."

"Damn it!" Reynolds shouted. "On screen."

The image of Captain Asya's ship appeared, and they zoomed in. A smoking crater was obvious about halfway down the hull. The ship's engines sputtered and died, the destroyer dead in space.

"I said wound, not kill, dumbass," Reynolds shouted.

"They maneuvered into the missile. Likely trying to

deflect it from their companion ship, but it hit flush. Nothing I could do."

"Well, if the Loranian captain didn't already think we were a bunch of killers, she most certainly does now."

"It's losing atmosphere, and life support is failing," Comm said.

"The ship's drifting off," Jiya reported. "Looks like the fleet is letting it flounder, preferring to take us down before they spare any thought for their wounded."

"And here we are, looking like assholes," Reynolds complained, growling at the screen. "The complete opposite of what we want."

"Orders?" XO pushed. "We can't sit here picking our mechanical asses."

"Close on that destroyer and tractor it," Reynolds commanded.

"Are you insane?" Tactical asked. "You'll make us a sitting duck."

"Do it!" Reynolds ordered. He spun in his seat and addressed the crew. "Jiya, get a team ready to board the *Valter*. If their people won't bail them out, we will. Maybe that will show them we don't mean any harm."

"Or maybe it will get us all killed," Tactical argued. "For the record, this is stupid."

"I hate to agree with Tactical," Maddox said, "but I think he's right. This is a mistake."

"Probably," Reynolds agreed, "but I'm out of options. We need to take the opportunity."

"Ship is tractored, and we're pulling it in," Helm called.

"Expand the gravitic shields over both ships," Reynolds ordered. "I don't want the *Valter* taking hits meant for us."

"The destroyer is shielded," Helm announced. "It's already costing us, though. Shields are taking a beating."

Reynolds jumped to his feet, waving to Jiya and the others. "Get over there and get power back to that ship, so she doesn't die out there. Do whatever you have to."

Jiya saluted and raced off, Maddox and Geroux at her heels.

"You sure this is a good idea?" XO repeated.

"Not really," Reynolds replied, "but it's what we're doing."

"Does this feel insane to anyone else?" Ka'nak asked as the crew crowded outside the boarding tube, armed and armored and ready to board the listing destroyer.

Geroux raised her hand.

"See? It's not just me," Ka'nak mumbled. "This is crazy."

"It's what we've been ordered to do," Jiya countered, "so it's what we're going to do. Period."

"Here!" Takal offered Jiya a belt with several small oval containers on it.

"What are these?"

"Screamers," he answered, "for lack of a better name. They'll be useful as distractions should you need them. Just make sure to keep your helmets on or your ears will hate me later. I've added baffles to protect you."

Jiya nodded and took the belt, strapping it around her waist. "Everyone know their job?"

"Convince the enemy that we aren't their enemy," Ka'nak stated.

The rest of the crew nodded, and Jiya sucked in a deep breath to steady her nerves. "Let's do this," she ordered and signaled for the boarding tube to be opened.

Weapons in hand, they raced down the tube with Comm's voice in their ears. "Boarding point is clear," he reported. "The crew is busy trying to save the ship, but you won't have long before they realize you're there, so stay frosty."

Jiya replied in the affirmative as the crew burst through the hatch onto the enemy ship. Smoke filled the air, and tiny electrical fires sparked in the electronics along the wall.

"Clean shot," Maddox whistled. "Too bad we weren't *trying* to take them out."

"You've got lifeforms headed your way," Comm told them.

Jiya turned to face her people. "Geroux, you and Takal get to engineering and try to resuscitate this wreck." She waved them off before turning to the remaining crew. "It's up to us to hold this point as long as it takes for Takal and Geroux to restore power to the ship."

She motioned down the hall to where the *Valter*'s crew would be coming from, the opposite direction from where Geroux and Takal had run off.

"Do what you have to, but stun only," she ordered. "We can't go killing them if we want to pull this off."

"I'll do what I can," Ka'nak complained. "Doesn't seem fair, you ask me."

"Life ain't fair," Jiya told him. "Let's make sure it works out the way we need it to."

Bolts of energy screamed down the corridor and Jiya

darted to the left for cover, Maddox and Ka'nak going to the right. They returned fire, snapping shots down the hall, grateful that Comm had led them to a place on the *Valter* that provided them with reasonable cover.

"I count twenty crew," Comm said over the communicator. "They're clustered at the bend at the end of the hall. No way to advance without making a target of themselves, so stay tight, and you should be fine."

Ka'nak loosed a few bolts in the general direction of the *Valter*'s crew to help them with their decision to remain behind cover.

"We're going to have issues when Geroux and Takal return," Maddox pointed out. "No cover down that corridor."

Jiya nodded, having realized that herself. She patted the belt that Takal had given her, letting Maddox see it. She had an idea what she'd do when the time came, but right then, she had her hands full trying not to get shot while they waited.

It'd only be a matter of time before Captain Asya figured out a way to come down the corridor and make this a real fight. Jiya didn't want to be there when that happened.

"How's it going?" she asked Takal over the comm.

Takal came back, breathing heavily. "There's a system-wide failure," he reported. "I'm trying to reboot it, but I'm having a hard time getting it to take commands. It's largely unresponsive."

"What does that mean?" she pushed.

"It means I don't know if we can bring her back online in time to save the crew or us," Takal told her.

"Not sure what the enemy crew is doing, but they're gathering," Comm announced. "Piling up behind one another, drawing closer to the corner."

"Shit," Jiya muttered, shaking her head. "They've either got something to deflect shots or they're willing to sacrifice some of their people to get close enough to take us out."

Jiya had to admire their courage, considering the *Valter*'s crew didn't know Jiya and her people were intending to immobilize them instead of killing them. She snarled into the comm. Ka'nak started to growl deep in his throat with the adrenaline surge of the impending fight.

"I need to know now, Takal," she said, "Can you fix this tub or not?"

"It's going to take some time," he came back.

Time they didn't have.

"Screw it, then," she told him. "You and Geroux get back here now! We're getting off this ship."

"What about the crew?" Maddox asked.

Jiya shrugged. She hadn't thought that far ahead.

Captain Asya didn't give her any more time, either.

The *Valter*'s crew pushed around the corner in a tight mass, looking like a Roman shield wall, bodies standing tall upfront and weapons poking out of every available cranny. They came down the hall at a brisk run.

Jiya swallowed hard. Even if she took out the lead crew members, the rest would be on them, and that'd be that.

But much like when she'd faced off against her father's guards, she knew she wasn't going to go out that easily.

Rather than yank a single screamer off the belt, she removed the whole thing and triggered the devices, hurtling the entire belt down the hall at the advancing enemy.

"Fire in the hole," she shouted, having no clue exactly what to expect.

The screamers went off when they struck the ground, and the effect was instantaneous.

True to their name, the screamers did exactly that: scream loud enough to shake the great struts holding the once-impressive destroyer together.

The *Valter*'s crew shrieked in response to the wailing-harpy pitch of the screamers. They stumbled, dropping their weapons and clutching at their ears despite the helmets they wore.

Jiya gasped as the sound stabbed her in the skull even through the baffles Takal had installed, giving her an instant headache she figured would last a week or more. She could only imagine how bad it was for the *Valter*'s crew.

"You used all of them?" Takal asked, coming alongside her, his eyes narrowed in pain.

"I wasn't supposed to?" Jiya asked.

He shook his head.

"Seems to have worked," she muttered over the comm, although she was sure he could barely hear her.

She turned back to the *Valter*'s crew, who were scattered about the floor. Only a few of them still moved, the majority of them unconscious. As the screamers died out one by one, the rest of the crew stilled and flopped to the ground.

"I'm going to need a hearing aid," Ka'nak shouted despite the devices having gone silent.

"Me too!" Maddox yelled, tapping the side of his helmet.

"What's going on?" Comm asked. "All of the *Valter*'s crew are down. How'd that happen?"

"We, uh, stunned them," Jiya shouted into the comm, also unable to talk at a normal volume.

"You don't have to yell at me," Comm complained.

"I really think I do," she answered, still yelling. "Get us some bots down here fast," she told Comm. "We've got twenty Loranian crew members who are going to need medical assistance."

"You want to bring them aboard?" Reynolds asked, cutting in.

"You wanted a chance to make peace, right?" Jiya shouted. "Here it is."

"Taking hostages wasn't exactly what I intended," he answered.

"Don't think of them as hostages, then," she replied. "Think of them as guests. Give them tea and cookies, and it'll be okay."

Reynolds growled. "Get back aboard," he ordered. "We're taking a beating here and can't hold out much longer."

"Yes, sir," Jiya replied and waved the crew through the boarding tube after the bots arrived to haul away their *guests*.

"Score one for the good guys?" Ka'nak asked.

Jiya shrugged. "Guess we'll see soon enough."

CHAPTER TWENTY-SIX

On the bridge of the SD *Reynolds*, the crew gathered around the still unconscious Captain Asya. The rest of her people had been placed in Pod-docs, being healed but kept asleep until there was some resolution to the current crisis.

"Why are we still hugging this heap?" Tactical asked. "We need to let the *Valter* go and defend ourselves."

"Gravitic shields are degrading quickly," Helm announced. "We're taking actual hull damage now," he reported. "It isn't much, but it'll add up quickly."

"Wake her up," Reynolds told the crew, gesturing to Captain Asya.

Jiya went over and gave the captain a quick sternal rub. The captain grunted and bolted upright as Jiya stepped back.

"Wha-what?" the captain asked, clearly still reeling from the effects of the screamers. Dried blood was visible in her ears. "Who?"

"I'm sorry to have brought you aboard under such difficult circumstances," Maddox told her, taking the lead since Reynolds looked like a murderous metallic skeleton, "but we need to make it clear that we are not your enemy."

The ship trembled as the fleet continued its barrage.

"Shields down to thirty percent," Helm warned.

"I'm...where?"

"You're aboard the SD *Reynolds*, Captain," Maddox continued, "And I'm sorry, but we don't have time to catch you up on everything. Your fleet's continuing assault is going to force us to make a decision we don't want to make."

Captain Asya clambered to her feet, swaying unsteadily. Jiya stayed close to steady her, remaining wary. Ka'nak also stood nearby.

"I don't understand," she said, finally appearing to gather her wits. "Why am I here?"

"Because your ship was dying," Reynolds said, stepping in, his impatience clearly getting the better of him. "It was struck down accidentally, and it was clear your fleet prioritized our defeat over your safety. We couldn't let you die for our mistake."

"But the Thra'kal scout ship..."

"Was a mistake, as I tried to tell you earlier," Reynolds replied. "We had believed it to be a Kurtherian ship and meant it no harm."

"We're not some invading force," Jiya added. "We're on a mission to find Kurtherians, gather intel on them alone, and make alliances. Believe it or not, we come in peace."

Captain Asya frowned. "Tell that to my crew and my ship."

"Your ship was an accident," Reynolds told her. "You

flew into a missile meant to disable another of your craft, not take you out."

"As for your crew," Jiya said, "they are alive and well in stasis. They're all fine."

"If we had meant to kill you, we would have done it from the get-go," Maddox told her. "We have weapons aboard this ship that would scorch holes in your planet."

"But we held back," Reynolds offered. "Even now," he gestured to the viewscreen and an image of the SD *Reynolds* hovering in space, still connected to the *Valter*, appeared. "We're taking a beating because we don't want to hurt your people."

"We boarded your craft to rescue it," Jiya said. "The only reason we stunned you was because there was no way you'd believe us in time to get you off that wreck before someone died."

Captain Asya spun in a slow circle, looking at the crew and the ship around her. "You kidnapped us to prove your peaceful nature?"

The screen altered and a readout of the *Valter*'s condition appeared alongside its image. It was clear from the data that the ship was dead in space, life support and all systems fried.

"You could fake that," the captain argued.

"We could, but do you feel that shudder?" Reynolds asked. "That's your fleet pounding us while we sit here with our thumbs up our asses, holding back our true potential. We don't want to fight you, and we're not here to invade, but we're going to have to fight back very soon. Now or never, Captain."

"Give us a chance to prove our capabilities. Show you

that we could have wiped your fleet out from the start but didn't," Jiya said. "Your life is as much at risk here as ours are, Captain," she explained. "If nothing else, call a pause to the battle so we can ship you back to your people. Whatever happens, we don't want you or your crew hurt."

Captain Asya growled and glared at the viewscreen showing her ship's stats. She stood there rigid for a moment, then she turned around and nodded at Jiya. "Can you open a channel?" She offered up a specific frequency.

"We're connected," Comm said a moment later, and the viewscreen shifted to an image of a man in a Loranian uniform.

"This is a restricted channel—" the man started, and saw the captain. "Captain Asya? Are you being held hostage?"

She sighed and shook her head. "Not exactly, Commander Ast."

"What is this, then?" he asked.

"This alien craft continues to proclaim its peaceful intentions, sir," she replied. "They claim they have no interest in invading our space and seek an alliance with us, and suggest they have been holding back this entire time," she told the commander. "If we continue to attack them, however, they say they will be forced to defend themselves to the full extent of their capabilities. Which, according to them, is more than the Loranian fleet can withstand."

Commander Ast chuckled. "How magnanimous. And all we have to do is not destroy them?" He shook his head scoffing.

"Release the *Valter*," Reynolds said over the comm speaking so no one but the crew could hear him. "This guy isn't going to give us the opportunity to provide an example, so we need to take it."

"It's loose," Helm replied. "Nudging it with boosters."

"What's that?" Commander Ast asked someone standing behind him. His eyes narrowed as he looked at the viewscreen, clearly seeing the *Valter* moving away from the SD *Reynolds*. "What are you doing, alien?"

"Proving a point," Reynolds answered, motioning to Tactical.

Tactical didn't hesitate, firing one of the railguns into the floating husk of the *Valter*.

The blast tore through the ship with ruthless efficiency, tearing its hull open as though it were made of paper. The ship exploded, a quick flash filling the screen and then vanishing. Debris and wreckage floated away from where the *Valter* had been.

Captain Asya gasped.

"That is only one of the many similar weapons we have aboard our ship, Commander," Reynolds warned. "I promise you, this is a fight you cannot win."

"Please don't force us to hurt anyone," Jiya added.

The commander stared wide-eyed through the viewscreen, swallowing hard as he contemplated his options.

"I believe them, sir," Captain Asya told her superior. "They could have killed my crew and me or left us to die in space, but they didn't. They risked their lives to board and bring us onto their ship before life support gave out." She glanced at Jiya and the others. "Why would they do that if they meant to invade us?"

"To gather intel," Commander Ast suggested.

Asya shook her head. "They never once approached the bridge, sir. Never asked us questions or anything." She raised her hands in the air, showing she wasn't bound. "I'm on their bridge, sir, and I'm not restrained in any way. While I have no doubt they could subdue me before I did any damage, they have no clue as to my capabilities. They don't know the threat I pose, and yet here I am."

Commander Ast grunted, taking in the information. After what seemed forever, he raised a hand. "Cease fire," he ordered, and the fleet immediately complied, the shuddering impacts of fire no longer crashing into the *Reynolds'* shields.

The crew let out a collective sigh as damage control raced into action.

"Thank you, Commander," Reynolds told the man. "I understand your concern, us appearing out of nowhere in your system. We had expected the opportunity to hail you properly, but that's clearly not how things worked out. Still, we hope to parlay with you and put all this behind us."

Commander Ast nodded. "I offer no certainties as to the measure of our talks, Captain…Reynolds, is it?"

Reynolds nodded.

"But if you return the *Valter*'s crew and captain without harm, I assure you that we *will* sit down and have a dialogue, however it might turn out."

"That's all I ask, Commander," Reynolds replied. "Thank you." He motioned to Captain Asya. "We'll provide a shuttle for the captain and her crew to return to your flagship immediately."

"I'll await their arrival forthwith. I'll be in touch with

directions to the meeting location soon," Commander Ast said, cutting the connection.

"I'll take her to the hangar bay," Jiya said, gesturing for the captain to follow her.

Captain Asya acknowledged Jiya but turned to Reynolds. "Could you have really wiped out my entire fleet?"

He paused for a moment, then nodded. "It would have been far easier than I like to admit," he told her. "I'm glad we could come to terms before anyone was hurt."

Asya stood there staring at Reynolds, seeming to contemplate something before finally accepting Reynolds at his word.

"Speak with you soon, Captain Reynolds," she said, walking off with Jiya and Ka'nak, the bridge door closing behind them.

"You think this Commander Ast will stay true to his word?" XO asked.

Reynolds shrugged. "If he doesn't, all bets are off. We can't afford to take another beating like that. New SOP: we enter these systems closer to the edge of the heliosphere and assess the situation before traipsing down the gravity well."

"So, stay ready?" Maddox asked.

"Exactly," Reynolds answered. "Once the captain and her crew are back with their fleet, we prepare for the worst."

"I'll get Takal and the rest of the crew working on restoring the shields and repairing the damage we took," Maddox said, triggering his comm and speaking into it.

Reynolds nodded and leaned back in his seat, watching

the viewscreen. A few minutes later, the Pod carrying Captain Asya and her crew departed the hangar bay on its way back to the Loranian fleet.

They watched it go, each thinking their own thoughts about what would come next.

CHAPTER TWENTY-SEVEN

Once Captain Asya and her people had been returned safely to their people, Commander Ast did as promised and arranged a meeting between the Loranian government and Reynolds' crew.

The SD *Reynolds* settled into orbit over Loran with the Loranian fleet arrayed around it. Maddox, Takal, and Geroux remained behind to oversee repairs along with the AI personalities, just in case the commander went back on his word of safe passage.

On the planet, Jiya was surprised by how much the meeting location reminded her of her father's compound. They had been directed to a similar area, set a distance outside the nearby bustling city.

"Guess they don't want us near their people," Jiya muttered as they exited the shuttle, which had been led to the landing area by an automated system.

"Maybe it's they who don't want to be near anyone," Reynolds suggested, glancing around.

"This place is pretty sparse," Ka'nak commented, tightening his grip on the butt of the weapon at his hip. He was nearly invincible in hand-to-hand combat, but this was a different kind of engagement. "You might be right."

"As long as we get what we came for, I don't care if we have the meeting in a broom closet," Reynolds told them.

The Loranian entourage met them on the tarmac, Captain Asya surprisingly at their head. At her back were a half-dozen soldiers, their weapons holstered.

"Hello again," she said, offering a slight bow.

"Thank you for having us," Jiya replied, smiling. Whatever happened, she wanted to put her best foot forward after the clusterfuck that had been Dal'las Tri.

Asya returned the smile. "Come this way." She waved them on, the rest of the congregation closing around the party.

Jiya felt the tension of the Loranian guards around her, but nothing made her feel threatened. They were simply being cautious, and she was okay with that. After the demonstration with the *Valter*, she knew the Loranians were wary of the hell that would rain down on their heads should they deviate from their guarantee of safety.

Jiya and Ka'nak had dressed in the battle armor Takal had adjusted for them, so the vibe they gave off was definitely one to consider.

Reynolds had insisted they show off in their meeting. They'd made the mistake of letting Jiya's father get the drop on them, and he didn't want that to happen again.

Jiya was just fine with that.

They followed Captain Asya to a small meeting room buried deep inside the compound. More soldiers met them at the door, and Jiya caught the eyes of each and every one, offering a friendly greeting as they passed.

It doesn't hurt to grease the wheels of the men who might be ordered to kill us soon, she thought with a chuckle.

A long table was situated at the back of the room on a short dais. It made it so the occupants looked down on the visitors. Commander Ast sat at the table alongside five other people, three women and two men.

While the commander remained in his military garb, the rest of the representatives wore long purple robes with sleeves that nearly covered their hands. They sat poised, hands clasped as Reynolds and the crew approached. Only the commander narrowed his eyes at their arrival.

Captain Asya ushered them to seats arranged in front of the dais. Reynolds and the crew sat without saying a word.

"Welcome to Loran," the woman seated at the center of the table announced. "I am Zal'a Gom, President of Loran." She motioned to the woman to her right, then the man at the end of the table. "This is Artan Sie and Golan Tor," she continued, then gestured to her left. "You, of course, know Commander Ast, and the last of our parliament here is Nor Kan."

"Pleasure to meet you all," Reynolds said as he stood to acknowledge the gathering.

"Please, sit," Zal'a told him.

Reynolds complied, and Jiya bit back a grin at the obvious psychological efforts being made to show up the crew. She wondered if Reynolds would play along or cut straight to the chase.

"We are told you seek information," Zal'a went on. "That you are not here in a military capacity."

"That's correct," Reynolds replied. "We are tasked by Former Empress Bethany Anne to seek out Kurtherians, an ancestral enemy of humanity. We've come here only because we caught wind of Kurtherian activity in the area."

"We know nothing of these Kurtherians," Nor Kan said, "Nor of your Bethany Anne."

Jiya stood, offering a shallow bow. "We would also like to establish a compact between the Loranian people and ours," she announced. "We could use a safe haven to dock when we are in the system and purchase supplies. We are willing to exchange limited technical knowledge for such a deal."

"We have a similar deal with those of Lariest," Reynolds added, "And we would like to add your planet as a sanctuary, should we need such."

"I'm not sure you'll find many systems nearby willing to trade with you, I'm afraid," Zal'a told him.

Reynolds stiffened. "Why's that?"

"Much like our Captain Asya here heard, leading to the unfortunate confrontation between you and our fleet, there is much chatter that you are a dangerous species bent on the destruction of all you come across."

"There are words, and there are deeds. Those gossiping about the great alien ship do so in fear. We said what we were going to do, and then we did it. That is the foundation of trust," Jiya explained.

"Your actions showed us differently, of course," Zal'a acknowledged, "but I'm afraid the word is already spreading."

"We will do what we can to disabuse our allies of your supposed hostile nature, but I'm not sure what we can do beyond that," Artan Sie said, shrugging. "Your example will have to shine the light on your character."

Reynolds nodded. "That's the best we can hope for, then," he told the assemblage, clearly not satisfied that someone was working to impugn their character but seeing no point in arguing. Those who listened to rumors were no better than those who spread them.

"As for the safe haven and supplies, we would be glad to discuss these options with you further," Zal'a continued.

The discussions went on for several hours after that, Jiya struggling to stay awake as Reynolds and the Loranian government got into the specifics of what equaled what. In the end, the Loranians walked away with more than they gave, and Reynolds got confirmation that they'd offer up any information regarding Kurtherians that they came across.

After what seemed like forever to Jiya, the meeting was called, and Captain Asya came over to see them back to their shuttle. As she walked them out of the building, Jiya noted the entourage of soldiers were no longer crowded around them. They hung back a good distance. Close enough if they were needed, but far enough to not appear hostile.

"I'm glad you came to speak with our parliament," Captain Asya told them. "It went a long way toward showing them who you really are by coming here personally."

"I only wish we'd gotten the point across *before* our confrontation," Reynolds told her.

"As do I." She nodded. "But like the president said, someone is spreading the word that you are dangerous and need to be destroyed." She glanced around as if she were suspicious. "Do you have any enemies nearby?"

"We are newly arrived in this sector, and it seems that fear is running rampant. That, to me, indicates the Kurtherians have preceded us. Misinformation is one of their greatest weapons. Turning allies against each other. Our enemies are secretive, and they could be anywhere," Reynolds admitted. "We may well have crossed them recently and not even realized it."

"Well, I'd be careful, since it's clear they have far-reaching access to have spread such rumors so widely and so quickly. They must be incredibly powerful."

Reynolds nodded. "They are."

Captain Asya went silent, leading them back to the shuttle. It was only when the crew was ready to board that she spoke again.

"I apologize for my part in the confusion," she told them, offering a curt nod to each in turn. "Had I been more receptive, none of this would have happened."

"No need to apologize," Jiya told her. "We understand." She smiled at the captain, doing her best to convey her sincerity.

"Perhaps not, but I still feel honor-bound to do so," she said. "It is the way of my people to repay a blood debt with service." She dropped to a knee. "While you had no reason to risk your lives to save my crew or me, you did exactly that. As such, I would be honored to serve at your side and join you in your mission against these Kurtherian enemies."

"Whoa! That is not necessary, Asya." Jiya muttered, going to help the captain up. Reynolds grabbed her arm and stopped her, shaking his head.

"While our people have no such expectations of you, Captain," Reynolds told her, "we would be grateful were you to lend your expertise to our crew." He offered her his hand.

The captain took it, rising to her feet. "Then we have a compact," she said, grinning. "I have cleared my intention with the parliament, and they are in agreement—my life in exchange for that of my crew. I am now indebted to you."

"Did I miss the kneeling ceremony when I got made part of the crew?" Ka'nak asked. "I don't remember having to kneel. Doesn't mean I didn't, mind you." He smiled broadly as he towered over the others.

Jiya elbowed him in the ribs. He grunted and went quiet.

"Welcome to the crew," Jiya told the captain as she joined them. "It'll be an...experience, no doubt about that."

CHAPTER TWENTY-EIGHT

After the crew returned to the SD *Reynolds* and settled in for the night—Captain Asya having been shown her quarters and given a tour of the ship—Reynolds sat on the quiet bridge with only his thoughts to keep him company.

Fully stocked from Lariest, the ship needed nothing from the Loranians, so they decided to stay only overnight in Loran orbit. He'd given the crew the night off, letting them rest and get comfortable after all they'd been through, but there was little rest for Reynolds.

He couldn't help but wonder how news of their attack on the Thra'kal scout ship had traveled so quickly and how it had been so misconstrued. He admitted that the attack didn't look good, boarding after he hailed the fleeing craft, but there was nothing in the gesture that pointed to the SD *Reynolds* heading up an invasion force.

"A single ship does not an invasion make," XO said, having clearly been listening in on Reynolds' thoughts.

"No, it does not, but someone is saying that's what we're doing here."

"Has to be Kurtherians," Tactical added. "Maybe that's who built up the security at Dal'las Tri and set up that neural web device."

"Could be, but wouldn't we have detected them there?" Reynolds asked. "There were no signs of anyone tapping to the Etheric."

"Maybe they've gotten better at hiding," XO suggested.

"We were a bit distracted, though," Comm joined in. "We could have missed something."

"Anyone with the power to lock down a system like that has to have powerful resources at their beck and call," XO went on. "They'd likely have communication arrays powerful enough to send out rumors like the ones that reached Loran."

Reynolds nodded. It all made sense, yet it didn't.

They'd cost the casino owners a great deal of cash by shutting down their scam and raiding their servers, but there wasn't an obvious connection to the SD *Reynolds* anywhere in that.

Someone would have had to have tracked them down as they fled to the shuttle and departed. Otherwise, it wouldn't be clear where the attack group had come from.

"None of this makes sense," Reynolds mumbled.

"None of what?" Jiya asked, stumbling onto the bridge with a steaming cup of coffee in her hand.

The bridge lights flickered and came up, Reynolds only then realizing it was morning—time for the crew to return to work.

"Just talking to myself," Reynolds admitted. He glanced around the bridge as Jiya settled and thought back to his decision to tractor the *Valter* and wait while the Loranian fleet pounded the ship.

"Are you sure you want to do this?" he asked her.

"Do what?" Jiya asked.

"*This.*" He gestured around the ship. "Be a part of the crew, fly off to random galaxies and hunt down Kurtherians? Is this what you see yourself doing?"

Jiya chuckled. "You trying to get rid of me already?"

Reynolds shook his head. "No, I just…" He paused for a moment, collecting his thoughts. "I just wonder if I'm needlessly putting you and the others at risk for my mission. Bethany Anne assigned this task to *me*, not to anyone else. Although she ordered me to get a crew, she doesn't know I've recruited anyone. I'd hate to have to report back to her that I got a bunch of crew members killed in my zeal."

Jiya hopped up and came over to stand in front of Reynolds. She set a hand on his metallic shoulder.

"We're all here by choice, Reynolds," she told him, meeting his gaze and not letting it drop. "While circumstances were a little questionable at the start," she said, chuckling, "you know, all that kidnapping crap and whatnot, we're all where we're supposed to be, and I speak for the crew when I say that."

"You don't speak for me," Ka'nak said as he trundled onto the bridge. "What are we talking about?"

"Whether we want to stay onboard as part of the crew," Jiya clarified.

"Oh, that," Ka'nak mumbled. "Sure. I thought you were discussing breakfast."

"See?" Jiya asked Reynolds.

The AI grinned. "I guess that answers that, then."

"Is that a no for breakfast?" Ka'nak pushed, grunting when no one answered him. "I'm off to the mess."

Maddox walked onto the bridge then, a young woman Reynolds didn't recognize coming in alongside him. Maddox took his position, and the young woman sat in Helm's spot.

"Meet your new helm," Maddox said, eyeing Jiya's coffee all the while. "You got another one of those hidden around here somewhere? A carafe, maybe?"

Reynolds turned to the woman at the helm and offered her a smile. She returned it, along with a crisp salute.

"Your orders, sir?"

"Take us to the next system, please," he answered, realizing then that he didn't even know the woman's name.

That's okay, he thought, *there's plenty of time for that.*

She was part of the crew, the same as Jiya and the others. He would learn everyone's name in time because they would make this journey with him. They were *his* crew now.

They were his family.

"Ready to go at your order, sir," the youngster at the helm replied.

There was no time like the present to get acquainted. "What's your name, Helm?"

"Tanirika, sir."

Reynolds thought for a moment. "In one of the Earth languages, that means 'a flower.' Apropos. If you would be so kind, Tanirika, activate the Gate drive and take us to the next stop on our search for the ever-elusive Kurtherians."

The End

EPILOGUE

Jora'nal stood in front of the altar, praying.

He had much to be thankful for. Phraim-'Eh had sent his messenger to him and had given him a path to follow, the path to ascension. Followers had gathered at the hem of his robes to serve him in his mission, spreading the word of the old god Phraim-'Eh across the universe.

There was much to rejoice about in such a journey.

Word had been spread of the virulent Etheric Federation ship and its crew, and it would carry far ahead of their travels, assuring that Jora'nal's master was satisfied. The Etheric Federation was an enemy of the old gods, of the beliefs Phraim-'Eh stood for.

"You did well, Jora'nal," a new Voice of Phraim-'Eh told him from the shadows. "Our god is pleased."

"Thank you, Messenger," Jora'nal replied, keeping his head low as the Voice approached. "I wish only to serve."

"And you shall get your chance," the Voice said, coming up to stand before Jora'nal.

He reached down and raised Jora'nal's chin so that their eyes met.

Jora'nal gasped at seeing the face of the Messenger so clearly.

The Messenger offered Jora'nal a broad grin, welcoming him to his feet.

"Phraim-'Eh has another mission for you, child," he told Jora'nal. "Do you accept?"

"Of course, Messenger."

"Good," the Voice said and then explained to Jora'nal the god's new expectations.

Once the Thra'kali left to do the messenger's bidding, the Voice pulled his hood from his head and stared out at the empty temple.

Commander Ast grinned as he imagined his plot playing out against the SD *Reynolds* and its pathetic crew.

AUTHOR NOTES - CRAIG MARTELLE
WRITTEN OCTOBER 8, 2018

Thank you for reading this book and you're still reading! Oorah, hard chargers. I really hope you liked this story. I was invested in it as soon as Michael Anderle broached the idea. It works for me. It's classic Star Trek with a twist and then some. I love the premise and the characters and all the good things that go into making a space opera great.

First and foremost, I want to thank Tim Marquitz for helping me get this off the ground. I had four other co-authors for this project which started back in March 2018, but each of them had quirks and issues that were insurmountable. I wanted this story to turn out a certain way and Tim helped me to realize that vision.

Micky Cocker, Kelly O'Donnell, and Dr. James Caplan

all provided in process feedback to make sure that the story was sound. They came through. We tweaked some flow and subplots and have what I think is a solid story, but what I think doesn't matter. It's what you think, now that you've read it. If you would be so kind as to leave a review, I'd appreciate it.

Of course, we always have Michael Anderle, the one who made all of this possible, by broadening the universe that he created so that other authors can fill a galaxy-wide void with stories. It's a cool thing and we all win, as long as the readers find our stories to be fulfilling, a journey away from everyday issues. Even better than all of the great stories, Michael is my friend and we do spend an inordinate amount of time on the phone.

I live in the sub-arctic and fall has come and gone (it was a long month). Winter is now upon us, but as I write this, we are distinctly lacking in snow, an odd occurrence, but the northern lights are out almost every night when it is clear, which is most nights. That's the benefit of cool weather in the high desert. Clear skies for the win.

Peace fellow humans.

BOOKS BY TIM MARQUITZ

Also Available from Tim Marquitz

Enemy of My Enemy
(with Michael Anderle)

Any Port In A War (1)
Refuge In The Stars (2)

The Demon Squad Series

From Hell (Novella)
DS1 - Armageddon Bound
DS2 - Resurrection
Betrayal (Intro short to At the Gates)
DS3 - At the Gates
DS4 - Echoes of the Past
DS5 - Beyond the Veil
DS6 - The Best of Enemies

DS7 - Exit Wounds
DS8 - Collateral Damage
DS9 – Aftermath
DS10 – Institutionalized
To Hell and Back - A Demon Squad Collection (books 1-3)

The Blood War Trilogy

Dawn of War
Embers of an Age
Requiem

Clandestine Daze Series

Eyes Deep (novella)
Influx

Standalone Fantasy

Dirge
Witch Bane
War God Rising

Sci-fi

Excalibur

Dead West

Those Poor, Poor Bastards

The Ten Thousand Things
Omnibus 1

Horror

Prey
Serial
Skulls
Heir to the Blood Throne: Inheritance

Collections

Tales of Magic and Misery

Non-Fiction

Memoirs of a Machine – w/John MACHINE Lober
Grunt Style: The Blue Collar Guide to Writing Genre
Fiction

Anthologies

Blackguards (Ragnarok Publications)
Unbound (Grim Oak Press)
SNAFU: Survival of the Fittest (Cohesion Press)
SNAFU: Hunters (Cohesion Press)
SNAFU: Future Warfare (Cohesion Press)
SNAFU: Black Ops (Cohesion Press)
In the Shadow of the Towers (Night Shade)
Neverland's Library (Ragnarok Publications)

At Hell's Gates 1&3 (Charity)
American Nightmare (Kraken Press)
Corrupts Absolutely? (Ragnarok Publications)
Widowmakers (Charity)
That Hoodoo Voodoo, That You Do (Ragnarok
Publications)

Craig Martelle's other books (listed by series)

Terry Henry Walton Chronicles (co-written with Michael Anderle) – a post-apocalyptic paranormal adventure

Gateway to the Universe (co-written with Justin Sloan & Michael Anderle) – this book transitions the characters from the Terry Henry Walton Chronicles to The Bad Company

The Bad Company (co-written with Michael Anderle) – a military science fiction space opera

End Times Alaska (also available in audio) – a Permuted Press publication – a post-apocalyptic survivalist adventure

The Free Trader – a Young Adult Science Fiction Action Adventure

Cygnus Space Opera – A Young Adult Space Opera (set in the Free Trader universe)

Darklanding (co-written with Scott Moon) – a Space Western

Judge, Jury, & Executioner – a space opera adventure legal thriller

Rick Banik – Spy & Terrorism Action Adventure

Become a Successful Indie Author – a non-fiction work

Metamorphosis Alpha – stories from the world's first science fiction RPG

The Expanding Universe – science fiction anthologies

Shadow Vanguard – a Tom Dublin series

Uprise Saga – an Amy DuBoff series

Enemy of my Enemy (co-written with Tim Marquitz) – A galactic alien military space opera (coming late summer of 2018)

Superdreadnought (co-written with Tim Marquitz) – a military space opera (coming fall of 2018)

About Tim Marquitz

Tim Marquitz is the author of the Demon Squad series, the Blood War Trilogy, co-author of the Dead West series, as well as several standalone books, and numerous anthology appearances. Tim also collaborated on Memoirs of a MACHINE, the story of MMA pioneer John Machine Lober.

Website: www.tmarquitz.com

Follow Tim on Facebook and Twitter.

Subscribe to Tim's newsletter and get up to date information on new releases as well as an Excalibur prequel story (exciting sci-fi) and Dawn of War, the first novel in the Blood War Trilogy (Epic Fantasy)!

http://www.tmarquitz.com/contact

Craig Martelle Social

Website & Newsletter:
   http://www.craigmartelle.com

Facebook:
https://www.facebook.com/AuthorCraigMartelle/

Michael Anderle Social

Website: http://kurtherianbooks.com/

Email List: http://kurtherianbooks.com/email-list/
Facebook:
https://www.
facebook.com/TheKurtherianGambitBooks/

Printed in Great Britain
by Amazon